Lies Beget Lies

a novel

by

rebecca mealey

"*I believe that unarmed truth and unconditional love will have the final word in reality. This is why right, temporarily defeated, is stronger than evil triumphant.*"

DR. MARTIN LUTHER KING, JR.

Chapter One

The South in 1965 isn't easy when you're biracial. You worry about things like which water fountain to drink from. Biracial pretty much means you're illegitimate too. What do you put on the line that asks for your father's name?

On a yellow-white afternoon in late February, Callie Gibbs Knight crossed the railroad tracks to the little bungalow where she lived, or existed rather, with Reggie Knight. The little cinder block house belonged to Reggie's granddaddy. He'd lost his wife years ago and stayed in it by himself until the time came for him to spend his last days in a nursing home. Despite scrubbing from sagging ceiling to chipped linoleum floors, and leaving the windows wide open on a mild, windy day last month, the odor of old people still lingered.

Reggie had promised to save money and fix up the place. They'd only been married since Christmas, but it hadn't taken Callie long to figure out he spent it on drinking and gambling. It didn't matter to him he was an officer of the law.

A scraggly old cat darted out of nowhere.

"Blackjack! You rascal, you came back. Come in and eat. I can see your ribs."

Blackjack snaked around her ankles while she fished for her key. The door was unlocked. Reggie must have gone to work the second shift. She loved it when Reggie worked the second shift because it was her chance to be alone.

Blackjack headed straight for the spot where his bowl used to sit. She found a bag of cat food and shook the last few crumbs into a cracked china bowl. "Sorry, buddy, that's it. You've been gone for days. I'll have to walk back to the store."

Blackjack turned to stare at her licking crumbs from his whiskers.

"Oh, all right, let me look." She pulled back the curtain she had hung over the pantry and searched through the rusting forgotten cans of beans and soup. "How would you like a nice bowl of tuna, Blackjack?"

She dumped tuna into his bowl and grabbed one of Reggie's Pabst Blue Ribbons from the fridge. She sat at the table drinking the cold beer and laughing at Blackjack munching tuna like it would be his last and purring at the same time. She leaned back, closed her eyes, singing.

In the middle of *Stop in the Name of Love,* the beads on the door between the kitchen and the rest of the bungalow rattled. She froze. The hairs on the back of her neck prickled. It wasn't Blackjack. Did he have a friend? How did it get in? She turned.

"Afternoon." Reggie threw an empty PBR can in the trash. Hard. He stood motionless except for his darting eyes. " Why you feeding that cat my lunch tuna?"

"I'll get you some more. I have to go get cat food. I thought you were working."

He fixed his eyes on hers. "Kenneth said he saw you get off the bus at that white girl's house."

Sergeant Kenneth Sawyers was Reggie's direct supervisor. His busty blonde wife left him six months ago. Already balding and thirty pounds overweight, he was a woman-hater.

"Why'd you get off there?"

"To help my friend Ruby Jean. She has trouble reading."

"And Ruby Jean has a brother. You expecting him to come over? Is that why you all happy and singing?" The tilt of his head was like a suspicious father questioning a guilty child.

"No, nobody's coming over, Reggie."

"You're lying. You're a lying bitch."

He slammed her beer on the floor. It splattered on the lime green kitchen wall. He slapped her, and she fell out of her chair. She couldn't tell if the ringing was in her head or if their older model Frigidaire was humming. Blackjack hissed and spat. Reggie left.

She pulled herself up just like she always did. Reggie didn't hit her that much in the beginning. A few times he'd even apologized.

After she met Reggie, Callie's life stopped going in the direction, she had planned. Her dream had been to leave Frogmoor and stay with her mother, Della, in Memphis. Della had gotten discovered by a talent scout while singing a solo at the First Baptist Church in Raleigh. He got her a job as a backup singer for groups like Martha and the Vandellas. But when Reggie bought her a princess ring and asked her to marry him, she had gone over the moon. She'd have a husband and younguns that knew who their daddy was. They planned to wait until she graduated, but by Thanksgiving, wedding bliss fever caught her in its grip. She thought about how pretty a Christmas wedding would be. She would wear the white linen dress she was saving for graduation, and they'd have a candlelight ceremony at the little church where she was baptized.

So that's just what she did. Candles glowed in polished brass candelabras. Lucy's sister, Aunt Lettie, decorated the sanctuary with sprigs of real holly, mistletoe Reggie shot down with an air rifle from the tall oaks behind the bungalow, and red, satiny ribbons.

But then like the candlelight the choir boy snuffed out, happiness went up in smoke. It turned out Reggie had a bad temper. He took it out on her in the form of slaps and punches. It could be jealousy one day and a cold supper the next. Reggie had said he didn't care if she went to the white school, but now, all it took was a sideways glance from a white boy to stir up trouble. Callie walked a mile and back to Frogmoor General Store to ride the bus with the white students to Wesley High School. Mr. Avery, the bus driver, wouldn't go past the railroad tracks and out to the bungalow, but when a representative from the State Board of Education came to Callie's school at the end of last semester to recruit volunteers, she had jumped at the chance to be one of the first colored people to register at Wesley. It would give her a chance to see how she fit in. The kids shunned her at school as long as she could remember, but she found Wesley to be no different. White kids whispered *nigger* behind her back and the few Negro students called her Mulatto and high yellow bitch. Ruby Jean, a white girl Callie called RJ was her only friend.

She got no sympathy from Lucy. She showed her a busted lip once after it had almost healed, but she only laughed and said, "As long as nothing's broke, you ought not to complain. You ain't got to make somebody else's beds and scrub their toilets like I did when I was your age. Anyway, Reggie's a cop."

Callie had believed her grandmother meant well when she set her up with Reggie. She could finally "find her place" with him. But the pieces of a giant puzzle had been floating around all Callie's life. Come to find out, it had all been a part of a plan—a plan Clarence had helped her understand. Her cousin Clarence grew out of his coke-bottle glasses and acne, drove a bread delivery truck part-time, and enrolled in criminal justice classes. His main goal in life was to be a private detective. The skill he had perfected first was eavesdropping. He told her stuff he heard Lucy and his grandma, Aunt Lettie talking about. Then it all came together like one of those thousand-piece jigsaw puzzles. The last piece was the letter. She found it a month after the wedding when she returned the cultured pearl necklace Lucy let her wear for something borrowed. Lucy hadn't been home when she went to put it back in the cedar box on her dresser. There it was, with the familiar handwriting.

The side of her face was on fire. She popped open a tray of ice cubes, put some in a washcloth and sat at the table thinking. She couldn't go back to Lucy's. If she did, she feared she would lose control of her life. As far as she could see, she had one choice. After graduation, she would leave and go to Memphis to find Della. She would be as free as a songbird to sing her way to stardom with Della in Memphis, amidst the music world where unlike here, biracial people were accepted and even admired.

But the problem was Lucy wouldn't tell her exactly how to get in touch with Della. Callie wondered if she even knew herself. Della didn't call that much. The last time she had been home was for Granddaddy Moses's funeral four years ago. She had secretly wished on the evening star that Della would show up for the wedding. *Starlight, star bright. I wish I may, I wish I might.* Maybe Lucy would call and they'd surprise her. It didn't happen. But she'd find her somehow. She'd get a job there and be on her own. First, she had to find a way to put some money aside. She hoped she would make it before she got herself killed.

∞ ∞ ∞

Ruby Jean Carson wiped the sweat from her mother's brow. She took her by the hand and whispered, "What is it, Mama? Are you hurting?"

"No, baby, I'm not. That medicine's working."

"What's wrong then, Mama?"

"Ruby Jean, did you tell your friend she'd better go home?"

"Yes, I did, Mama. She left."

She had watched as her best friend Callie walked the rest of the way home. Poor Callie. It didn't look like she cared much about Reggie. Not like on TV where Laura loved Rob. Or Lucy loved Ricky.

Mama closed her eyes. "I'm sorry, honey. Call Roy home from work. Tell him it's an emergency and to get here as quick as he can." She opened fearful eyes and looked at Ruby Jean.

"Then when he gets here, tell him to hide them kitchen knives he sharpened the other day. Tell him to hide them good."

"You saw a picture again, didn't you?"

Her mother nodded.

Seeing a picture was how Ruby Jean had been explaining Mama's gift, as she called it since she was twelve years old. Mama said Ruby Jean didn't have good control of her emotions sometimes. She used it sometimes to keep Ruby Jean from doing something she might have to spend time in prison for. In other words, to keep her from killing her daddy, Raeford Lee Carson, a man everyone called Snake for a reason. She knew it frightened her mother more than anyone's worst nightmare.

Roy had given their mother her afternoon medications and a bowl of soup with crackers before he left for his job at the grocery store. She gave her mother's hand a squeeze wondering where their daddy was. It was a slow time of the year for tobacco farmers. The only thing to do was to keep checking on what was curing and when it was ready. That and planting seedlings to set out in the fields in the spring. Easy. Why wasn't he home to help take care of their sick mother? There was only one answer. He had been at Ledford's all afternoon. Ledford's was a gas station that sold cigarettes, soft drinks, a few groceries, motor oil, live bait and the Ledford brother's homemade liquor. They sold it in pint jars under the counter to certain customers from two other surrounding dry counties. The station also had a secret room in the back where the men gambled.

Ruby Jean swallowed and promised she would call right away with a message about an emergency.

"Call who?

Ruby Jean turned. Snake Carson leaned against the door jamb. It didn't take more than a gnat's brain to see he was tanked.

"I saw that nigra leaving. What did *she* want?"

"She was helping me with my schoolwork, Daddy."

Callie and Ruby Jean sat beside each other in chorus and English. She got off the bus with Ruby Jean that afternoon after she caught her spilling tears over her homework on the long ride home. Miss Wilson picked Ruby Jean to read Juliette in Romeo and Juliette Act II for tomorrow. Callie had helped her a little, but she had to leave before Snake came home. The only other time she had gone home with Ruby Jean, he had yelled at Callie to *git off his property and stay off.*

"Ruby Jean, you can't learn nothing. The school said so. Face it. You might as well get to hoein'." Snake snorted an ugly laugh. "Come here, and I'll show you how to stay out of the fields."

Ruby Jean's mind left her body. She brushed past Snake and walked the few steps to the kitchen. Mama didn't say anything about hiding Grandma's old iron skillet. She grabbed it blindly and went into the bedroom with it behind her back. She whacked Snake over the head with it. Since he was already ten sheets in the wind, it didn't take much to knock him to the floor.

"Come here, Ruby Jean." Ida Carson ran her fingers through Ruby Jean's hair and kissed her on the forehead laughing and crying at the same time.

She had never seen her do that.

"Ruby Jean, leave. Go to your Aunt Peggy's. Her number is in my Bible. The boys will be okay with their daddy. You won't be," she added softly.

Ruby Jean ran the half-mile to Frogmoor General Store where Roy worked. She went through the line and bought a pack of Juicy Fruit gum with a dime she dug out of her pocket. Roy recognized her look. He ran her a receipt, gave her back three pennies and told her to wait for him. He'd be on a break in fifteen minutes

She took her gum and sat outside on the brick wall behind the store. Roy would come here to smoke. She opened a piece of gum and rolled it up jelly-roll style like Mama showed her to do when she was little. She sat chewing the gum, thinking. Mama had kept her out of trouble a lot, she guessed. But not this time. She hadn't been able to stop herself from whacking Snake on the head with Grandma's cast-iron skillet. What if she had killed him? The gum lost its flavor. Ruby Jean opened another piece, rolled it up, and popped it in her mouth. She thought of what Mama said about the knives. She knew her mother was using her gift to warn her. Losing your temper could be a very bad thing. Now her mother was dying. The gift would die with her.

Her mother had tried to make her understand the gift. She had been about fourteen she guessed. "Close your eyes and pretend you have another eye in the middle," Ida Carson would say, "Think about a problem. Ask for a picture to help you with it." Ruby Jean stopped chewing. She sat still thinking about the third eye on her forehead. She did not want to go to her Aunt Peggy's house. She didn't like Aunt Peggy or her cousins. They treated her like she was retarded. She wasn't, she just had to work harder to learn stuff. That was the biggest problem besides her mother being so sick. Think. Then she saw them. The pictures that flashed like a movie in her head didn't stay long. But she saw enough. It was like Mama had said. Callie. She had to warn Callie.

Chapter 2

The knocking on the glass of the door startled her.

"Callie, it's me, Ruby Jean. Can you come out a minute?"

RJ. What was she doing here? Callie opened the door holding a washcloth full of ice cubes to her mouth. Another busted lip. She had looked in the bathroom mirror, and it seemed like her eye wasn't turning black.

"Come on in, Ruby Jean. Reggie's not here." Funny how she called her Ruby Jean now that she was in her own house. "I didn't think you'd walk all the way out here. Sit down."

"What's wrong, Callie? What's wrong with your lip?"

"I fell. What're you doing out here? It's a long way for you to walk."

Blackjack jumped up on Ruby Jean's lap. She stroked the cat's black fur, so black it was almost blue.

"Callie, Mama's dying."

"I thought she might be. I'm sorry, Ruby Jean."

"Mama has a gift. It's a gift she's leaving to me."

Callie could only think of rings, or a watch, or maybe a rare copy of the Bible. "A gift?"

"Yeah. She sees pictures. Not everybody does."

"What do you mean, she sees pictures?"

"She sees things that will happen. Just when she needs to, though."

"You mean things that will happen in the future?"

"Yes, and she stops bad stuff from happening, like me killing Snake. But I might have already killed him."

"What?"

She told her about the ugly things Snake had said and how she brained him with her grandmother's skillet.

"Oh, my, gosh. What did you do then?"

"I left to go get Roy. He's working, but he knows something's up. He'll go home. But listen. Now I can do it."

"What do you mean, you can do it?"

"I tried to figure things out. That's when I found out I can see pictures, too. I have the gift."

"Okay. So what did you see?"

"For some reason, it was about you. Reggie was dead, and you were sitting in jail."

Callie laughed. "You're not serious, RJ." She was back to calling her chum RJ since she had gotten over the initial shock of her coming all the way out to the neighborhood across the railroad tracks.

"Yes, I am, Callie. I'm not smart in reading, and math, and all that, but I promise you, I know what I'm talking about."

"How can you be sure it's not just your imagination?"

Ruby Jean tightened her forehead and squinted. "I've done seen it before. I remember one time when the Thompsons from down the road's little boy got lost in the woods. Mama saw a vision and walked down to tell them. They found him a few hours later."

Callie's eyes widened. "Really?"

"Yeah, and that's not all. She packed everybody up and got on the bus with all of us for Tennessee three days before her mother died. She knew."

Callie had heard of things like that before. She remembered hearing Aunt Lettie, Lucy's sister, talk about a friend that had dreams about people dying, and then they died not long after. Ruby Jean might as well hear the truth. Somebody needed to. "RJ" she began. "Maybe it's time we talked." She locked the doors of the bungalow and sat across from RJ.

"Are you sure Reggie won't be home before midnight?"

"He was already home. He left." She reached over and picked up the washcloth with the ice cubes melting inside of it. "He did this."

"What? Oh, no, Callie. I better leave."

Callie shook her head, agitated. "No. Don't go. We need each other."

Ruby Jean looked toward the kitchen door and at the beaded entrance from the back.

"Don't worry. If I hear him at one door, I'll let you out the other. Anyway, he either went back to work or to Ledford's."

"Why'd he hit you, Callie? Has he hit you before?"

"Yeah, he has a temper." She sighed. "His sergeant saw me get off the bus at your house. He knows you've got a brother that's old enough to—well, Reggie's real jealous of white boys. You've probably noticed I'm, well, different."

"I know, you're mixed. Why'd you marry him? You never seem like you're in a hurry to go home to him."

"The answer to that is the first part of what I have to tell you." Callie got another one of Reggie's beers. Heck, she was already in trouble over the tuna. He wasn't here to knock this one out of her hand. "RJ, do you want one of these?"

Ruby Jean scrunched her nose. "Unh-unh."

Callie pulled the tab on the aluminum can, and beer spewed like an erupting volcano. She mopped up the sudsy foam with a dirty kitchen towel. "I can remember when I didn't think there was a difference. My granddaddy used to take me all kinds of places in his little orange truck. Most of the people we visited were always darker than me, but it didn't seem to make any difference. As I got older, it did. Then Grandpa got hit by a train, in his truck, crossing the railroad tracks."

Callie grew quiet, thinking about how much she still missed Moses Gibbs. She wouldn't be sitting here today if he was alive. "Della, my Mama, had already taken off for Memphis, so I was left with Lucy." She told Ruby Jean about Della getting a job out in Memphis after a talent scout heard her solo in church that time. "She sings backup for popular groups out there like Martha and the Vandellas, when they come to town, and a few others."

"So that's why you can sing so good. It runs in your blood."

Callie shrugged. "But you've got a nice voice too, RJ."

"Nothing like you, though. It sure don't run in my blood. But Mama's gift does. And like I said, I'm smart in the ways of the world and people. Now I find out that boy's been hitting you. Can't you leave and go stay with Lucy?"

"I wish it was that easy." She hugged herself against the chilly kitchen. The only space heater was in the back room. She looked at RJ. It was hard to begin.

"I remember when I was about ten I found an envelope and a check laying on the dining room table. It had both Lucy and Della's name on it. A few months after that I saw the same thing again when I went to get chewing gum out of Lucy's pocketbook. We were at church, and she'd gone to the bathroom. I got to watching and seeing mail come from the same address in Raleigh. They always had a classy look—cream-colored with nice handwriting and pretty stamps. After a while, I asked Lucy and Della about it. At first, they would tell me it was none of my business. Finally, one day my mama, Della, told me. It wasn't long before she left to go to Memphis. My daddy is a white man. He's the son of the people Della worked for. Rich people, right outside of Raleigh. And today I know just who those people are."

Callie finished her beer and tossed the can into the trashcan by the door. She stopped talking; she needed to see RJ's reaction.

"Well, I know what was in the fancy envelopes. Money. And it should have been. Mama's niece had a baby out of wedlock. I remember her talking on the phone with my grandma about it. They got blood tests these days that'll tell who the daddy is. They had to pay your Mama support." Ruby propped an elbow on the table. "But what's that got to do with you and…" She didn't say his name but nodded toward the door.

Callie looked up at the sagging ceiling tiles and sighed. "Well, you see, things just didn't happen overnight. The older I got, the more I understood what was going on. Then when Clarence stopped being a bratty kid, he told me stuff he heard Aunt Lettie and Lucy talk about. One time he told me Aunt Lettie told Lucy she ought to stop spending so much money on herself and spend it on me. Later I found more than checks. I found a letter. Since I'm married, these people want to pay for me to go to the Negro college. That's my only choice. They're bribing Lucy to keep me with colored folks.

"What does bribing mean?"

"It means giving somebody money to make them do what you want them to do."

Ruby Jean looked puzzled. "What did they not want you to do?"

Callie slammed her fist on the table. "They want to keep me a *secret*!"

Blackjack arched up and hissed. Callie unlocked the door and let him out. She turned to RJ and lowered her voice. "Because of who they are. And that's all I can say."

Ruby Jean shifted in her chair. "I understand. But still, what about Reggie? And you said there was another part of what you wanted to tell me."

Callie stood up and walked over to the kitchen door, pulling back the curtain. Stars winked in the late winter dusk.

"Oh, RJ. Look how bright that evening star is. That's Venus." Without turning around, she said, "I don't want anybody making me go to any school, let alone the Negro school. That brings me to what I really need to tell you, RJ."

Ruby Jean sat as still as a cornered animal. "What?"

"I've been planning to up and run away. Heck, I'm almost nineteen years old, I should call it leaving home. I can be on my own if I get away from Reggie and Lucifer. I had planned on heading out toward Memphis and find Della after I graduated. But now you've got me spooked with all this talk about seeing me in jail and Reggie dead."

"I'm sorry, Callie, but I can't help it. Something's going to happen. And now Mama's dying and wants me to go live with my Aunt Peggy. I told you about her, remember? Her and my stinking cousins that always look down on me. I can't stand the thought of doing that. And if I stay here, with Mama gone, I'll end up killing Snake. I know that. But the picture I saw of Reggie dead, and you in jail tells me you and I are in this together."

Callie opened a can of Campbell's tomato soup and turned on the eye of the two-burner stove.

"I say we need to head on out together. That's about the only way you can get away from Snake and keep from going to your Aunt Peggy's. And my fate is as bad as or worse than yours if I stay around here much longer."

"You mean us run away together?

"Yep."

Ruby Jean's winter pale skin flushed. "I was hoping maybe you'd say that." She smiled. "I feel safe with you, Callie."

Callie told RJ to call the store and see if her brother Roy went home. He did. Snake wasn't dead; he had come to, drank the rest of the liquor, and gone to bed. She turned on a green plastic radio and tuned to a station in Raleigh.

Ruby Jean and Callie ate bowls of hot tomato soup with Zesta saltines crushed into it listening to hit songs on the radio. The Temptations sang about my girl, the Zombies said to tell her no, and Gary Lewis and the Playboys sang about a diamond ring that didn't shine anymore.

Callie said the best thing to do was act like they were going to school next Monday morning and just leave. They could pack bags the night before and leave them in the Carson's barn. Their plans included getting Clarence to help them and staying in touch with Clarence and Roy without telling them exactly where they were. And she would stay home tomorrow and go to Lucifer's house and look around for money. If she had to, she'd tell her grandmother she needed money to go to the doctor.

They'd get to Memphis, get a motel room, and get jobs. Anything to begin with, and then she'd look for Della Gibbs. Callie would find a way to convince her mother to help her get a job singing. After all, she had the letter.

Chapter 3

Ruby Jean got up on Monday morning when the first rooster crowed. She dressed in her newest dungarees and a black sweatshirt Roy outgrew. Her other jeans and shirts and five school outfits were packed and waiting in the barn as planned. Clarence took Callie to the Army surplus store on Saturday in Raleigh and got Army duffle bags for them. She thought she heard rain pattering on the roof, but she tiptoed in the kitchen and saw bacon and eggs sizzling in the same skillet she knocked Snake out with. Roy had gotten up early and started breakfast.

"Good morning, Baby Girl. Are you sure you still want to go through with this?"

She looked around the tiny kitchen. Home was hell, but it was familiar. She thought how much she'd miss Roy. He turned twenty in January and was the closest in age, only eighteen months older than her. The twins, Bobby and Ben, were fifteen, and Junior, Raeford Lee Carson's namesake, was eleven.

"I've just got to, Roy. I don't even want to know how life would be for me here with Mama gone."

"I was hoping you'd go to Aunt Peggy's for a while. I should be able to get my own place soon. You'd have a place to live."

"I can't go stay with her, Roy. Not even for a minute. Aunt Peggy treats me like I'm retarded, and them stinking girls of hers make faces at each other about me. They're too stupid to know I see it."

Roy sighed. "I understand. I wish they wouldn't do that. Are you gonna eat breakfast before you go?"

"How many more minutes is it until six o'clock?"

Roy glanced at the clock. "About ten."

"I'd better not. I want to see Mama."

"Well, here." He sat a brown bag on the table. "I brought stuff home from the store last night and made ya'll sandwiches."

"How sweet, Roy, thank you. I'll call you. I've got my money I've been saving up, and we'll get jobs."

Ruby Jean had rolled up her life savings, thirty-eight dollars and seventy-two cents in one of Mama's hankies and shoved it into the bowels of the army duffle bag out in the barn.

"You better. Call me on the way if you can."

"I will, Roy, I promise. It's not like I'm disappearing. I have to get out on my own, and this seems like a good way. I trust Callie. She'll be good to me."

Even though she didn't tell Roy about the vision, she knew that was the truth. She'd been afraid Roy would think she only wanted to help Callie escape. She gave him one last hug and picked up the bag of sandwiches.

"I'm gonna go kiss Mama bye, and then I'm gone. I love you, Roy."

"I love you too, Ruby Jean."

The only light in the windowless room was the glow of a nightlight by the bed. She watched as Mama slept. The medicine the doctor gave her kept her comfortable, but she slept a lot. Ruby Jean had known Mama was sick for a while, but she kept hanging on to the belief she would get better. She prayed. Roy prayed. And she could see in the twins' faces, and Junior's too, that they weren't giving up hope for Mama to get better. But the last time Doc Turner came out, he said she would need to go to the hospital soon. Ruby Jean knew it wasn't for her to get better.

She leaned and whispered, "Mama, I'm leaving now. Don't worry about me, okay? I'll be all right. I love you, Mama." The tears came like salty rivers flowing down her cheeks to splash on her lips. She hugged her mother one last time.

She walked out on the porch past the swing with its rusty chains and peeling paint, the swing where just a few days ago she sat with Callie wrapped up in a dingy blanket against the February chill. It was the day she knocked Snake out cold with the skillet.

She'd never forget how Mama half laughed and half cried. *Ruby Jean, go away. Call my sister in Tennessee.*

That's what she was doing, leaving. Just not to Aunt Peggy's. She gave the swing a little push and ran to meet Clarence and Callie at the barn.

Daylight had yet to break, but a full moon lit the long path from the house to the barn. In only a few minutes, Clarence's bread truck, headlights off, crept up the dirt road that turned in from the highway. He parked and turned the engine off.

Callie jumped out, whispering. "You made it! Let's go. Clarence has a delivery near Charlotte, so he's taking us to the bus station there. We'll be two hours closer to Memphis."

They tossed the duffle bags in the back with a load of bread and got in the front. Clarence took off, and Frogmoor disappeared behind them. Soon the back roads turned into the interstate. Their plans became real. Ruby Jean Carson and Callie Gibbs had left home.

∞ ∞ ∞

The Charlotte Trailways station was even bigger than the one in Raleigh. They walked past rows and rows of silver buses hissing and puffing like huge dragons with different cities printed on their foreheads. Ruby Jean turned when Callie turned, following closely. When Mama took them to Tennessee, they lost Junior and had to have him called over the loudspeaker. She didn't intend to start life on her own that way. Thank goodness, though, Callie knew what she was doing. She wouldn't begin to know how to get the tickets.

Callie stopped and pointed. "Okay, that's where we need to go, right over there. She sat her bag down, dug into her pocket, and pulled out a twenty-dollar bill. "This ought to get us two one-way tickets to Memphis, but we'll have to make a couple of transfers. And these buses stop at every Podunk town along the way. You stay here with our things, and I'll go get the tickets."

Ruby Jean watched Callie wait in line until a man called her to the window. The man looked at the clock behind him and said something to Callie. Ruby Jean saw something was wrong the minute she saw Callie turn and walk back.

"What's wrong, Callie?"

She sighed. "Oh, nothing, except the bus we needed pulled out fifteen minutes ago. The next one doesn't leave until six o'clock tonight. Crap."

"Well, we'll just have to wait here until then."

Callie looked around. "I don't think that's such a good idea. Maybe not you, you're covered because they think you left for your aunt's, but I'll be a sitting target for Reggie when he figures out I'm gone."

"But Reggie thinks you're in school."

"But I won't be coming home from school. By six o'clock he could have gotten with his buddy Sawyers and put a lookout at bus stations."

"What'll we do? Can't we hide or something?"

Callie looked around. "We need to be moving. I've got an idea. Follow me."

She followed Callie across the busy street and up the highway. "Where are we going, Callie?"

She pointed ahead. "We're going back to that truck stop we passed on the way here."

"What for?"

"You'll see."

Callie took her hand, and they walked past stores with big windows weaving in and out of the crowds. Ruby Jean wished they hadn't missed the bus to Memphis. What was going on?

Why were they going to a truck stop? But she trusted Callie, so she didn't ask.

$$\infty\infty\infty$$

The truck stop had a grill in the back with a few booths. A short-order cook in a dirty white shirt flipped burgers and eggs at the same time. They ordered waffles, coffee for Callie, and a Pepsi for Ruby Jean. Callie's plan was to hitch a ride with a truck driver. She started talking to the man sitting beside them. She lied. She told him her name was Nellie Wilson. Nellie Wilson was one of their teacher's names. She said Ruby Jean was her sister and that they were too late to get tickets for the bus in Charlotte after their Cousin Clarence dropped them off. That was true, but then she lied again. She told him their grandmother passed and they left to go stay with their mother who had gotten a job a few months ago singing in Memphis. She became a backup singer for popular soul and blues groups. That part was true, according to Callie, and Ruby Jean had no reason to doubt it. But Callie's mother, Della left for Memphis years, not months ago. And Ruby Jean didn't look a thing like Callie except for her toffee-colored eyes. Straight brown hair and floppy bangs framed Ruby Jean's face and her lips were thin. Callie's was like coffee with extra cream and surrounded by curly reddish hair. Her lips were full and pouty. He looked at them funny a few times, too nice to mention it, Ruby Jean guessed.

His name was Matthew Prescott. She'd been afraid of him at first. He wore his curly black hair down to his collar, and he hadn't shaved in a while. That reminded her of Snake on what Mama called a bender. But then he told them he was a preacher on Sundays in a town outside of Tuscaloosa.

"Preaching doesn't pay much," he explained. "They provide a nice house for us, but the salary is small."

The preacher trucker had a wife and two little girls. Ruby Jean wished for a sister for as long as she could remember. She imagined two little girls in pretty dresses tied with sashes, clean faces, brushed hair, and lacy socks with shoes. They would run to their daddy when he came through the door calling their names. He'd pick them up one at a time and hug them while their mother watched, smiling. He'd reach into his pocket and pull out little boxes with necklaces in them while they squealed with delight.

Matthew Prescott traced a route in the air with his finger. "Tuscaloosa is south of Birmingham. I'm headed home, so you'll need to leave me in Birmingham. There's a truck stop outside the city with a bus station inside. You should be able to get a ticket to Memphis, it's only five hours from there. It's not even a station, really, but I'd get my tickets right away if I were you."

"We will. I'm glad we missed that bus," Callie said. "Instead of sleeping on the bus tonight, we'll be checking into a motel in Memphis."

Sleeping on a bus sounded romantic to Ruby Jean, but Callie looked relaxed and happy. She knew it was because of Reggie, but she wished she hadn't lied about her name. Mama always said lies beget lies.

Chapter 4

Matthew Prescott, the preacher-trucker, pulled into the Esso truck stop in Birmingham's outer city limits. Behind a row of big rigs, an oversized gas station boasted clean bathrooms, hot showers, and home-cooked food. A yellow sign you had to look for marked the Trailways Bus Station.

"Here you go. You shouldn't have any problem getting the tickets, but I'll wait here just in case."

Both girls hopped out, and Callie went to get the tickets. Ruby Jean checked out a shelf of souvenirs like Little Black Sambo statues and Aunt Jemima salt and pepper shakers. A white-haired man roused himself away from a portable TV and told her the next bus to Memphis was due in one hour and fifty-five minutes. She looked at the money she was about to pull out of her wallet. It had been so easy to hitch a free ride. What if they could do it again? She stuffed the money back in her wallet.

Back out front, they waved, hands high. Matthew Prescott blew his air horn.

"Come on, RJ, I'll treat you to a burger and fries. It's past lunchtime, and I'm starved."

They used the truck stop bathroom to spruce up, taking turns at the toilet and splashing cold water on their faces at the rusty sink. Callie dug into her duffle bag for her wallet and bought a pack of Salems and a roadmap on the way out.

They both had cheeseburgers and took their time sharing a large order of fries swirling them around in piles of ketchup they poured out on the empty cheeseburger wrappers. With the last fry gone, Callie pulled out a cigarette and lit it.

Ruby Jean fanned the smoke. "How much time do we have left, Callie? Are you keeping up?"

Callie squinted to see the clock above the bus ticket window. "Almost an hour."

"Did you get the tickets?"

"Not yet."

"Why didn't you get them right away, like you told that man we would?"

"Don't worry, RJ, I'll get them." She spread the map out on the table. "See here? This is where we are. It's not that far to Memphis. What if we found another ride? Think of the time we'd save from the bus stopping at all these little towns." She flicked her ashes into the little tin ashtray. "It's like this. I only have so much money. The more on our own we can be the better."

"But what if—"

"We won't miss the bus again, I promise. If nothing happens in thirty minutes, I'll go buy the tickets."

It was late for lunch and early for supper. Only a young couple sat in a booth in the back.

Callie fished a five-dollar bill and a driver's license from her wallet. The driver's license said she was Nellie Wilson, born on August 3, 1943. She had used her own for the last time when she cashed a check she stole out of Lucy's pocketbook last Friday. Clarence took her over. Lucy was busy frying chicken, and Clarence walked down to Aunt Lettie's house. That's when Callie saw it: Lucy's black patent leather pocketbook sat on the mantle. She took it down and opened the snap lock. It was full of dirty handkerchiefs, Rolaids, Wrigley's spearmint gum, and Lucy's blue checkbook full of blank checks. Callie tore one off and snapped the purse shut. She folded it and put it in her pocket. It had been no problem cashing the check made out to for three hundred dollars. She signed it C. Lucy Gibbs and showed the teller her own driver's license, the one she left behind with Clarence.

She tucked Nellie Wilson's driver's license into the pocket of her jeans in case she needed it for the tickets. For now, she was officially Nellie Wilson, and it was time to explain that to RJ.

Callie took one last drag on her cigarette and stubbed it out. "Once we get to Memphis, we'll get a cheap place to stay. I'm old enough to do most anything legally now. And for those I'm not…" she paused and opened her wallet, "I've got this." She laid the driver's license on the table.

Ruby Jean picked it up and examined it. "That's Miss Wilson. How did you get that?"

"One day when you had the flu, she got called to the office to fill out some kind of paperwork. She took her driver's license out and left for a few minutes. When she came back in, I saw her lay it on her desk and forget it. I snuck in at lunch and took it. I told you, I've been planning this a while."

"You did the ink?"

Callie nodded. "She has olive skin, and with the ink smudge, I can pass for her. And she's not that much older than me."

"That wasn't a nice thing to do. What if she needs it?"

"She can get another one. It's easy. Besides, I'm not going to use it for anything bad. What if I get a singing contract in Memphis and need to be at least twenty-one? This way, I'm covered. I'll tell everybody you're my sister and we'll have it made."

"Callie, I don't think we much look like sisters."

"We can pass it off. I'm half white, and it's Memphis. The music industry loves mixed. For once I'll fit in. Don't you want to break into the music business someday? You can sing, you know. Like a little lark."

"Gosh, I'd love to, but it would be scary. What if I'm not good enough? Hey, Callie, I saw a phone booth outside. Do you think I've got time to call Roy?"

"Sure. We'll get the tickets after you do that. And listen, if we get around people be sure and call me Nellie, not Callie. Nellie Wilson."

"Okay." Ruby Jean started to open her bag, but Callie stopped her.

"Here." She gave her a handful of coins. "Remember, don't

tell him exactly where we are. And tell him to call Clarence."

Outside, Callie lit a cigarette and stood around waiting on RJ. She pat the pocket of her jeans with Nellie Wilson's driver's license in it. Reggie Knight would likely issue a search for her. Having a different ID would make hiding easier. One good thing about the bus, it took the back roads. Reggie wouldn't figure out where she was. She could start a new life, and he wouldn't be able to do anything about it.

∞ ∞ ∞

Ruby Jean picked up the clunky receiver, dropped a dime in the slot and dialed. Nothing happened. She opened her hand and looked at the pile of change Callie gave her. She deposited another quarter. Mr. Jones at Frogmoor General answered and called Roy to the phone.

She smiled big when he answered. "Hey, Roy. It's me."

"Hey. Where are you? Did ya'll find somewhere to stay?"

"Well, no, not exactly."

A heavy sigh came over the phone line. "Where are you then?"

"I can't tell you. How's Mama?"

"About the same. Listen, Ruby Jean, ya'll need to get off the road. Reggie's already been over here looking for Callie. Can't she ask that mother of hers to help?"

"She's got plenty of money, Roy. It's just that we've had good luck hitching. We're saving money to get a motel room in Memphis. Then we'll find Della."

Ruby Jean watched from the phone booth as a couple in skinny jeans, boots, and heavy sweaters talked to Callie. She was lighting their cigarettes with her matches. Something didn't seem right. The operator's voice came on. *Please deposit fifty cents for the next five minutes.*

"I gotta go, Roy. What did you tell, Mama?"

"I told her Callie's cousin put you on the bus in Raleigh to go to Aunt Peggy's. Ya'll get off the road soon, you hear? If Reggie catches up with ya'll you better let me know."

"We will. I promise. Oh, and call—"

The phone went dead. She wished she could have talked to Roy longer, but she didn't want to take advantage of the hefty pile of change Callie had given her. She pushed the phone booth open and watched Callie and the couple for a minute before stepping out of it. She tried concentrating, wanting to connect with that third eye she had experienced, but nothing would come. She looked down at the change in her hand and put it inside her shoe.

Ruby Jean approached the three of them cautiously. She remembered them now. They had sat in the back booth making out. Callie hadn't seen them because they sat behind her.

"Hey, RJ. Everything at home all right? Is everybody okay? Did you tell them *Nellie* said hey?"

Ruby Jean knew to play along. " 'Bout the same."

"RJ, this is Babs and Dale. Guess what? They're headed to Tupelo. And they know all the back roads. Once we get there, it's just a hop and a jump up to Memphis." Callie clapped her fists together. "Yay! I told Dale I'd even buy his gas, but he said nonsense. He asked if we were lost or something because of how hard I was looking at that map. Oh, and they needed a light." Callie laughed, and the others joined in. "And this is my little sister, Ruby Jean."

Ruby Jean waited while they finished smoking and talking. Callie told them the same story about their grandmother and going out to stay with their mother, a singer in Memphis. She laid it on thick.

"Yeah, Granny's gone. Time to go start a new life." Callie tossed her Salem on the ground and stomped on it.

Dale and Babs looked like a nice couple. Babs had short, cute dark curls poking out of a corduroy beret. Dale was clean-cut, a red and white University of Alabama ball cap hiding a head with not a lot of hair. What seemed odd to Ruby Jean was that Dale and Babs didn't look at them funny like the preacher-trucker did. Maybe she shouldn't be so nervous. They crawled into a Volkswagen van that had seen better days.

∞∞∞

Dale drove the battered green and white van away from the outskirts of Birmingham. Businesses disappeared, and traffic dwindled. One of those ugly plastic troll dolls with pink hair and a half-dozen tarnished chains dangled from the rearview mirror. Callie and RJ bounced around in the back seat. It would be a rough ride. But all the way to Tupelo! One short journey away from Memphis.

"Bad shocks," Dale said.

"That's okay. I'm okay. You okay, RJ?"

Ruby Jean looked sideways at Callie. "I hope so," she said quietly.

After an awkward few minutes of silence, Babs spoke up. "So, going to Memphis, huh?"

"Yep," Callie answered.

Ruby Jean nodded.

Babs turned around in the van's passenger seat. "How long has your Mama been in Memphis?"

Callie and Ruby Jean spoke at the same time. Callie told them her mother left when she was fourteen and a year popped out of Ruby Jean's mouth.

Callie thought quickly. "Well, it's been a year since her last visit." She saw Babs and Dale exchange glances. The highway roared not far beneath their feet. Several rusty spots would soon give way to a view of the asphalt beneath them. The van's radio crackled between two stations. Roger Miller crooned about being King of the Road while a reporter talked about Malcolm X's assassination in New York.

Dale shushed them while tuning into the news. "Listen.

They shot that nigger causing all the trouble. Blew him straight to hell." He and Babs shrieked with laughter.

Babs had her window down, smoking. But more than the cold air blowing in made Callie shiver. She wasn't all that fond of Malcolm X or Malcolm Little. She learned his real name writing a report on him at her old school. But Dale and Babs's cackling made her fidget. She didn't listen to the news a lot; none of that crazy stuff happened in Frogmoor, North Carolina. But Raleigh wasn't far away. You couldn't help hearing about the big stuff, like when the FBI admitted that white terrorists like the Ku Klux Klan blew up the church where four little innocent Negro girls had their heads blown off. It had happened in Birmingham, Alabama. And they were in Alabama.

Callie glanced over at RJ. She sat as still as a stone statue like she was trying to meditate or something. Dale turned the radio back to music, and he and Babs sang along to the next top country tune.

It occurred to Callie she had been too quick to trust these two. She'd be glad to get the hell out of Alabama, hit Tupelo and then head for Memphis. She settled back to watch for the Mississippi state line. Something wasn't right. She was no world traveler, but the landscape was growing flat and swampy. She dug out her map and checked the past road numbers she had seen. It hit her like an asphalt road had slapped her in the face. They were headed south of Birmingham. Way south. And they wouldn't be mixed-race friendly like Memphis with its music industry.

Callie saw Dale's dark eyes watching her in the rearview mirror. "Checking out them back roads?" he asked.

She swallowed, folded the map back up, and stuck it in the pocket of her duffle bag.

"So who you running from, Nellie Wilson? Why'd you want to go on the back roads? You're in some kinda trouble, ain't you? And that moron you're traveling with ain't your sister any more than I'm Bab's sister."

Babs got the giggles, and they both guffawed for a minute.

"Okay, look, we appreciate the lift, but we'd better get out. We're headed the wrong way."

"Just so happens I got to pee." Dale took out a cigarette and stuck it behind his ear. "I'll pull over in a minute, Miss Daughter of a Nigger Lover."

Babs stifled a laugh.

They drove in silence for a while. Later Dale pulled into the graveled parking lot of a little white clapboard church. He opened the door, stepped out and stretched.

"Come on, RJ, we need to get out here."

"We're in the middle of nowhere, Callie."

"I know. But we got to head back the other way. Somebody will come along. A trucker, maybe."

The girls each picked up their duffle bag and slid out of the van. They turned and walked toward the lonely road in the direction they had come from.

"Hey, look," Dale yelled after them.

They turned around. He had a pistol pointed at them.

"I decided to take you up on that offer for help with gas," he snickered.

Callie froze. Ruby Jean cried.

"Ah, hush, honey. I ain't gonna hurt you," Dale crooned. He turned to Callie. "Let me have that fat wallet you got."

Callie still didn't move.

He waited a second. "Throw it on the ground. Now!" he shouted.

Callie took her wallet out and tossed it toward him.

He walked over and picked it up without taking his eyes or the pistol off them. "Hey, Babs. Get your ass out here and help me."

Babs was brushing her hair. "Oh, okay already." She pulled her beret back down over her curls and got out of the van. "What do you want me to do, Dale?"

"Go through their stuff."

Babs easily found the change from the five-dollar bill at the diner in Callie's jacket pocket. She skipped her jeans pockets and ruffled through Ruby Jean's jacket, then her duffle bag missing the money she had tied up in the handkerchief. Callie drew a silent sigh of relief, glad too that Nellie Wilson's ID was still in her pocket.

"Well, I found a little over two dollars, Dale. Yoo-hoo. I hope you got some loot in that wallet."

"Why didn't you check their pants pockets, dumb ass?"

"I don't see anything sticking out."

"Check anyway, stupid."

"Don't call me stupid." Babs checked RJ's pockets, and then Callie's.

Callie's heart sank when she pulled out Nellie Watson's driver's license.

"Just her stupid driver's license." She tossed it on the ground.

"Pick it back up, dummy, and bring it here."

Callie cringed as she watched Babs pick up Miss Wilson's license and hand it to Dale.

Dale dusted off the license in its plastic sleeve and looked at it an arm's length away like he was farsighted. He glanced at Babs and then back at the driver's license again. "Damn, girl, you could get away with this ID. And it says you're twenty-two. We can buy liquor with this." He tucked it into his shirt pocket and grinned.

"Oh, yeah," Babs said.

Dale ruffled through the bills in his pocket. "Come on, honey, let's go to the liquor store."

"So now I'm honey instead of dumb ass."

"Bye, ya'll. Ruby Jean, you ought to get away from that half-breed." Dale cranked up the van. Gravel spewed as he pulled out of the parking lot of the little white church and headed back toward Birmingham.

Callie picked up the things from her bag they had scattered on the ground. All of her money was gone. So was Nellie Wilson's ID. But she still had the letter.

Chapter 5

The hum of Dale's van faded into the distance leaving only the lonesome cry of a mourning dove in the trees. They calmed down after the shock of having Dale point a gun at them and sat on the church steps trying to figure out what to do. Ruby Jean noticed that Nellie Wilson's driver's license getting gone upset Callie almost as much as losing the money. Thank goodness she still had her hankie full of money, and even Dale hadn't thought of having them take their shoes off. Callie grinned when Ruby Jean showed her the change in her shoe.

Callie looked at the map and said she knew where they were. It was nowhere near Tupelo, but civilization was not too far away. If you call Southern Alabama civilization, she said, and it beat heading back in the other direction.

Ruby Jean didn't argue about not heading back toward Birmingham. It was the way Dale and Babs went. She didn't want to run into them again.

So with the best decision made, they headed for Selma, the next biggest town. Callie said, like Raleigh, there would be stores, communities, even little towns. She called them suburbs.

"We'll use what money we have and find a cheap motel," Callie said. "If they ask for an ID, which I hope they don't, we'll just have to tell them what happened. Then we'll either have to call Roy and Clarence or find jobs. Jobs would be the best thing. Memphis and Della ain't going anywhere."

They drifted through the woods alongside the road shuffling through last year's leaves. The woods weren't as thick as they were before but they stayed hidden between the pines and scrubby oaks as they followed the highway. Both glanced up at the sky often. A few clouds blew by, puffy white ones edged in gray drifting back towards Birmingham. They walked in silence for a long while, each lost in her own thoughts.

Maybe she should call Roy and see if he could wire her the money to get to Aunt Peggy's. Aunt Peggy sent Mama money that way one time. But should she take off for Tennessee on her own? Probably not. She trusted Callie even though they were in a real mess right now. Callie had taught her so much. More than any teacher she knew.

Ruby Jean knew she was different not long after she started school. She couldn't do what most of the other kids could, like write her name and say her letters. By the time she learned, the others had moved on to reading almost anything. It got to where Vonda Ramsey and Shirley Sikes stopped playing with her at recess. And they'd been best friends since first grade. She glanced over at Callie, thinking how glad she was to have a best friend again.

She went to a special class until the eighth grade. Mrs. Shooks helped her patiently. But once she got to high school, she was pretty much on her own. There was a special school, they had told Mama, but it was far away, and Ruby Jean didn't quite fit in. Most of the students were more handicapped, they said. Ruby Jean knew Aunt Peggy would sign her up for a special school as fast as she could say jackrabbit. She heard her tell Mama more than once that the government sent a paycheck to those kids. She decided she should stick with Callie.

Callie broke the silence. "Let's sit down over there on those stumps." She checked the sky again. "For a minute, anyway."

They both took long drinks from the canteens inside their Army bags.

Ruby Jean pulled out the lunch bag Roy had packed. "Look what I threw in, Callie."

They opened bologna with mayonnaise, livermush with mustard, and peanut butter and jelly sandwiches cut in halves and wrapped in waxed paper.

"I'm so glad you thought of this, RJ. I'm starved. Why didn't I think of this?"

"Actually," Ruby Jean began with her mouth full and swallowed. "It was Roy. He brought home a bunch of stuff from the grocery store."

"You're not sorry you came, are you?" Callie asked. "I'd understand if you wanted to go back home."

Ruby Jean took another swig from the canteen. "No, I don't. I'm never going back to that hell hole. We've got that money in Mama's handkerchief."

Callie scoffed. "Well, it might get us a night or two. What exactly did Snake do to you anyway besides work you like a mule in the fields?"

She picked up a stick and poked at the ground, avoiding Callie's eyes. "He just put his hands all over me when he was drunk. Mama pretty much put a stop to it." She flung the stick with a hard backhand. "It's the way he talked down to me all the time. I mean *all* the time."

A few stray raindrops splattered around them.

Callie screwed the lid back on her canteen and dug into her duffle bag. "Bless you, Clarence," she said as she pulled out a yellow plastic poncho. "And I thought he was nuts for buying camping gear."

They had only rifled through the Army duffle bags enough to find the canteens of water, basic first aid kits, and a compass, none of which had interested Dale. Ruby Jean had been playing with her compass twisting and turning it in different directions.

They both opened ponchos ready to put them on as needed and packed the leftover sandwiches back in the paper bag. Ruby Jean wanted to leave a couple of the peanut butter and jelly sandwich halves behind.

"What on earth for?" Callie asked.

"I don't know. A squirrel or raccoon might be hungry."

Callie talked her out of it. "We don't have much money left, remember, RJ?"

"Oh yeah."

They pulled on the ponchos as a few more droplets of chilly rain began to fall.

∞∞∞∞

Ruby Jean and Callie headed for Selma like troopers in yellow ponchos and carrying green United States Army bags. The rain didn't get bad enough to slow them down much. They sang the latest top hits as they trudged along.

The same evening star she had pointed out to RJ through her curtains appeared on the horizon. But tonight, she couldn't heat soup up on the two-burner stove or laugh at Blackjack eating Reggie's tuna and purring. She hoped Clarence meant it when he said he'd take her cat. "Let's get closer to the highway, RJ. I won't be able to see any signs from here in the dark."

Traffic had picked up which was a good thing because it meant they were getting near town and possibly a motel. But it was a bad thing because they would be more likely to have a cop or concerned citizen stop and ask questions. While a ride would be nice, the last thing she wanted was a cop to drive by and question them. Reggie was a cop. She didn't want anything to do with cops. Not now.

The rain picked up. Callie wondered what they would do. Find the thickest trees and hunker down, she supposed.

As if reading her mind, RJ spoke. "What are we gonna do, Callie, if we don't get somewhere soon?"

"Well..." Callie stopped. "Look," she said pointing to the horizon.

"The sunset."

"No, it's not the sunset. Get your compass back out, RJ. The sun, sets in the west."

"Oh. What is it?"

"It's the glow of buildings and businesses."

"You mean the sub…"

"Yeah. Let's go!"

The wooden sign welcomed them to Coosa Springs, Alabama: population, 7,110. Lions, Kiwanis, and garden club signs dangled from it. The lights turned out to be a car dealership. Eager salesmen lingered out front hoping to make a last-minute deal before heading home to supper.

"Boy, it'd be nice to just walk in there and buy a car."

"It sure would, RJ. Someday. Someday, somehow, some way."

Past the car dealership, they saw it: The Blue Moon Motel and Grill. A neon blue crescent moon flashed above a sign that said, Blue Moon. The l in Blue was burned out, and the M in Moon flickered. The place looked perfect.

∞ ∞ ∞

They took the rest of RJ's sandwiches out, stuffed them in their pockets, stashed the duffle bags behind the motel, and went into the friendly-looking little café. The stools were chrome and Naugahyde, and you could twirl around on them. If you were a kid. Callie remembered doing that when she went places with Granddaddy Moses.

A pretty white girl with a blond pixie cut greeted them. "Hey, girls. Rough night to be out, isn't it? I'm Vivian. What can I get you?"

"I just want a glass of water. What do you want, RJ?"

Ruby Jean hesitated and looked at Callie. "Me too."

"Well, in case you change your mind, here you go." Vivian laid down a menu and put her pencil and order pad in her pocket. "Be right back," Her voice was sweet with a lilt like a songbird.

Callie heard the sizzle of short orders cooking behind the swinging door, and the aroma of fried food was thick. She could see on her face that RJ would have given her right arm for a Pepsi, and Callie herself would almost kill for a cup of coffee. But every cent Callie had was gone except for the telephone change RJ had stashed in her shoe. RJ's money rolled in a hankie that would have to get them through until they figured something out. Coffee and Pepsi money would have to be for food.

Callie pulled a peanut butter and jelly half from her pocket. "RJ, did you stick that change in your shoe because of seeing a picture as you call it?"

Ruby Jean opened bologna with mustard. "Something like that."

Callie nibbled at the sandwich half. "I figure a motel room will be at least ten bucks a night. But we've got to have food. We can put that change with what's left and buy a little food at a store somewhere."

They crammed the last bites of the sandwiches in their mouths as Vivian brought them their water.

"Thanks," Callie said. "Hey, what do we do to rent a room for a night or two?"

"I can take care of it. Just you two?"

"Yeah."

"Got an ID?"

Callie's heart sank. It was all too much. She had tried to stay so strong even if only for RJ. She broke down as silent tears slid down her cheeks.

"What's wrong, sugar?" Vivian asked. She handed her a napkin. The only other customers, an elderly couple with two young children got up to leave. A blonde guy that might be Vivian's brother or husband rang their bill on a register near the door.

Callie dabbed her eyes. "We don't have IDs, but we've got cash. I'm Nellie Wilson from North Carolina, and this is my little sister Ruby Jean. Our grandma died, and we've got to go stay with my mother in Memphis. She's a singer out there. A backup singer for Martha and the Vandellas."

"Wow!" Vivian looked at Ruby Jean a little curiously and

turned to address Callie. "Did you drive? Do you have a license plate number?"

Callie shook her head. "We've been hiking—well, hitchhiking and hiking."

"I thought ya'll look a bit drenched. Why?"

"We were supposed to catch a bus, but we missed it. We hitched a ride with a really nice truck driver on his way back to Tuscaloosa. But a couple we met outside Birmingham lied and said they were headed to Tupelo."

Callie's voice quivered, and RJ took over.

"Callie figured out we was going the wrong way, so she told Dale, the guy, that we needed to get out. We got out at this church, and he pulled a gun on us. He told Babs, the girl, to go through our stuff. They robbed Cal, uh Nellie blind and took her driver's license."

Callie flinched at RJ's slip with her name, but Vivian didn't seem to notice.

"I don't have one yet," RJ continued. "But I have money tied up in a handkerchief, and they didn't find it. So we've got thirty-eight dollars and seventy-two cents. We can pay for a room."

"Oh my God. Well, girls, I'll put you up for a night on the house. You poor things. Tomorrow, we'll see about making a police report and contacting your mother to help you get to Memphis from here." She smiled at RJ and pat Callie's hands. "Hey, Jerry, bring me the key to room seven. How's that girls, lucky seven? And I'll get Sammy to cook you up a bite to eat."

After grilled cheese sandwiches, French fries, a Pepsi for RJ and hot coffee for Callie, they got their bags from behind the building and followed Vivian to room seven, a cozy room out of the rain. It felt wonderful. Callie sacrificed a Salem in celebration, turned on the little television and laid back on the bed wondering what they would do next. How would she explain that she didn't want to make a police report and why she couldn't call her own mother?

Chapter 6

The next morning Vivian invited Callie and Ruby Jean to breakfast. Vivian explained that the café closed after breakfast each morning and opened back up at lunch. It gave them a chance to do checkouts and ready rooms for new guests. Jerry bounced back and forth from the motel office to the back booth where they sat.

Callie had never had coffee so good, and RJ sucked on a huge Pepsi through a straw.

"So everything was okay in room seven?" Vivian asked.

"Oh, yes, wonderful," Callie said.

RJ nodded, her mouth glued to the soda straw.

"We'd like to pay for it tonight if it's available. It might be a couple of days before my cousin can send us money." Callie told them how Clarence had always wanted to be a detective and drove a bread truck part-time to pay for school. "And Della moved again. She's hard to get in touch with sometimes."

Vivian offered to let them stay at the Blue Moon until something worked out. Vivian and Jerry Robinson turned out to be a married couple. They could have passed for twins. They both had the bluest, friendliest eyes Callie had ever seen.

Vivian's parents lost their lives in a car wreck a few months ago, and she left college up North to come back to Coosa Springs. She married Jerry, and now they ran her family's business. They managed the small motel single-handedly and lived steps away from the Blue Moon in a matching bungalow.

A handsome boy came from the back carrying a tray loaded with plates of buttered grits, toast, and scrambled eggs. He had skin like shiny milk chocolate and one of those new Afros. He had a red rag flung over his shoulder, and Callie couldn't decide if the way he balanced a toothpick on his bottom lip looked haughty or playful.

Vivian introduced Sammy Lucas, and he served them their plates and sat down. She told Sammy about the robbery and how they had to wait for their family to send them money to get to Memphis. "They're staying in room seven." She turned to Callie. "Sammy's a friend from college. He's on sabbatical and down here for the civil rights campaign."

He popped a triangle of toast in his mouth. "Well, it's what I hope is a sabbatical, instead of getting kicked out. Please to meet you two," he grinned.

"You know what, Vivian, maybe we can let these girls help us out around here," Jerry said. "Don't get me wrong, not to earn their way. They're welcome as guests for as long as they need to stay. We can't put them on the payroll, but Ruby Jean can wait tables for tips. Nellie can help Sammy in the back. Or clean rooms. We'll pay her cash. Since Jimmie Lee Jackson got shot over in Marion, all hell is about to break loose. Word is MLK himself wants to organize a march in his honor. I think we're about to get bombarded with people. TV cameramen, activists, you name it."

Callie pulled her clean blue sweater tightly around her. It had been heavenly to shower and change clothes. She thought about RJ waiting tables. Could she spell well enough to take orders? She took a deep breath and spoke. "It might be better if I wait tables and RJ—I call her RJ—cleaned. I bet she could help Sammy cook, too. Right, RJ?"

"Oh, yeah, for sure. I'd be way better at that."

Jerry looked at Vivian. Vivian looked at Sammy. Vivian squirmed and cleared her throat. "Uh, we haven't quite done away with Jim Crow down here, ya'll."

"What's that supposed to mean?" Callie asked.

Sammy turned to Callie. "It means once we open the door, I gotta go in the back and cook—so all the *white folks* can come in and eat." He paused. "So RJ's your sis, huh?"

"Yeah."

"Wow, you look so different. Sisters. Same mom and dad, right?"

"Right."

Sammy Lucas chuckled and shook his head. "No, you're not. Half-sisters, maybe." He folded his arms and leaned over the table. If you both had the same parents, you'd both be caramel-colored instead of just one of you." He stared straight into her eyes.

Callie stared back and looked away. She could kick herself. RJ was right; they didn't look anything alike. Why had she wanted to claim her as a sister? Now she had just one lie left to worry about. And lots of stuff to explain.

∞∞∞

Ruby Jean looked around at the empty tables and stools around the counter that would soon fill up with people. Customers they wanted her, Ruby Jean Carson, class dummy, to wait on. Take orders, count change. She prayed Callie would just tell the truth. Mama always said the truth was best. The silence was as thick as fog. Vivian broke it.

"Sammy, bring us all more coffee, and get Ruby Jean another Pepsi."

Silence again, then Sammy brought their drinks.

"Talk to us," Vivian said. "What's going on?"

Callie began telling their story. She told them everything except that her real name was Callie. She told them all the mean things Reggie and Snake had done to them. Ruby Jean could hardly breathe as Callie told them about Mama dying and leaving her the gift.

"Oh. It's called clairvoyance, extrasensory perception, one or the other. I've heard of it." Vivian had tears in her eyes, and Sammy and Jerry looked sad. She knew then that Vivian, Jerry, and Sammy cared about people and their feelings.

Callie explained how she found out her daddy was a white man Della had worked for, and how she didn't want the choice of being white or colored taken from her. Her only chance in life was to get to Memphis and make Della help them.

"She has a responsibility to you," Jerry said.

"She sure does," Vivian said. "I can't believe she never calls or anything."

"I guess she thinks Lucy needs to take care of everything since she's the one getting the shut-up money from them white folks."

"Tell you what," Vivian began, "Ya'll use what you've got for spending money. But we've got your room and board covered. That'll help you get to Memphis. We've got three rooms checking out of the motel today. There's nothing to learn there: change the linens, clean the bathrooms, take out trash, vacuum. I'll pay you two dollars a room, together. Later, I'll help Ruby Jean get started taking orders and Nellie, you can wash dishes and help Sammy. Fifty cents an hour. It doesn't sound like much, but it'll add up."

Ruby Jean sighed with relief, glad the Robinsons would let them make some money. Then they wouldn't have to bother Clarence and Roy. Roy was always strapped for cash; he had a family to help. And Clarence had school to pay for. But two things bothered her: Callie didn't tell them she wasn't really Nellie Wilson, and that she, Ruby Jean, was nineteen years old and struggling to make it through high school.

∞∞∞∞

That afternoon Vivian walked them through the basics of cleaning a motel room, pointing out nooks and crannies to sweep and dust that were easy to miss. Ruby Jean saw it as being like life itself—dusting and constantly cleaning to keep the dirties out. She loved how the rooms looked. The big windows had pretty drapes and matching chenille bedspreads. She couldn't help being excited about their own room, lucky room seven, she hoped.

"Okay, that's it, girls. One short lesson. You're on your own for the rest of them." She picked up the phone and sprayed the receiver with Lysol, "Gotta keep the germs down, or we'll get sick." She wiped it down with a cloth and put it back in its cradle "Oh that reminds me. We'd better call in and report that robbery, the money, and especially your ID."

"I already did," Callie said.

"Really? When?"

"Oh real early this morning. Outside from the phone booth."

"You should have called from the room phone, silly. Local calls are free."

Ruby Jean knew she hadn't called. She hated Callie had to resort to lying again, but she understood. Reggie was a cop, and she had to be careful about using her real name. And it wasn't really her ID that Babs got. What a mess.

Callie and RJ helped each other change linens and make the double beds in room nine. The soft yellow chenille bedspreads were identical to the ones in room seven, and the patterned drapes matched. RJ dusted and took out the trash while Callie scrubbed the bathroom and vacuumed.

"Mama always says lies beget lies."

"I know, RJ, and I'm sorry."

RJ scrunched up her nose in that funny way she sometimes did. "Why don't you just tell Vivian and Jerry the truth? They seem nice as can be. Sammy, too."

"I'm just scared, I guess. I don't know what to do. I'm just taking it a minute at a time. That robbery shook me up bad."

Room nine was ready for the next check-in. A line of dust particles danced in the rays of the sun seeping through the blinds. Callie sat on the edge of the bed and lit a precious Salem, the blue smoke swirling and mixing in with the dust.

RJ flopped back on the bed and sighed. "I tried to tell Roy to call Clarence, but the phone cut off. Do you think we ought to call and tell them what's going on?"

Callie finished her Salem, stubbing it out in the ashtray to save for later. "It's like this. I want to call. I promised Clarence I would, but the less Roy and Clarence know, the better. If they send us money, it might cause a paper trail, and we don't want Roy to have to lie to the police. I don't trust Reggie. He's liable to be looking for me. And Clarence says they have ways of tracking people we don't even know about."

Ruby Jean decided not to tell Callie about Reggie coming by. She figured it would just make her more nervous. "What should we do then? Roy will worry."

"We'll walk to town and call. Soon as we can. They'll be okay. You talked to them yesterday, right?"

RJ nodded. "Yeah. Seems like forever ago now."

"At least the call won't come from here. I got to hold my breath and pray we can head on out before Reggie can track me down. I didn't plan on us getting stuck in a small town." Callie wiped the ashtray clean with a paper towel from their cleaning supplies and stuck the half-smoked Salem back into her dwindling pack. "Oh yeah. The phone." She sprayed the receiver with Lysol, wiped it with a rag and hung it back on the cradle.

They breezed through cleaning the next room with little conversation knowing just what to do. Back in their own room, Callie lit the last of her Salem and turned on the room's portable TV. The local news was on. Jimmie Lee Jones was in a hospital. The TV station ran a review of the events leading to his injuries. He was beaten by Alabama state troopers; one of them shot him.

"Just think," Ruby Jean said. "That guy's fighting for his life in a hospital not far from here."

"And it's on national TV," Callie added. "That makes it pretty important."

"Why'd they want to beat him and shoot him?"

"He's a civil rights leader. White folks down here don't want Negroes to be able to vote." Callie explained.

"That don't seem fair, does it?"

"No, it doesn't." Callie thought about it. She was old enough to vote now. She and Clarence had talked about it once. He said she might get by with eating in a white restaurant or sitting with whites at the movies, but she would have a hard time voting in the south. Clarence said it was because of the not one drop rule—not one drop of colored blood. She might not be able to vote for any of her own country's leaders. She sighed and turned off the TV. "Let's go see about lunch, RJ."

Jerry was unlocking the glass door that led from the motel office to the café when Callie and RJ walked in.

Callie turned over the keys to the rooms they had cleaned.

"Come on in, girls. Sammy's got hot dogs in the back."

Vivian sat at the counter with Sammy. The café's TV was on.

"Hey, Nellie. Hey, RJ. How'd it go?"

Callie gave a thumbs up.

The anchorman went into more detail about the shooting of Jimmie Lee Jackson showing a big smashed camera and another beaten reporter in the hospital.

Jerry came in to watch. "If that boy dies and they don't charge that cop with murder, no telling what might happen."

After watching the news, Callie wondered if Jerry was right about their business picking up because of what happened. That would make it good for her and RJ too. They'd make more money. But what happened was awful. Jimmie Lee Jackson was trying to protect his mother. His own mother had gotten beaten. His grandfather too. An old man.

"Sammy, you'd better be careful at those meetings over in Marion," Vivian said. You could have been one of them."

"Somebody's got to change things, Vivian. I just hope Jimmie doesn't have to die."

Sammy went through the swinging doors to the kitchen and

brought out hot dogs and fries for Callie and Ruby Jean. He sat the tray down and left quickly.

The little girls at church, Callie thought. But aloud she only said, "Man, these hot dogs look good, don't they, RJ?"

"Um-hum," Ruby Jean mumbled. She had already taken a huge bite. Chili oozed from the sides and fell to her plate.

"It's Sammy's special chili that makes them so good," Vivian said. "I'll get ya'll some Pepsis."

Jerry had gone back to the motel's little office. Vivian tied on a starchy apron ready for any lunch customers. The door opened to the café, and two elderly couples walked in. They all wore street-length coats, even the men. The men took off hats that matched their coats and hung them on the brass hat rack by the door. Both the ladies wore pillbox hats and gloves.

"Hello, ladies, and gentlemen," Vivian said. "We're open for lunch. Sit anywhere you'd like."

One of the ladies gasped. "Oh, my God."

Callie and Ruby Jean stopped eating and turned around. One of the women grabbed the other woman's arm. "Look, Margaret." She pointed at Callie.

"We're not eating here, Fred. Let's go," Margaret said. Both couples turned and walked out.

Callie wanted to shrink and disappear. She'd lost customers for the Robinsons. Please, God, don't let it be like this in Tennessee. "I guess I'd better leave sooner from now on. I'm sorry, Vivian."

Vivian's face was red. "Me too, Nellie. But they're old people. Things are going to change. Someday. Someday soon."

Chapter 7

Ruby Jean was thankful for every room they could clean and for every minute that Vivian didn't ask her to learn how to wait tables. They needed to make back that $300 and get to Memphis so Callie could find her mother.

They all watched the news at noon now after they finished cleaning rooms and before the café opened for lunch. Somehow it helped to watch as a group. Jimmie Lee Jackson wasn't doing well. It looked like he might die. Ruby Jean kept wondering how his mother and grandpa was, but most of the talk was about what would happen if Jimmie Lee died and how marches were being organized.

It looked like what Jerry said about business picking up might be true. Ruby Jean couldn't help being excited when Vivian told them some guys from the *Jackson Journal* and the *Birmingham Times* checked into rooms eleven and twelve.

On Thursday, Ruby Jean panicked when Vivian told them she wanted Nellie, or Callie, working in the back with Sammy over the weekend and Ruby Jean helping her upfront.

"You won't have to ring up the customers or give change right away. One of us will do that," she said.

Right away? She said right away. That meant she'd have to later. Ruby Jean glanced at Callie like when they were in school, and she froze up at an assignment the teacher had given.

"We'll all pitch in together and cover the rooms. Gosh," Vivian said. "We might even have to hire people. Ya'll sure came along at a good time."

Ruby Jean figured that just like herself, she felt bad but glad at the same time for more business.

"If we're gonna be real busy, maybe RJ and I ought to go do some shopping. You, know personal items and stuff. We've still got our spending money."

Vivian began clearing away the dishes. "Jerry's going into town later. A couple of our delivery trucks are delayed, probably because of all that's going on around here. Ya'll can ride in with him. One of you, anyway. I might need somebody here for cleaning rooms."

"Well, if it's not too far, we can walk after supper."

"Nonsense Nellie. You and Ruby Jean don't need to be walking around here by yourself. Ruby Jean spoke up. "We really need to call home."

Vivian stuck an order pad in her pocket and a pencil behind her ear. "For heaven's sake, call them from your room. It doesn't cost that much. If you're worried about it, you can pay me back. Run on out to the laundry room and fold linens. Jerry will wait and take you with him."

∞ ∞ ∞

Ruby Jean volunteered to stay behind and help Vivian ready rooms for what promised to be a busy weekend. They had booked all but room twelve. Vivian said Jerry always insisted on leaving one room vacant in case something broke down.

Just after three o'clock, Callie took off with Jerry—her purse packed with plenty of change for the payphone, a pretend list from RJ of things she needed, and a promise to call Roy.

Callie watched as the tiny town of Coosa Springs expanded to include a couple of gas stations, a post office, and a hardware store. She made it a point to pay attention to the route they took. She noted landmarks at each turn and tried to estimate how long it would be by foot. If calls could get traced from payphones at least they wouldn't be from the Blue Moon. Reggie was only a rookie traffic cop, but he had friends in higher places, like Sargent Kenneth Sawyers. After two lefts and a right, they turned into a shopping center with an A&P grocery store. Callie noted three telephone booths along the strip.

Jerry pushed the buggy and Callie walked alongside helping fill it with several gallons of milk. "The dairy truck doesn't come until Tuesday," he explained.

While Jerry compared prices on restaurant-size canned goods and condiments, the wheels in Callie's mind turned, looking for the best way to talk to Clarence without getting caught. It would be the perfect time to call. All his classes were in the mornings, and he didn't deliver bread on Thursdays. "Hey, Jerry, I'm gonna go shop around for some uh, personal stuff, if you don't mind."

Still looking at giant cans of green beans, he laughed. "That time of the month, huh? You don't have to be embarrassed. I buy Kotex for Vivian all the time." He tossed two cans of beans in the buggy. "They've got them here. Just go get some and toss them in." He took a stubby pencil and a list out of his shirt pocket and busily ticked off items.

"I saw a Rexall drug store pulling in. I'll bet they're cheaper there. Plus, uh, RJ needs these drops she puts in her ears. She has earaches. Can I just meet you back at the truck?"

"Well, okay. In that case. I wouldn't want Ruby Jean's ears to hurt." He looked slightly amused.

"Thanks, Jerry."

Callie started to head straight for the phone and then thought better of it. Instead, she hurried into the drugstore first and came out with a bag of Kotex, shampoo, deodorant, and some kind of ear drops. She scrambled to the phone booth farthest from the A&P and made the call after dropping a quarter twice. The operator got Clarence on the third ring. She crammed in a handful of change, and they were connected. She had been granted fifteen minutes to find out what was going on.

"Hey Clarence, it's me. We got jobs outside Tupelo." Not really a lie, she thought. "We're okay. We're saving up money and then heading for Memphis."

"I thought you had money. But that'll have to wait. I got bad news."

Callie clutched the receiver. *Lucy*?

It wasn't Lucy. Reggie had been shot and killed. Sawyers found him in the bungalow early Wednesday morning when he didn't show up to direct traffic. There were no signs of a struggle.

A chill crawled from Callie's neck down her spine. Reggie had a dark side that she only became aware of after living with him. But this news was still a shock.

"Shot and killed? My God. Did they find who did it?"

"No."

"They have no idea?"

"They're investigating. That's all I know. But I've got a couple of hunches of my own."

"Like what?"

"Word on the street is Reggie owed money from gambling. And he owed money to old man Ledford. He's been running liquor and cigarettes into Virginia. Ledford fronted him the goods and never got paid."

"Does the Law know that?"

"Probably, but the thing is, Sawyer's been asking about you. He kept going by Reggie's place and you weren't ever around, so he went looking for you at Lucy's. She spilled the beans and said ya'll had been fighting. She thinks you ran away."

"I did run away. To get away from Reggie."

"It ain't that easy, Brown Sugar. It's looking like you might be a suspect. And when Lucy gets her bank statement, she won't be too happy."

"But he got shot after I left."

"Don't matter. I know their games. They're not gonna let anything that looks bad come out about Reggie. Did you keep your bus ticket stubs?"

The answer to that was no, of course. They hadn't taken the bus. "Maybe. I'll look," she lied.

Callie hung up the phone and hurried toward Jerry's car idling in the A&P parking lot getting ready to head back to the Blue Moon. Just like normal. She would apologize and say thanks for waiting. They would drive back to the Blue Moon as she silently digested what she found out from Clarence.

She opened the passenger door and hopped in with her bag from Rexall. "Sorry, Jerry. Thanks."

"No problem. Did you get everything you needed?"

"Sure did." Did she ever. She just found out the husband she hated and ran away from had been shot dead. And she might be a suspect. She had wondered what she'd do about getting away from Reggie legally. Clarence had mentioned it more than once. But she'd figured she would cross that bridge when she got to it. Well, that problem was gone. But now she had to face the fact that she might be a suspect. *Might.* Life couldn't be so cruel as to have her locked up for a crime she didn't commit.

Chapter 8

The afternoon sun shone through open drapes. Room seven was cozy, and Ruby Jean had grown fond of it. The carpet was worn but soft, and the butter-colored drapes and spread were cheery. A round table with two chairs made a little sitting area.

Callie sat the bag from the drug store and the menu and order pad on the table and fell into the chair nearest the door.

"What's up with the ear drops thing, Callie? Why'd you lie this time? Did you talk to Roy?"

Callie picked up the bottle of ear drops and acted like she was reading the directions. "No, RJ, I'm sorry. I didn't get to call Roy. I used the ear drops as an excuse to go over to the drug store and use the payphone. I had to use all my time to talk to Clarence."

Callie told her about Reggie getting shot and killed and Kenneth Sawyer asking around about them.

Ruby Jean shot straight out of her chair. "Reggie got shot? And killed? Oh, no! My vision was right then. Roy told me on the phone the other day that Reggie came around asking if he had seen you. And where I was. He told them I went to Aunt Peggy's."

"Why didn't you tell me?"

"I forgot." She hesitated. "Well, no, I didn't forget. I didn't want you to be all nervous."

Callie slammed a fist on the table. "Dammit, RJ, we can't keep secrets from each other. We're in this together."

Ruby Jean flinched. "I'm sorry, Callie."

Callie sighed. "No, don't be. I'm sorry. It doesn't matter, anyway. Reggie's dead. He must've got shot right after that." She told Ruby Jean about the gambling and the liquor running.

"Well, they'll figure out it wasn't you that shot Reggie."

"It might not be that easy. I mean for me not to be a suspect."

"People like that always get caught."

"Yeah, on TV they do. Or in big cities. It's different in places like Frogmoor. Ledford's brings in a lot of revenue. Politicians overlook it and expect the cops to do the same. Anyway, let's practice you being a waitress." Callie handed Ruby Jean a piece of paper and a pencil out of the nightstand drawer. She looked over a menu like a customer about to order. "Okay, I'll have this here Salisbury steak, ma'am, with green beans and mashed potatoes. And mushroom gravy. Does that come with hot rolls?"

"Yes, ma'am. Hot rolls come with all the plates."

"Eeexcellent, my dea'."

Ruby Jean giggled. She carefully printed SS, GB, and MP on the ticket. Vivian taught her that afternoon how to use abbreviations: FF was French fries, HD a hot dog, and HB meant hamburger. Put a C in front of HB and you had cheeseburger. She scrunched her nose and asked, "What's the abbreviation for mushroom gravy?"

"Uh, I don't see it on the list. Some things you may just have to spell out."

"Hell, Callie, I can't spell mushroom gravy."

"Heck, draw a picture."

Ruby Jean drew a picture of mushrooms swimming in a bowl and showed it to Callie. They both doubled over, laughter a tension reliever for them. Ruby Jean scrunched her nose up again and sat down.

"You're not supposed to sit with the customer. You're the help," Callie said.

But RJ had grown serious. "Since Reggie's dead, couldn't you just go back to using your real name?"

Callie thought for a minute and shook her head. "No. It's safer this way. Because of that ID getting stolen. I'd have to admit it to Vivian and Jerry, and they might get really mad and make us leave."

"What're we gonna do now?"

Callie dug through the ashtray for a half-smoked Salem, lit it and took a long drag. "Same thing as planned. Stay here, work. We're not doing anything wrong. We're both over eighteen. And if I panic, it'll just look bad." She finished the stub of a cigarette and lit another one. "I don't think anybody's gonna come looking for us here. Not right away. The only thing I can see happening is if they somehow trace payphone calls to Aunt Lettie's. I don't know if they can. But we can't use the phone here. I checked out the way to Coosa Springs Mall. It's close enough to walk. We can make it in about half an hour."

Ruby Jean perked up. "Does that mean we can go call Roy? When?"

"We can probably go between lunch and supper tomorrow."

Vivian and Jerry let them take breaks between two and five each day. Ruby Jean smiled with a sigh of relief. It would be good to check up on Mama, and she needed to pretend she was calling from Aunt Peggy's all safe and sound. Mama wouldn't try to call her sister, Peggy. Snake wouldn't let her make long-distance calls. It cost too much. She had tried hard to see a picture of Mama, pictures like the gift she now had. She did it in the bed every night right before she fell asleep. She would smoosh her face into the feather pillow and wait until those weird swirly patterns disappeared. Then she would see Mama's face, wide-eyed and smiling. Ruby Jean wasn't sure if it was a sign or her own wishful thinking.

The weekend that followed the Thursday Callie found out Reggie was dead caught them by surprise. For the first time in a long time, the No Vacancy sign glowed bright orange beneath the neon Blue Moon sign. Guests clearly from out of town joined the few regulars. They spotted well-dressed gentlemen coming and going carrying camera cases and notebooks.

On Friday morning at breakfast, Vivian turned on the news. Jimmie Lee Jackson was dead. The reporter said gunpowder on his chest proved the shot came from up close. Then they started in about how the cop said it was self-defense. Jimmie acted like he was going for a gun.

"That's a lie!" Sammy cried. "He was a deacon. He had no gun. He just wanted to lead a peaceful prayer vigil to support James Orange. James is locked up for leading a voter drive. Some technicality they made up about contributing to the delinquency of a minor."

Vivian turned off the TV. They said a prayer for Jimmie Lee and his family.

By noon Callie could see there would be no time for them to get away to call Frogmoor, North Carolina. She and RJ spent all morning taking out the trash and changing towels in rooms with leather luggage and hanging dress shirts and pants. Papers, coffee cups, and notebooks sat on the tables. One room even had a portable typewriter set up.

Vivian sent Ruby Jean out on the floor to take a few late afternoon lunch orders. Callie became Sammy's sous chef, as he called it. She wasn't quite sure what that meant, but she figured it was a fancy name for an assistant.

Callie tied on an apron and started peeling potatoes and carrots for Sammy's huge stew. Old Time Alabama beef stew was the special of the day.

"Wow, you sure look ready to serve a bunch of food."

He had made hamburgers and hot dogs earlier, and a pot of his yummy chili simmered on a burner. Pans of Salisbury steak and baked chicken sat in warmers by the burgers and dogs. Breaded catfish fillets, hush puppies, and French fries waited to be dipped in hot grease.

"Girl, I was up all night."

"Think we're gonna be that busy?" Callie asked. Sammy either didn't hear or didn't answer. But that was Sammy. He wasn't rude, nor was he a racist. His day-to-day actions went right along with the activist he said he was. Vivian said he had been going to meetings over in Marion.

Sammy fixed himself a hot dog and an order of hushpuppies. "Better grab something before we get slammed."

Callie stopped peeling and chopping vegetables and wiped her hands. The Salisbury steak sure looked good, and a pot of mushroom gravy simmering nearby reminded her of playing waitress with RJ. "Oh, can I get a little of that Salisbury steak?"

Sammy pulled a white oval plate off the shelf above the grill and forked up a piece for her topping it with a ladle of the mushroom gravy. "Here you go, Miss." He handed her a fork. "You won't need a knife. It's that tender."

Sammy led her into the back to a card table and chairs and motioned for her to sit first. He took off his hairnet, letting his afro spring to life and sat down across from Callie.

Callie took a bite of the steak and raved. "You were right about not needing a fork."

"Oh, let me go get us two big old Pepsis." He winked at her.

Callie watched him leave thinking how polite he was. It felt like a tiny butterfly fluttered somewhere inside her.

He came back and set the Pepsis down. "So, Miss Nellie, eat fast and talk fast. Tell me about you."

She sipped on the Pepsi and then asked, "What do you want to know?"

Sammy took a huge bite of his hotdog and gulped it seemly without chewing. "So let me get this straight. You left home to go find your mother because you wanted to be a singer. Or, did you leave to get away from an abusive relationship?"

Callie thought for a minute. "Can't it be both?"

Sammy thought even longer, polishing the hot dog off in two more bites. "Well, I guess you'd have to figure out if you'd still go for the singer-mother thing if you weren't in a bad relationship."

"I think it's both." She changed the subject. "So what are you studying in college?"

"I'm in pre-law."

Her status as a high school dropout reared its ugly head "It's not like I wouldn't *like* to go to college. But I don't want to be forced to go to an all-black one. That's what Lucy wants me to do."

"And you shouldn't have to." Sammy had been polishing off hush puppies while Callie talked.

Something about Sammy seemed to make her want to open up. A little. "I guess Lucy, my *grandmother*," she said as she rolled her eyes, "figured it would be the only way I'd get to go to college. Boy, you sure eat fast."

"And you'd better too. You'll learn."

Callie scarfed up her steak. Leaving the half-finished Pepsis for later, they went back to work. They'd need them, Sammy promised.

Three tickets hung limply from the rotating rack when they got back to the grill.

"Told ya," Sammy said.

Callie pulled the three tickets down and recognized RJ's block printing: HDs on one and HB on the other. Two with FFs. They filled the three orders. It was still early, not yet four o'clock, and they had a few more minutes to talk.

"So what're your plans?" asked Sammy.

"Stay here, work, and save money. Then head to Memphis. On a bus, this time. No more hitching and hiking."

"I hear that. Vivian and Jerry sure can use you two right now. There's no telling when things will get back to normal."

"Yeah, me and RJ noticed some of the rooms are occupied by the press."

Sammy nodded. "There's going to be a march soon. Martin Luther King, Jr., himself is leading it. We're right here nearby it all."

"Because of Jimmie Lee Jackson?"

"Yeah, him and others, too. It's supposed to be in their honor. People like Jimmie Lee shouldn't have to pay with their lives for the right to vote. Dr. King demands that it be peaceful."

Vivian came back with one of the plates. "Hey, ya'll, this was supposed to be a hamburger, not a hot dog. And it's for one of the journalists." She sounded slightly annoyed.

Fifteen minutes later, they were slammed. Ticket after ticket came up. More than once, Vivian came back to exchange a hot dog for a hamburger, or the opposite. Sammy grew curious and began looking back at the tickets that had already gone through. He chewed on a toothpick and shook his head. "Your girlfriend's writing these down wrong."

Callie panicked for RJ. She must be having a hard time.

Things got worse before they got better. Customers started complaining about having to wait too long. Vivian came back to reassure them it wasn't their fault. "Thank God you had the foresight to cook all this."

Callie and Sammy yanked off tickets with Vivian's curvy scrawling and RJ's neat block letters, filling them furtively.

Sammy grabbed one and stopped. "What the—what the heck is this?"

Callie looked at the ticket. RJ's block letters: SS for Salisbury steak, GB, green beans, and MD. Mashed potatoes? And at the bottom of the ticket RJ had drawn a bowl of mushroom gravy just like the one she had drawn back in their room. Callie's heart laughed and cried at the same time. All she could say was, "it's mushroom gravy, silly."

Sammy looked back at the ticket and then back at Callie. He filled the order with no more questions.

Around ten-thirty, things finally slowed down. Their drinks were waiting on them, watered-down but still cold. They both sat down and took long swigs.

"I'm beat," Callie said. "I know you must be after being up all night."

"Nah, I'm okay. I wasn't really up all night, just late. We need to talk to RJ. That girl had me messed up. I mean, she's new and all, but Jeez. And where did drawing gravy come from? Vivian needs to give her some more training."

Callie had been thinking about what went wrong. She re-

membered RJ telling her she had a hard time telling single letters apart. She decided to trust Sammy. "Well, RJ would die if she
knew I told you this, but she has a bit of a learning problem. I
mean, don't get me wrong, she's not stupid or anything. She just
has a hard time reading and a little trouble with math. I played
waitress with her. When she didn't know the abbreviation for
mushroom gravy, I told her to just draw it. I was joking, but she
tends to take things literally, and I guess she decided it was okay
to draw it." She watched for Sammy's reaction.

"Oh, so she confused HD with HB. I see. I understand. Poor
kid."

At least he was sympathetic. "I'll help her some more. Please
don't tell her I told you. It would really embarrass her."

"You know, that's what Vivian was studying before she had
to drop out of school. Special education. She's very understanding. I'll bet she has a way to help RJ. It's nothing to be ashamed of.
I remember Vivian talking about people with reading problems
being normal, or even super smart. She said even some famous
people were like that."

"Yeah, but, like I said, RJ would just die if ya'll know."

Sammy pat her on the hand and looked at her with those
soulful eyes. "Sometimes, Miss Nellie, the truth can set us free."

Chapter 9

Friday night at the Blue Moon Café had been a whirlwind, unlike anything Ruby Jean ever experienced. Lots worse than working in the tobacco fields or helping Mama give the house a good scrubbing. She guessed it was because she'd had to do so much thinking. Brain tired, Mama had called it when she did their taxes every year. Mama graduated from high school, so Snake depended on her for things like that.

The job started easy enough, but then she got an order wrong. It wasn't too bad, a hot dog had to be exchanged for a hamburger. Vivian had called her aside and told her to be more careful. But it happened again and again. Impatient customers kept asking her when their food was coming. Ruby Jean had to hold back tears for most of the shift.

They served coffee and icebox pie to a handful of customers until close to midnight. Jerry took care of them so she could sit in the back booth with Vivian, Callie, and Sammy to discuss what went wrong.

They all fell into the booth.

Vivian began. "Whew, what a night! Thanks, guys, for all your hard work. Sammy, the food got rave reviews."

Sammy nodded. "I'm glad. But I couldn't have filled all those orders without Nellie." He glanced at her and smiled.

Callie's cheeks flushed. "Thanks. You had enough food cooked for an army."

"That saved us," Vivian said. "We were understaffed and overworked. We need to hire a couple more people, but we've got some kinks to work out."

Sammy spoke up. "Ruby Jean, I love you, girl, but we kept getting mixed hot dog and hamburger orders."

Ruby Jean focused on her folded hands on the table. "I'm sorry, Sammy. I guess I wrote them down wrong. I got in a hurry and mixed up my Bs and Ds.

"And what about that bowl of mushroom gravy you drew? What happens when I make catfish stew? Are you going to draw a fish and a cat in a bowl?" He chuckled.

Ruby Jean noticed Vivian watching her reaction.

"I can see that happening," Vivian said.

Ruby Jean knew then that Vivian knew. She felt embarrassed but relieved. She decided Vivian was one of the kindest people she had ever met. Thank goodness Callie changed the subject.

"Vivian, Sammy told me you were studying to be a teacher before you had to leave college."

She didn't say a teacher for special students, but Ruby Jean bet that was it—like Mrs. Shooks.

"Yeah, and I think we can fix the problem with a few tricks. But that can wait until tomorrow. We're all exhausted."

Callie and Sammy finished cleaning up in the back. Jerry locked the door to the café after the last customer left. Vivian and Ruby Jean restocked napkin holders and refilled salt and pepper shakers. Finally, the time came to call it a day at the Blue Moon.

Jerry met them at the door to let them out jangling keys and holding two envelopes stuffed with money. He handed one each to Callie and Ruby Jean. "You deserve this and more. Here's to helping you get to Memphis."

Back in room seven, Callie helped Ruby Jean add up her money plus the tips she pulled from her apron pocket. She totaled all their money together.

"We've still got some of that money you had, too. We could get bus tickets, but we need more. And we can't leave now anyway, at least not until Vivian and Jerry hire some help."

Ruby Jean agreed. Her first real job felt good. Vivian would help, and she would do a better job tomorrow. She wondered if

Callie was glad too. Somehow she thought she was.

∞ ∞ ∞

Saturday turned out to be as busy. Callie carefully watched the tickets coming through at lunch. Vivian had sat down with Ruby Jean before the café opened. They must have done something. Ruby Jean did better.

Being busy kept Callie's mind off Sergeant Sawyers and Reggie. But she desperately needed to know what was going on.

Late Sunday afternoon they got their chance. Since business had picked up, Vivian and Jerry decided to close the café after lunch every Sunday to have time to themselves. They went to see a movie. Sammy said he planned on sleeping all afternoon. Just after two in the afternoon, Callie and Ruby Jean set out on foot for Coosa Springs Mall.

A bone-chilling wind replaced the spring-like weather, they had hiked into in Alabama. They both put up the hoods of the warm army jackets Clarence had picked out for them and set out for Coosa Springs Mall, their jacket pockets lined with quarters from RJ's tips.

RJ brimmed with excitement at calling home. "Mama's feeling better." She told Callie about the visions she'd had of her Mama smiling.

"I hope so, RJ. I'm glad we're getting the chance to call." But Callie dreaded the call back to Frogmoor. She would rather be safe in the madness of the Blue Moon Café with Sammy.

"You go first, Callie. Bad as I want to talk to Roy, and Mama, I'm not worried about being wanted for murder."

Callie rolled her eyes. "Thanks, a lot."

"I'll wait outside."

"No, you won't. Stay here with me."

Callie propped the phone booth door open. Ruby Jean turned to watch the cars going in and out of the A&P parking lot.

Callie made her call. Lucy answered. *Shit.* What was *she* doing there? A split second passed by in which she almost hung up. "Hey, Grandma. What are you doing there?"

"Girl, where you at?"

"I can't tell you that, Grandma."

"Oh, Lord. That does it. You shot Reggie. What you gone do now?"

"I didn't shoot Reggie, Grandma."

"Well, what are you running from?"

Callie let loose. "You, Grandma, and Reggie, too. Everybody. I've got to find myself."

"Oh, Lord. You're on them drugs young'uns has been taking."

"No, Grandma, I'm not on drugs. Reggie was mean to me. He hit me."

"Well, he won't hit you no more. He's dead. And they think you shot him."

"Why? They who? Let me talk to Clarence, Grandma."

"Kenneth Sawyers came out here asking about you. He must think something. Listen, you need to come on back here and finish your schooling. I can get you some kind of car, and you can go on to college and make something out of yourself."

"What college, Grandma. Any college?"

"Well, now no, Callie, you need to go to the Negro college."

"Why, Lucy? Is it because of them?"

"Them who? And I don't like it when you call me Lucy."

"You know who. Look, I didn't shoot Reggie. I'm sorry he got killed, but I'm not running from a crime I didn't do, so I'm not gonna stop what I'm doing. I'm close to Memphis, I'm working a job, and I ain't on the street. I'm going to find Della and make her help me get a singing job like her. Then I can pick my damn college. Or none at all. Let me talk to Clarence."

"All right. But Della called. She ain't in Memphis no more. That record company she works for sent her to Detroit. Here."

Lucy stopped talking and handed the phone to Clarence. She didn't even get to ask if Della left a phone number.

"Hey, Brown Sugar."

"Clarence, what's going on?

"Sawyers talked Lucy into filing a missing person's report. They sent your name along with a description to the FBI. Lucy told him she didn't have any picture of you any later than when you were five."

That sounded about right to Callie. Lucy had never been big on memorabilia.

"Reggie was shot with his own gun, Callie. And the gun is gone. Maybe you'd better come on in and clear your name."

"There isn't anything to clear, Clarence. Tell Sawyers to go find the killer. It's not me. See if Lucy got a phone number from Della. I'll call you back."

"Okay. Let me know if you change your mind. Sawyer's trail is cold right now, so stay put. Don't do anything funny."

"Like what?"

"Like shoplift or something."

"I wouldn't do that."

Callie dumped some change in RJ's hand and took the rest of the money she saved on her phone call to the A&P and bought a pack of Salems. She met RJ walking from the phone booth.

"Guess what? Mama's better. My vision was right. Roy said the doctor said that sometimes happens right after they take you off that cancer medicine. But still, it was good to hear her sounding like her old self. What did you find out from Clarence?"

"Lucy said Della left Memphis. They sent her to Detroit."

Ruby Jean cupped her hands over her mouth.

"Don't look so shocked. Me and Clarence are gonna find Della. I'll get to her. In the meantime, we work and save money, save money and work. Like I said before, we're in this together. You don't want to go back, do you?"

"No, never. Do you want me to go back?"

"Of course not. We're like family now. It's like we really are sisters."

Callie reached for RJ's hand, and they walked side-by-side back to the Blue Moon. The Sunday afternoon traffic was light.

People in cars passing by turned to stare at them. A blue Ford Fairlane overloaded with teenagers turned around and came back. The car slowed down. Hateful words spewed from the passengers: "Hey, lover of a nigger lover. Ya'll queer, too? Who's the man?" Laughter. Boisterous laughter.

"Just keep walking, RJ."

Cans and bottles flew, none hitting them. The car sped away.

So Della was in Detroit. Callie bet this crap didn't go on there. It sure would be good to get the heck out of Alabama. But there was no way, not now. Clarence was right. It was best to stay put for now.

∞ ∞ ∞

Back in the cozy safety of room seven, Ruby Jean took a nap. Callie lit a Salem and took out the letter reading it again for the hundredth time taking in the message it carried. The message she wasn't acknowledged by her own flesh and blood.

January 26th, 1965

Dear Mrs. Gibbs,

I trust this letter finds you well. Enclosed is a check that should cover your granddaughter's expenses nicely for the next six months. Mrs. Gibbs, I know you are aware that my political reputation, as well as my son's, could be ruined if the public should learn the truth about young Miss Gibbs.

However, keep in mind that extortion is a crime punishable by law. We have learned that Miss Gibbs is over eighteen and married. My son is no longer legally responsible for providing child support. However, our offer for full tuition at a Negro college remains.

Should you request additional funds, we will be forced to make a public announcement revealing Miss Gibb's identity. This will not mark the beginning of any family ties but merely acknowledgment and admittance of my son's past mistake.

More simply, Mrs. Gibbs, our offer for tuition stands good only if you demand no more funds and keep Miss Gibb's identity confidential.

Sincerely,
Winfred Fitzgerald Whitfield
United States Senate
Raleigh, North Carolina

Callie folded the letter and slid it back in the envelope. She stuck it between the pages of the King James Bible in her nightstand.

She had always imagined what her daddy was like. He was one of Della's old boyfriends. He didn't love Della anymore, but he had at one time. He just found somebody new—a woman white like him. Whenever she went to Raleigh, she would watch couples walking down the street and try to guess which one might be her daddy. She'd seen the name on the checks, but did that really prove anything? Maybe the checks had been for some other reason. But then she had found the letter. She hadn't known exactly what she would do with the letter, but she had to have it.

Grayson Whitfield was Senator Whitfield's only son. And Callie had the proof he was her daddy. The senator, *her* Grandpa, wanted to run for president in the next election. President of the United States. She'd seen it on the news. And Grayson Whitfield, *her* father wanted to be a congressman.

This will not mark the beginning of any family ties but merely acknowledgment and admittance of my son's past mistake.

So was she a mistake? What was the real story between Della and him? Had they been sweethearts, or had he taken advantage of her one night? She pondered the question and fell asleep dreaming of Granddaddy Moses.

∞ ∞ ∞

Ruby Jean opened her eyes. Dusty rays of light cast shadows in room seven. She called it the purple time of day. There were two of them, one in the morning and one at night. She sat up and glanced over at the alarm clock on the nightstand. Four past seven. The four really stood for another number like ten or fifteen or something. Was it morning already? She got her bearings and decided it was still Sunday. She'd been dreaming about something. That's what threw her off. She usually only dreamed at night.

Callie slept like a log beside her all wrapped up in the chenille spread. Suddenly aware of the room's chill Ruby Jean did the same. The phone rang. Ruby Jean jumped, and Callie stirred.

"Hey, Ruby Jean. It's Vivian. What are ya'll up to?"

"Nothing much. How was the movie?"

"Long. Dr. Zhivago. My butt's still numb. You two come over. Sammy will be here. We're ordering pizza."

Vivian and Jerry's little house was an extension of the motel, painted yellow with blue trim. Vivian had told them she grew up there, even helping her parents run the little motel back then. The bungalow didn't have a lot of sitting space. Callie and Ruby Jean found a place on the gold shag carpet.

Sammy dished out pepperoni pizza on paper plates. "No dishes to wash!"

Ruby Jean couldn't wait to sink her teeth into the hot cheesy topping. Pizza had been rare in the Carson household. Beer was the beverage of the day, and Ruby Jean accepted the one Sammy popped open for her. She sipped on it and relished the pizza wishing for an icy Pepsi. But she didn't want to be an oddball. Besides, something from one of her dreams this afternoon kept bothering her. A few sips might help her remember. Snake sure seemed to remember plenty when *he* was drinking—the first few chugs, anyway.

Vivian told them a little about the movie. "What did you guys do?"

"Slept," Sammy reported. "And watched a little TV. The weekend was wicked."

Vivian swallowed her pizza and took a long swig of Budweiser. "No shop talk," she declared. "I want to watch the Sunday night news, though. There's a special on CBS about stuff happening around here. I guess that will affect our business. The time may be right to look for extra help."

"I thought you said no shop talk," Jerry said.

"You're right. What about you girls? What did you two do?"

Ruby Jean and Callie looked at each other. Callie took the lead. "Pretty much the same."

Vivian turned on the TV and got another slice of pizza. "There's more, everybody. Eat up."

After a few commercials, Walter Cronkite's familiar face bid them good evening on Sunday, February 28th, 1965. Vivian, Jerry, and Sammy pointed out places they recognized as the story unfolded of all the efforts of organizations working to register black voters in the south. Ruby Jean shuddered at the dark stories that unfolded. Ones like last August when three civil rights workers, two whites and one black had gone to investigate the burning of a black church in Mississippi. The police pulled them over for speeding. After spending time in jail, they were released only to be killed by a group dressed in white sheets called the Ku Klux Klan.

Ruby Jean took a few more sips of beer. What was that she had dreamed?

Then came the heartbreaking story of Jimmie Lee Jackson. He was a deacon trying to register to vote for years. Every time he tried, he was met with hard questions he couldn't answer. Ruby Jean knew what that was like.

"Will they put me through that when I go to vote?" she asked.

"Probably not back in North Carolina, but here they would,"

Sammy said. "You're white, which makes a difference. Here, it's the South's way of keeping the vote from black citizens. They ask impossible questions and ask for stupid documentation. And it goes against everything Abraham Lincoln declared in the Emancipation Proclamation. Not to mention the Civil Rights Act of 1964. This is some crazy messed up shit."

"Amen," Vivian and Jerry said together.

Scene after scene flashed on the screen as Mr. Cronkite said even reporters were getting hurt. Governor Wallace ordered protesting at night against the law.

"That means more people going to jail," Sammy said.

Jail. The afternoon dream came into focus. She remembered seeing Callie in jail again, but this time Babs was with her. She had something in her hand, and she was laughing. It bothered Ruby Jean. She wished she could ask Mama if dreams were sometimes the same as seeing a picture.

Back in room seven, Ruby Jean couldn't get the dream she'd had out of her mind. She had decided earlier not to say anything, but if she did she could quit thinking about it, she might not have it again. She told Callie.

Callie shrugged. "So you had a bad dream. That's not the same as having a vision, is it?"

"That's what I don't know."

"Well, it sounds like just a dream. You'd been asleep, right?"

"Yeah, but it was a different sort of dream. I don't usually dream in the afternoons."

"Ruby Jean Carson didn't get afternoon naps, RJ, remember? You always had to work on that tobacco farm or take care of your brothers after your mama got sick."

"What bothers me is Babs and what she was holding in her hand. Maybe you ought to report the robbery and tell them your money and ID got stolen."

Callie walked over to draw the drapes against the darkness. She turned and faced RJ. "I can't—I don't—think I can.," she stammered. "I'd have to tell them I was traveling. They'll want to know where I was and everything. I'd have to give them the address. They might try to contact Miss Wilson. That might lead to getting caught. No," she nodded. "I can't do that."

Frogmoor, North Carolina

February 26, 1965

The annoying humming of the fluorescent lights was the only sound in the office. Sergeant Kenneth Sawyers had his feet propped up on his desk, leaned back in his new office chair, half asleep. He'd been out at Ledford's and drank two beers for lunch. He didn't mean to. The chief sent him out again with more questions about Reggie's killing even though Al Ledford had a perfectly good alibi for his whereabouts during the time frame of the shooting.

"Yeah, Reggie owed me," he'd said, "but we worked it out." *Damn.* Reggie told him he paid off his debt to Ledford and swore he hadn't joined in any of the poker games after closing hours in weeks.

The phone blasted two short rings. *The chief.*

"Yeah, Chief?"

"Afternoon, Sawyers. How'd it go out at Ledford's?"

"I didn't get anything new, Chief."

"Well, take your mind off that for a while. I've got a little assignment for you."

"What's that, Chief?"

"I got a call from Alabama, somewhere around Birmingham. From a detective Henry Stephens. It seems a few days ago, a young Bonnie and Clyde type held up a liquor store on the outskirts of town. They got away, but the stupid girl left her license on the counter. They'd gone in and picked out a shit load of liquor, the owner said. They'd looked young, so the girl showed an ID saying she was twenty-two. Name, Nellie Wilson. DOB,

September third, 1933. Address, 2205 Pine Street, Frogmoor. The ID had an ink smudge over the picture. The detective got a little suspicious. When he called her, he found out she was a teacher at Wesley High and had never set foot in Alabama. He figures somehow Nellie Wilson's driver's license was stolen and ended up in Alabama."

Sawyers picked up a pen. "What about a description?"

"Auburn hair, olive complexion." A close fit to Nellie Wilson's description.

"What do you want me to do, Chief?"

"Go see Nellie Wilson. See if you can figure out some way her ID might have ended up in Alabama."

"Will do, sir." He hung up the phone. Olive skin. Ink smudge. Wesley High. Where the mixed girl Reggie married went to school.

Chapter 10

On Monday the first of March, Ruby Jean and Callie worked together cleaning the check-outs and getting rooms ready for any new guests.

Stripping dirty linens and replacing them with fresh ones appealed to Callie. They would haul the dirty ones to the laundry room and pull the clean ones from the dryer to fold. Mundane, mindless work like folding sheets and towels was the perfect time for thinking—unlike the weekend frenzy helping Sammy. Callie decided she was proud of herself for standing up to Lucy and refusing to go home. Heck, an eighteen-year-old girl deserved to be on her own. She left home, got a job, had a goal, and didn't need to clear herself of anything. She picked up the corners of a sheet RJ tossed and smiled thinking about Sammy. He acted so cool but still like a gentleman. A far cry from Reggie.

As if hearing her thoughts, RJ broke the silence. "You like working in the back with Sammy, don't you?"

"Yeah. It's kind of fun. I like Sammy. He's a terrific guy."

RJ raised her eyebrows. "Um-hum."

"Not like that, silly. I like what he's doing down here with that organization he belongs to. It's called the Student Nonviolent Coordinating Committee. I admire him for that."

"Me too." RJ filled the empty laundry hamper while Callie filled their cart with supplies.

Together, she and RJ made the beds in no time flat. RJ didn't tell time all that well, so she made it a game, timing their work in each room and seeing if they could beat themselves.

"Okay, we're starting at 9:20. Every mark after that twenty

is another minute. There are five minutes between each number. You already know twelve means o'clock, so just count by fives. By the way. You never told me how you did so much better with your orders the other night."

RJ explained how Vivian helped her with her letter reversals. She made a four-fingered fist with each hand and stuck up her thumbs. She held up her left fist. "This is the head of the bed." Then she held up her right fist. "And this is the foot of the bed." She picked up a notepad and a stubby pencil from the table and scribbled b—d.

Callie smiled. "That's cute!"

"Yeah, but I still need you to help me practice with the menu. And counting change. Vivian knows about my reading problem. She said a lot of people do. But she don't know I'm dumb in everything else too."

"RJ, you're not dumb in everything else. Reading's a part of the whole picture. We'll get the money out tonight and practice." They kept their money in a folded pillowcase underneath the mattress of Callie's bed.

They had one room left, the room that one of the newspaper guys had checked out of.

"RJ, you go on ahead to our room and get ready to help Vivian. I won't be seeing people, you will. I'll get this last room."

"You'll see Sammy," RJ said with a tease.

"Oh, go on, girl."

RJ laughed and left to go shower and change in room seven.

This room would be a breeze. Callie unlocked the door to room twelve where a journalist from Birmingham had stayed. One bed was undisturbed, not slept in. She made the empty bed and put in fresh towels and toiletries. The only trash was a scattered newspaper on the table. The New York Times. Not that she read many newspapers, but Callie found it intriguing. She glanced through a few pages of the first section. She read an article about how a woman's complaint of no heat for five days had stirred city action. *Jeez.* She turned the page. A headline caught her eye:

NC Senator Publically Opposes Democratic Liberal Plank On Civil Rights.

At the end of the half-page long article was a picture of the senator with his son. The caption read: *Senator Winfred Fitzgerald Whitfield to Seek 1968 Presidential Nomination While Son Grayson Vies for Congress.*

Callie looked at the picture for a long moment. "It's *them*," she whispered. She read enough to learn that her grandfather had opposed the Civil Rights Act of 1964 and was now in opposition to any voting act for black citizens. She folded the newspaper and stuck it on her maid's cart. She slipped from one blue door to the next gutting rooms of dirty linens and trash. A few of the guests had their telltale cameras with huge flashes strapped to them. She didn't intend to end up in the background of a photo splashed around the country. She thought about the picture in the New York Times of the senator and his son walking side by side up the Capitol steps seemingly unaware of being photographed. And unaware of having their secret offspring stare at it in the dim light of a motel in Alabama.

The way Callie saw it, she was in Coosa Springs for the long haul, at least until Clarence could pin Della down. She wasn't even there when Reggie got shot. Maybe that's the blessing from the first vision RJ had of her sitting in jail. The second vision involving Babs had to be nothing more than a whacky dream.

Coosa Springs, Alabama, might not be the best place for a mixed-race girl to be, but she couldn't complain. North Carolina wasn't that much better. Their senator, *her* grandfather, was against any civil rights bill and had been for years. She had read the article in the New York Times folded underneath the Bible in her nightstand again and again. The senator believed each state should be free from Federal civil rights laws regardless of voting rights. If the South wanted blacks to be equal but separate so be it. Callie wondered where that left her, being half of each.

She carted the linens to the laundry room by the office. Jerry always came by and collected the trash bags they left by the door. RJ would be down when breakfast slowed, and they could do their speedy bed-making routine. She hummed along with the Motown tunes in her head while folding warm sheets and towels in the stuffy little laundry room. She wished she'd had the forethought to pack her old green plastic radio it in her duffle bag, but no doubt Dale would have taken it too. What would have happened if she hadn't gotten robbed? Would she be going on interviews in Memphis?

RJ was right; Detroit was a far cry from Memphis, and she had no ID now. What she did have was a job and a place to stay. Yep, she would stay put. For now.

She finished room twelve and put the cart back in the storage room. She took the newspaper to room seven and stuck it in the nightstand drawer underneath the Bible with the letter inside.

Ruby Jean came bouncing in from breakfast, her pockets jingling with tips. "Sammy said hey, and to hurry up and get your fine ass up there."

"No, he did not. Fine ass?"

"Yes, he did," Ruby Jean laughed.

Callie had time to shower and put on her best jeans and a white blouse that was fairly new. She pulled her damp copper ringlets into a ponytail. Hazel brown eyes stared back from the mirror, eyes not quite as dark as Negro eyes. *Negro.* Sammy had said they were lobbying to get that word done away with. It's derogatory, he said. We should be called African-American or Black American.

She tied a pink scarf, she had found and washed, around her ponytail and went to be Sammy Luca's sous chef.

∞∞∞

"What smells so good?" Callie asked.

Sammy turned, stirring a big pot of bubbly heaven. "Texas

chili. Special of the Day.”

"RJ should have fun with that.”

"Vivian already talked to her. Just X for Texas.” Sammy laid the spoon down, yanked her ponytail, and tossed her a hair net to match his. " 'Bout time you got here. I need chopped carrots, celery, and onions for the second batch, Miss Sous Chef.”

"Carrots and celery? For chili?”

"Yep, it gives it crunch.” He handed her a knife sharp enough to cut paper.

Callie chopped while Sammy made batches of burgers.

"So, Miss Nellie, any idea when you're heading to Memphis?”

She started to lie, but she was living with enough of those. "Della's not in Memphis anymore.”

"She's not? How did you find out?”

"I called home last Sunday, and Lucy—Grandma told me.” Callie had sworn when she found out Reggie got shot not to tell anyone at the Blue Moon about it. She made RJ do the same. RJ was good at following directions. "Ouch!”

Red droplets splattered the carrots.

"This knife is sharp as hell.”

Sammy led her by the other hand to the spacious sink and ran warm water over the cut. "A good chef always has a sharp knife. A little of that.” He poured mecurachrome over the wound. "And a little of this.” He added a dot of salve and wrapped her index finger with a Band-Aid. "Now clean up and get to chopping.”

"Aye, aye, sir.”

Three tickets were up: two CBs with FF and one X. Callie got the fries and chili while Sammy assembled cheeseburgers.

"It's the lull before the storm,” Sammy said. "So did you find out where your mother is?”

"Della?”

"You call her Della?”

"Yeah, well, she wasn't around much when I was growing up, so I call her Della like Grandma did. Anyway, *Mother* is in Detroit working for a recording station.”

"Ah, Motown. Think you'll make it there?"

"With any luck. I've got my cousin working on getting a phone number. Like I said before, sometimes Della's hard to reach." She chopped carrots to replace the bloody ones. "You're from up north, right? Where up north?"

"New York. Brooklyn."

"And you're going back?"

"Pretty sure. I vowed to make this activist thing the basis of a thesis."

"So you just picked the Blue Moon off the map and ended up here?"

Sammy laughed. "Not exactly. I met Vivian and Jerry last year during Freedom Summer in Mississippi. Snick was a big part of it. That's what we call the Student Nonviolent Coordinating Committee. I found out Viv was a student at Framington State College near Boston, home for the summer. Jerry was a local boy. I was a student at Boston University. We got to be friends. Then Viv's folks died last semester, and she had to leave college. When Snick needed volunteers to work voter registration drives in the area last January, I jumped at the chance. I knew Viv and Jerry were struggling. The organization offered me ten dollars a week, and I could stay at the motel and help out for room and board."

"I remember hearing about Freedom Summer on the news."

"You're a North Carolina girl, right?"

"Born and raised an hour or so outside of Raleigh."

Sammy held up a hand for Callie to slap. "That's where Snick got its roots—from sit-ins and boycotts at lunch counters in Greensboro. They paved the way for a change."

Tickets were piling up on the carousel. Callie saw RJ peeking in. Vivian threw open the swing doors. "Wake up, guys!"

The storm had hit. The air grew thick with the smell of fries and burgers. They began a tango of cooking and serving with no time for talk. She wanted to hear more. What did he do with the organization? This mess in Alabama made her problems at Wesley High seem trivial. She got bullied, but at least she didn't have to worry about white men in bedsheets killing her. Not yet. She didn't know of anyone dying to vote in Frogmoor, but they should have the right. It triggered a spark of fear deep inside her. She wouldn't be there, but Clarence was, and Aunt Lettie—and Lucy.

Callie watched Sammy work, his dark, muscular body glistening in his white t-shirt. She'd felt that way looking at Reggie in the beginning. He had been her man. Even though they didn't hold off until their wedding night, he was her first, her only. She'd been proud of that. But after the sarcasm and slaps took over, it seemed he didn't want a roll in the hay any more than she did. She couldn't imagine Sammy Lucas being mean to a fly. He smiled so much, like now. He glanced her way and smiled all through the busy shift giving her the thumb and finger okay sign.

The tickets coming through began to dwindle. "Whew, finally. I'm gonna go get a refill." He held up his empty cup. "Want one?"

"Sure." If that were Reggie, she'd be getting them. She was serving the last order when he came back. She took the risk of sounding stupid. "What exactly do you do with the organization?"

Help with a little of everything. When I can get away, I hop in my DoodleBug and go over to Selma and Marion to work for the cause. We go door to door, talking to folks, helping them get prepared to register to vote, organize sit-ins at public places, that sort of day-to-day stuff." He shrugged and grinned. "So tell me about your town—or the one you left. What's the name of it?"

"Frogmoor. It's a corny sounding name, but it's a corny town. The blacks live on one side, and the whites live on the other. The black school uses the books the white school decides to toss. I was an integration project, the first Ne—black at the white high school."

"That's progress. We're still working on cases of pure neglect of the Civil Rights Act last year. Brooklyn has its problems too.

Some schools flat out try to ignore Federal law. It's ridiculous."

Orders coming through came to a virtual standstill. They started the nightly cleanup.

Jerry came back and told them to scram. "Out, guys. Go. Me and Viv will take care of this."

Sammy got them a big bowl of chili. "Head for the little table in the back."

"This chili has had me bouncing all night wanting some."

Sammy waited, ever-smiling until Callie took the first bite.

She parked the bite of Sammy's chili a moment and swallowed. "I love it!" She wondered how he had learned to cook so well if he was studying law.

"I'm glad you like it. Tell me. Is being a caramel girl hard for you?" His wink made the question inoffensive.

"It never was when I was little." She told him about Granddaddy Moses and going places in the orange truck. "As I got older, things changed. It seems like I did better by myself. I drank at the white water fountain and used the bathroom. But with other black people around, I didn't."

Sammy pretended to hold up a picket sign. "Heidy Ho, Heidy Ho, Jim Crow's got to go."

They both laughed.

"Seriously. I was cleaning the room of one of those press guys last week, and I came across a New York Times newspaper. There was this article about our senator. It seems like he's always against any civil rights bill."

"A North Carolina senator?"

She nodded.

"What's his name?"

She forced out *Winfred Fitzgerald Whitfield*. Saying the name out loud made it seem more real, and her cheeks burned. "And his son Grayson is a lawyer running for Congress."

"Oh yeah. That sucker. The senator, I mean. I don't know anything about his son. It's all politics. Whoever can vote him in is who he's gonna side with. He knows the Deep South doesn't want integration. He switched from Democrat to Republican because Democrats were too liberal with the civil rights law. They call themselves Dixiecrats. They preached states' rights. Years ago, he held a huge filibuster against integration laws. He called us Commies. He's against what people died for in the Civil War. Here in the South, those rights are not being honored. And people are still dying today." Sammy shook his head, his smile gone.

Callie felt as dumb as RJ must have felt in class. She wasn't sure what a filibuster was, but it was enough knowing her own grandfather fought so hard against civil rights. She knew Commie meant Communism, and she'd learned what that was. In grade school, they had air raid drills against what the teacher said was the Communists, and they had to duck underneath their desks whenever the siren sounded. She thought of something intelligent to say. "I did a paper not long ago about Malcolm X. I heard on the news on the way down here he was assassinated."

Sammy sighed. "Live by the sword, die by the sword. We all want change, but Malcolm went about it in the wrong way. He preached too much about using whatever means necessary. An attitude like that turns into violence. Snick works with Martin Luther King. Our way is a peaceful way. It's hard, and some of our members are getting frustrated. But we have to do things peacefully and politically. Violence is not the answer." He shook his head. "Not the answer," he repeated softly.

Callie breathed deeply, taking in all Sammy had said. Where had she been all her life? In Frogmoor, her head buried in the sand with Lucy, and then Reggie. She grew aware of how quiet the café had grown.

"And there's going to be a march soon," Sammy said. "Led by Dr. King himself. An important one."

Callie could usually tell when a guy was flirting with a girl. But she had to admit that as they worked side by side and talked, she wasn't sure about Sammy. One minute she thought he was just a really nice guy. And the next…Well, it didn't matter. She would soon leave for a different world, and he would go back to his college.

She found herself wanting to ask him more about his work. She hoped he wouldn't be one of the ones getting hurt or locked up. Times were not good. But to her advantage, she figured Kenneth Sawyers would be none too anxious to search for her on this part of the planet.

Frogmoor, North Carolina

March 1, 1965

Sergeant Kenneth Sawyers cruised down Main Street and turned left at the First Baptist Church. Nellie Wilson lived on Pine Street, a quiet street three blocks out of downtown Frogmoor. He had driven by her house twice over the weekend, but she hadn't been home. This time he had called ahead, so Nellie Wilson was expecting him.

Sawyers adjusted his cop's cap and rang the doorbell of the duplex where Nellie Wilson lived alone, he presumed, but you never could tell these days. Women were tramps anymore. When a petite brunette answered the door, it occurred to him that he was a free man now, and had been ever since his wife ran off with the Electrolux vacuum cleaner salesman.

"Come in, Mr. Sawyers."

He glanced around at the neatly kept living room.

"Please, sit down. Can I get you something to drink?"

A cold beer would be nice. "No ma'am, that won't be necessary. I don't want to take up too much of your time."

They both sat on opposite ends of a worn burgundy sofa.

"As you were told, Miss Wilson, your driver's license showed up in Alabama. In the Birmingham area."

"Yes. I'm aware of that, Sergeant, and I assure you, I have no idea how that happened."

"When did you first notice it was missing?"

"Actually, only after the detective called. I assumed it was in my wallet. I hadn't needed it." She gave a little laugh. "I didn't realize I was driving without one. I replaced it immediately," she added.

"That's fine. Miss Wilson, can you remember the last time you *did* use it?"

"Umm, let's see." She looked around the room as if a clue would fall out in front of her." Oh, yes. I had to go the office one day at school to change my address on some paperwork, and they needed a copy of it. I'd moved here to this apartment over Christmas."

"So you went to the office, used your driver's license, and then straight back to class?"

"That's right."

"Did you put it back in your purse? Do you remember?"

"Well, I remember it was right before lunch. I take my purse to the cafeteria to buy lunch every day." She shook her head and shrugged. "I guess I can't say for sure."

"Do you remember the date you signed those papers?"

"No, but I should have a copy. If you'll give me a minute."

Sawyers admired Nellie Wilson's rear view as she searched through a briefcase sitting in the corner.

"Yes, here it is." She held the yellow copy under a desk lamp. "The nineteenth of January."

"And you didn't use your driver's license again?"

She slowly shook her head. "No."

"Miss Wilson, do you think one of the students could have gotten your license?"

"I don't see how."

"Maybe you dropped it in the hall that day."

"Well, I could have dropped it at the supermarket for that matter."

"Miss Wilson, what can you tell me about Callie Gibbs Knight, the Negro student they put in your class?"

"Callie Gibbs? She doesn't go by the name Knight. She is a bright girl, and a brave one. I know she got teased, and she took it well." She looked at him with a determined eye. "I don't think we should judge anyone because of their race."

Sawyers shifted, uncomfortable. "Neither do I, Miss Wilson." He decided it best not to mention the girl had been married to the recently murdered deputy. He asked about Ruby Jean Carson instead to see where the conversation would go. "Don't you find it odd that they both left school on the same day?"

"Not really. I talked to one of Ruby Jean's younger brothers. He told me she left to live with her aunt in Tennessee."

"That checked out with what old man Carson had told him. He'd gone back to ask questions again, but the old guy they called Snake had met him at the door with a sawed-off shotgun. According to the boys at Ledford's, Snake was capable of anything if he was drunk enough. Kenneth Sawyers wasn't about to take any chances. "One more thing, Miss Wilson. Mrs. Gibbs, Callie's grandmother, doesn't have a recent picture of her. Would the school?"

"I don't know. Maybe in her permanent records."

"Do you think you could find one for me?"

"Mr. Sawyers, I'm really very busy with my own job." She pointed to a stack of papers on the coffee table, the top one with lots of red marks and the number sixty-five circled at the top. "Maybe you should do your own job."

"Fine, Miss Wilson." Women. They were all bitches. As far as he was concerned, the chief should change Callie Gibb's status from missing person to person of interest wanted for questioning in the murder of her young husband.

Chapter 11

On Tuesday morning, Vivian called a meeting. Sammy served waffles with maple syrup and sausage, and they all sat down at the back booth to a late breakfast.

"Ya'll meet the new help." Vivian introduced everybody and asked them to talk about themselves.

"What is this, school, or something?"

The question came from a skinny white boy with shaggy brown hair. Something about Ricky Cooper didn't sit right with Callie. For one thing, he pulled up a chair and sat at the end of the table even with room in the booth. Vivian was about to say something, but Ruby Jean interrupted.

"Vivian's practically a teacher."

"Oh. Well, I'm a senior at Thomas Jefferson High. I get to leave at two every day on a work-study release if I have a job."

"Ricky's going to take a big a big load off of us in the kitchen. Dishwasher and assistant sous chef. Sammy's thrilled. Sammy's our wonderful chef. He was in college up North where I went to school."

Sammy smiled and winked at Callie. Her cheeks grew warm.

"Trudy?"

"I'm Trudy Marshall, high school dropout." Trudy, short, spunky, and dark flipped her long braids over her shoulder. "Had to," she said glancing at Ricky. "They found my daddy dead last month behind the church where he was a preacher. He'd been involved in the voter drive. Me and my mother and three little sisters moved here from Birmingham to stay with my grandmother. We won't make it if I don't work." She smiled at Vivian.

"Thanks so much for this job. Oh, and I'll be cleaning rooms, not working in the kitchen." She glanced at Ricky again.

"Oh my God, I'm so sorry," Vivian said.

Callie saw Sammy hang his head, pinching his nose between his eyes. She and Vivian looked at each other, shaking their heads.

Callie told them she was Nellie Wilson and Ruby Jean was her friend from high school. "We're dropouts, too, Trudy, so don't worry about it."

"All right, well, go team," Vivian said cheerfully. "Ricky, get here as soon as you can after your last class. Trudy, you can start right away."

By the end of the day, Callie and Trudy were a team. Besides getting rooms done in record time, they had shared the basic facts of their lives. Callie told her about Reggie getting shot, swearing her to secrecy. However, she stood by the name Nellie Wilson, her last lie, and she was beginning to wish she hadn't stolen the ID. She told her about finding the letter, but that her daddy and granddaddy were well-to-do white men, not a judge running for Congress and a senator who wanted to be the next president.

Trudy shared the spooky story of her daddy found dead.

"The Klan murdered him, I'm sure of it. He led a big group at the church where he was a minister on campaigns to get Negroes registered to vote. He went to church late one night to do some work and didn't come home. The police found him dead behind the church, shot to death."

"I'm so sorry, Trudy. Can't they find out who done that?"

"Humph. Not around Birmingham. It all gets covered up. It was a bummer. Still is." She sniffed and pulled the corners of the sheet on her side of the bed they were making.

They finished up room ten and sat on the rusting porch chairs outside, sharing a Salem.

"So what're you gonna do?" Trudy asked.

"About Reggie?"

"Well, that, too. Think you'll find Della in Detroit? That's an awfully big place."

"What I have to do is get to the phone over at the mall. I told Clarence to try to track Della down. And he'll know what's going on with Sawyers. But I'm innocent, and I'm not going to act like I'm guilty." She puffed on the Salem and passed it to Trudy. "Ruby Jean needs to call home, too."

"Why did Ruby Jean run away?"

Callie told her about Snake, Ida Carson and her illness, and the gift she passed on to Ruby Jean.

"She seems kind of weird."

"She's just shy." As close as she was getting to Trudy, Callie didn't want to betray RJ by talking about her disability. "Anyway, her vision of me being in jail and Reggie dead is one of the reasons we're here. But I would have left sooner or later."

"So when was the last time you called home?"

"Last Sunday. That's when I found out this guy Sergeant Sawyers came out asking about me."

"I wouldn't go walking, even to the mall. We're too close to Selma, and all hell has broken loose over there. Folks around here don't like half-breeds, as they call them, because they hate mixed marriages. Look. My grandma has a big old white Impala. We don't drive it much, we can't afford the gas these days. I fight the bus crap and just sit in the back."

"Gosh, I thought all that mess was over with after Rosa Parks."

"It should be, but not around here. Anyway, what I'm saying is, if you've got a few bucks for gas, I can come pick ya'll up and take you to the payphone. We'll go Sunday after we get the checkouts done. Since the café closes after breakfast, RJ can help. We'll get the rooms done in no time. How does that sound?"

"Perfect." Callie smiled. "Thanks, Trudy."

In the lull of the early afternoon, RJ came to help them finish. She bounced with joy when they told her about the planned drive to Coosa Springs Mall on Sunday. "The Blue Moon's going to be slam full all weekend, Jerry said. And Vivian said Sammy's gonna be late. Real late. He drove to Camden for his activist work. She wants to know if Trudy can help in the kitchen an extra few hours."

"Gosh, for a little while. But then I've got to get home and watch the girls while Mama goes to work."

No Sammy thought Callie. And then after Trudy left she'd be stuck in the back with Ricky Cooper.

Friday afternoon Ruby Jean could feel it coming on. Tonight she would have to make change. A steady flow of traffic streamed by the Blue Moon. The booths had been full since not long after she started the early supper shift, and only a few stools at the counter were empty. She couldn't get the tables cleared off at her station fast enough. Customers ended up with fresh drinks sitting on dirty tables. Food came out slower than it did when Sammy was there. The jingle of tips in her pockets stopped growing.

She kept hearing the same thing over and over—"Miss, can we get our table wiped down?"

A while later, Vivian carried plates of hamburgers to one of her customers and replaced hot dogs with them. *Be more careful,* she mouthed. She'd forgotten to stop and think about the bed sign.

Jerry came back and pulled her and Vivian aside. "Let's stop serving food at the counter. I'll seat them and bring their drinks. You two can show them to their table when their order is up. I've got Nellie cooking. Ricky and Trudy are filling orders. But

Trudy has to go soon."

Ruby Jean had a table that still needed drinks. She filled a round tray with two sodas, three iced teas, and one water. She balanced the tray carefully on upturned palms like Vivian taught her.

Snake used to laugh and say she could trip over her own feet. That's the first thought she had when she looked down and saw tea, ice, Pepsi, and water in a puddle on the floor. Then she thanked God the glasses were thick red plastic. Tears stung the back of her eyes like hot pepper, and her face burned. She stood in shock while Trudy came out and began cleaning up the mess.

"Don't just stand there. Go get them more drinks."

What were they? She knew it was one water. Was it two teas and three sodas? She fixed another tray of sodas praying she had it right. Trudy had finished and disappeared. As she set the freshly filled glasses down, she heard a voice behind her. "Are they letting the negras work in white restaurants now?"

"I guess. It doesn't bother me as long as one of them ain't sitting down eating with me. We let them clean and cook in our houses."

The supper shift became a nightmare like the one where you look down at school, and you're in your petticoat. Vivian tapped her on the arm. "Look, I've got to go in the back. Ricky walked off the job, and Trudy had to leave. Jerry will help you. Sammy should be back before long." She hurried away.

"Miss, this Pepsi is supposed to be tea." She turned and saw the lady at the end holding up her drink glass.

The nightmare got worse. Jerry said she needed to go ahead and ring up her own customers.

She did her best. Some of the people didn't bother looking at the change. A few said she owed them something like forty cents more, or a dollar. She gave it to them. Some just looked at her funny and left. She hoped she hadn't given them too much back.

Mama used to say she felt like a house had been lifted off of her when certain troubles passed. That's how Ruby Jean felt when Jerry locked the door to the café and turned the sign to closed. She didn't know what time it was, but she knew it was earlier than when they usually closed.

The horrible night was over. This time it was Callie who served hot dogs and chili. Sammy had made it back, and they all sat wearily in the quiet of the night as Sammy told them all about his day in Camden.

"About two hundred of us showed up. We marched two miles from the church to the Wilcox County Courthouse. The mayor, two police officers and a bunch of unofficial officers made us turn back. A few of them had guns. They all had night-sticks, and I even saw a few with cattle prods. That blew my mind. We asked them to let us demonstrate peacefully and make our case. But then the mayor told us nobody, black or white would vote today."

"Whites? How can he do that?" Vivian asked.

"They claim to only open at certain times. So another group of us tried all day to get into the café in town to test the public accommodations act. The door stayed locked except to let a few whites come in."

"Why don't we do that here?" Callie asked. "Trudy and I could try it."

"No," Sammy said. "Jerry and Vivian aren't against the act, to begin with. It would just hurt business, and they would be the victims."

Callie remembered the older couple that walked out the day she was eating a hot dog at the counter with Ruby Jean.

"We need to focus on the ones that are fighting it first. What exactly happened to Ricky Cooper?"

"I don't think he liked working with black people," Callie said.

"We probably got too busy to make the job worth it to him," Vivian said.

"I'm sorry, guys."

Jerry spoke up. "Don't be. You're doing what you're supposed to do. We'll hire somebody else. We don't need people like him."

"An interesting march is planned for tomorrow. A white minister from a black Lutheran church is leading it. He's a native of Selma, and he wants to show that some whites, too, are against this injustice. But I'm going to sit that one out. I'll be here. I have a duty to this job."

Sammy Lucas was working for a cause. In a way, they all were. Last night Ruby Jean had the dream again—the same picture of Babs sitting in jail beside Callie, laughing, holding something in her hand. It was different, somehow, from her other dreams. Maybe it was all the violence they watched on TV. Every night after showering and tucking themselves into bed, they watched as people got hosed down with huge fire hoses and forced back with billy clubs.

Chapter 12

Vivian had Ricky Cooper replaced by Saturday afternoon. Miles Young, tall, slender, with baby cheeks and blonde hair had been her second choice while hiring. She called him and he agreed to come in. Vivian declared it as no less than a miracle. He had graduated high school, worked in the grocery store as a stock clerk, and wanted to become a chef. Callie liked him right away, and Sammy did too.

Vivian told them Press and white activists occupied most of the rooms. "The motels will be last to integrate, wait and see," she said. "Right after restaurants."

Callie found another abandoned copy of the New York Times while cleaning rooms. She flipped through it furtively but didn't catch a headline or photo concerning Winfred or Grayson Whitfield. Dated February 28, she scanned the scattered articles related to the goings-on in Alabama. One headline caught her eye. She stopped and read it. Twice. It was an incident beyond frightening. A Negro preacher at a church involved in voter rights reported that during Sunday services, several truckloads of white men with shotguns interrupted service, calling the deacons out. They told them to get that nigger out of town, or somebody would kill him. The deacons, out of fear for his life, gave him one hundred dollars for the next three months' pay and let him go. She shuddered and thought about Trudy's daddy. Grandpa Moses was never a preacher, but she thought about him, too. She folded the paper neatly, placed it back on the night table, and finished straightening the occupied room.

Once again, she couldn't see Sawyers looking for her here. She envisioned him kicked back, watching the news, and being glad all of this wasn't going on in Frogmoor.

∞ ∞ ∞

Heavy rain the night before left the Blue Moon shrouded in fog. Trudy had the low beams on her grandma's Impala on. She pulled into room seven's empty parking space and hopped out. Callie, sitting outside drinking coffee and smoking, got up to throw her cigarette away.

"No, don't. Let me have that. Grandma would kill me if I smoked in her car. She saved up forever to buy it."

"Want a cup of coffee? Jerry gave us an old percolator he found."

"Nah. Don't you want to get started?"

Together, the three of them stripped linens and cleaned checkouts, made beds, and delivered fresh linens to the stay overs. Ruby Jean did the vacuuming and cleaned the bathrooms. Callie and Trudy talked while making the beds. Trudy asked about the new guy, Miles.

"He's okay. He works good with Sammy. By the time I got up there, he'd done told Miles about his activist work. I worried, but Sammy told me later Miles brought it up first. Turns out, Miles's dad teaches history at the high school over in Selma. He's working on a secret committee to start plugging for integration later on."

"That's interesting," Trudy said, holding a pillow by the chin and tucking it into its case. "But they need to wait until this voting mess is over."

"Sammy says it's a struggle that'll take a while. As he puts it, it's trouble that has to take place. This thing is getting all kinds of attention around the whole country." Callie told her about the articles she'd seen in the New York Times, but she didn't say anything about the Negro minister. "Anyway, there's a big march for today. He wouldn't say anything except that there would be around five hundred people, and MLK was leading it himself. Sammy's organization, like Dr. King's, doesn't want any violence."

"Humph. Well, they've sure been getting it."

They finished one bed and moved to the second.

"I say King's right," Trudy continued. "We ought not to judge people by the color of their skin. Sometimes, I'm guilty too, like with Ricky Cooper."

"He was a jerk, anyway."

After finishing, they signed their time cards on the board in the laundry room and threw in the wet linens to dry. Callie and RJ each took their supply of quarters, and they piled into the car.

"I would take ya'll to the house, but Grandma's there, and she'd freak out. But times are changing, just not very fast around here."

Callie draped the same pink scarf she had found around her questionable hair and tied it under her chin.

"Here, I know." Trudy dug in the car's glove box and dug out a pair of huge sunglasses. "Put these on."

Callie put them on and looked in the visor's mirror.

"You look like Jackie Kennedy," Trudy said laughing.

Ten minutes later, they pulled into Coosa Springs Mall. Trudy dropped RJ off at one phone booth and drove the short distance to the other. "I'm going to the A&P and pick up some stuff for Grandma. Keep your scarf on, Jackie."

Callie shot her a bird, and they both laughed. Trudy drove away and left her staring at the phone booth. She had to admit she was nervous despite her decision to act normal. Part of it had to do with RJ's dream and all that freaky stuff about her vision. There had been something to it after all. Reggie was dead. She opened the door of the phone booth, stepped inside, and made the call.

"That line's busy, ma'am. Would you like to try again later?"

"Okay, thanks, operator." The phone spat out her change. She picked it up and hesitated, thinking. It was Sunday, not long after church. Lucy and Aunt Lettie were probably talking about people from the church that morning while they cooked dinner. She stepped out to have a smoke and wait. Maybe it would take Trudy a while. Or maybe she wouldn't mind waiting. She paid for three dollars' worth of gas. At thirty-one cents a gallon, that was almost ten gallons.

Callie watched the phone booth up the street where RJ was. She had gotten through and was talking. She'd said she'd try to ask her mother about the double dreams. Callie hoped she got the chance. She finished her cigarette and stepped back into the phone booth.

"Sorry, ma'am, that line is busy. Would you like to—"

She hung up the phone. Outside the phone booth, she paced back and forth. She heard the gunning of an engine behind her. She turned, expecting it to be Trudy. A carload of kids, either the same hooligans from last week or their cousins and neighbors were they instead. But they barely glanced at her before speeding off. She decided to stay in the phone booth and pretend to be talking.

Come on, Aunt Lettie, hang up. She deposited the money and crossed her fingers. The line was still busy. She tried again and again until Trudy drove up.

Trudy rolled down the window yelled, "I'll go get her first." She pointed up the sidewalk where Callie saw RJ walking toward them. Her body language said the news wasn't good. Oh God. Callie hoped her mother didn't die. Sure, she was dying, but not yet, she hoped. She gave up trying to get through to Clarence. Damn Lucy and Aunt Lettie.

Trudy pulled up with RJ sitting solemnly in the back. "Her mother went to the hospital last night," Trudy said quietly.

Callie slipped in the back beside her, taking off the big sunglasses. "I'm so sorry," she said hugging her friend.

The tears trickling from the corner of her eyes turned to sobs as she leaned against Callie. "I knew it was coming—I just—wanted to talk to her one more time."

Callie cried too. She took off her pink scarf and handed it to RJ. Then Trudy cried. They all sat crying. Trudy pulled herself together first. "What did you find out, Nellie?" Ruby Jean handed the scarf back to Callie. She dabbed her eyes and spoke.

"The line's busy."

Trudy pulled McDonald's napkins out of the glove box, kept one, and passed the others back. "You'd better put your scarf back on, Jackie." They all three laughed through their tears. "Did you try again?"

"Over and over and over."

Trudy sniffed. "Go call again and tell the operator it's an emergency, and will she please cut in. They can do that."

"Good idea." She pat RJ on the arm. "I'll be back in a minute."

This time, before the operator asked if she wanted to try again later, Callie interjected and declared an emergency in a desperate tone.

"Certainly ma'am, I can do that." She heard a click, then another click. "Ma'am, was that number 704-657-6640?"

"Yes."

"Ma'am, that number is out of order at this time."

Callie hung up the phone, opened the glass door, and threw up her hands.

"What happened?" Trudy asked.

"Phone's out of order."

"Oh, I bet it was the storm. Roy said they had a bad storm up there last night. He said it made Mama going to the hospital especially awful."

"Ruby Jean," Callie said, skipping her nickname, "Look.

I've got enough, or we've got enough money to send you home on a bus. You could go to the hospital and say good-bye to your Mama. I'd get Clarence to meet you." There was no Carson family car. "We'd get a round-trip ticket, and you could come back."

"I can't," RJ said. "I can't do that. Not after being here on my own. I'm afraid Aunt Peggy would be there. It would be her chance to snatch me up. She'd go get my school records and tell everybody it would be best for me. She wants me declared stupid, so she can be my guardian and get a check. Besides, I don't want to mess things up for you, Nellie. Roy said Sawyers had been snooping around again. Snake got out his shotgun and told him to leave."

"Good Lord," Trudy said. "Looks like ya'll have your own brand of violence. What about your brother Roy? Can't he take over?"

"Roy's not twenty-one yet. Besides, she'd still be around Snake." Trudy didn't seem surprised to find out about RJ's learning problem. Callie was glad. Trudy was a bit blunt sometimes, and she didn't want RJ's feelings hurt.

"Twenty-one. Twenty-one. Damn, twenty-one." Trudy slammed her fist on the steering wheel and accidentally blew the car horn. They all jumped. "They'll ship your ass off to Vietnam when you're eighteen, black or white. But you can't do this, and you can't do that until you're god-damn twenty-one. And if your ass is black, you got to fight the war without a vote."

Callie thought about it. Twenty-one was the whole reason she'd stolen Nellie Wilson's ID. So she could get a singing contract. And twenty-one was the reason Babs and Dale got it too. To buy liquor. She couldn't stand it any-more. It was time to tell Trudy the truth. They were too close now not to tell her. "Trudy," she began, "I have some-thing big to tell you." She squeezed RJ's hand. "Everything I've told you about me is true but one thing. My name's Cal-lie Gibbs, not Nellie Wilson. You see, I stole my teacher's driver's license when I started thinking about running away. I wanted to be over twenty-one."

Callie told her about the ink stain, and leaving her ID behind, and about how Babs and Dale laughed when they stole it, planning to pretend it was Babs's and buy liquor with it. "Please don't tell Vivian and Jerry. They're nice and all, but I still don't feel like I can take a chance on them getting mad at me and throwing us out. I don't know what we'd do since Della's not in Memphis."

"Of course I won't tell. But I know good, and well Vivian and Jerry wouldn't throw you out. I think you're mainly embarrassed. Sure, you shouldn't have taken the ID, but I understand why you did. But your man getting shot is the worst part. And since you ran away about the time he got killed, it might look fishy."

"But he was murdered two days after I left."

"Do you have proof? Did you keep your bus stub or anything?"

"No. We missed the bus and hitched."

"Humph! Well, if they try to pin the murder on you, your best bet may be to 'fess up to stealing the ID and then hope to find a way to prove when you left town."

The wailing of sirens caught their attention. Cop cars were screaming down the road—a lot of them. Callie paled. RJ gasped and ducked down in the back seat.

"What in the world?" Callie asked.

"It looks like every cop in Coosa Springs," Trudy said.

RJ sat back up after the last one sped by. "What do you think happened?"

"I don't know," Trudy said, "but it looks like they're headed over the Coosa Springs Bridge into Selma."

"Oh my God, Sammy's march is today," Callie cried.

They sat until the sound of sirens vanished into the distance and then drove in silence back to the Blue Moon. Trudy parked in front of the café.

Jerry opened the locked door and waved them in.

"Come on in, girls. We were looking for you. We were over here working when my brother called. Things aren't good over in Selma. State troopers met the marchers at the bridge. They didn't even get across. They got tear-gassed big time and even clubbed."

He led them to the kitchen where Vivian sat huddled over a radio. An announcer was urging everyone to stay home. "There are injuries. I repeat, injuries. Ambulances need to get out."

Callie's heart all but stopped. Sammy was there.

$$Chapter\ 13$$

No longer did it matter that Callie hadn't been able to find out anything from Clarence that day, or that she had told her new friend about pretending to be Nellie Wilson. Jerry and Vivian hadn't asked why they were riding around with Trudy, and RJ hadn't even told Vivian and Jerry about her mother.

"The best thing to do is to sit by the phone at the house. Sammy will call us when he can." Jerry grabbed the keys and shooed them out the door. "Trudy, you'd better stay put for a while. I'd say the roads you have to go through are closed."

They met Miles on the way out. "I guess ya'll heard. Any news from Sammy?"

"Not yet," Vivian said. "We're praying for a phone call. Come on and wait with us."

They all gathered around the radio in the tiny kitchen waiting for the phone to ring and the evening news to come on, hoping the phone call would come first. With heads down and hands folded, they listened to reports coming in from a Montgomery station. There were injuries, most treated at the scene. Others had been serious enough to be transported by ambulance to Good Samaritan Hospital. They looked up and glanced at each other anxiously.

Trudy called her grandma. "She said my mother planned on marching with her friends from church but got roped into baby-sitting for her boss, the Duncans."

"This is such a shame," Miles said. "I learned some stuff talking to Sammy while we worked. Selma has a population of roughly 20,000, and only a little over a hundred African Americans are registered to vote. It's not right. And then there's what happened to Jimmie Lee Jackson. Dad says protesting is within everyone's constitutional rights. Everything around here—Jim Crow laws, school segregation, all of it goes against Federal regulations now."

"Right," Jerry said. "The whole state of Alabama is getting to be an embarrassment. And my brother said the uppity whites at the golf club won't even turn on the TVs anymore. They just want to ignore it and hope it goes away."

"The problem is, too many people around here are against doing away with separate but equal, and that disenfranchisement thing is keeping the right to vote away from blacks," Vivian said.

Disenfranchisement. New word, but the situation for blacks here in this part of the country was becoming clear to Callie. They basically weren't free. Not entirely. Not until they could vote, and eat, sleep, and play wherever they wanted. Blacks. African Americans. Callie had noted right away how Vivian, Jerry, and Miles avoided the word, Negro. Like Sammy told her that word was on its way out.

Callie noticed that RJ was quieter than usual. She normally piped in with lots of questions. Then she remembered what RJ had found out that afternoon. She turned to read what was going on in RJ's head.

Her eyes were filled with tears. "I hope our Sammy is okay," she said quietly.

∞∞∞

Black and white pictures flickered on Vivian's portable TV. They hadn't turned on any lights yet, and it was another purple time of day. Ruby Jean thought of the afternoon dream. But that didn't matter right now. Sammy hadn't called yet, and they all worried. She thought about Callie's offer to send her home earlier, but she'd rather remember Mama like she was before she left. Like when she laughed and cried at the same time when she cracked Snake's skull.

Ruby Jean could tell Callie wasn't anxious to leave the Blue Moon, and Sammy, and Jerry and Vivian now. That was okay with her. The three girls held hands, Callie, in the middle and watched the horror as Jerry flipped back and forth between a station in Montgomery and Mr. Cronkite's news way up in New York. It made her feel like she a part of it all when she thought about the newsmen and photographers staying at the Blue Moon. She wondered if Roy was watching. She listened as she had never listened before, not since President Kennedy got killed.

Mr. Cronkite said 525 marchers, young and old, started that morning from a church in downtown Selma. They carried backpacks, bedrolls, and lunch sacks and wanted to cross the bridge over the Alabama River to walk fifty miles to Montgomery, the Capitol.

"Their intention," he said, "was a protest to dramatize Negro voter rights. They planned a peaceful demonstration led by civil rights leaders and Martin Luther King. They battled a cold wind whipping across the Edmund Pettus Bridge only to be stopped on the other side. CBS has live coverage of the scene. Take a look."

"They came like a moving blue wall," a reporter said, "as more than fifty-uniformed Alabama State troopers stood shoulder to shoulder across the divided highway. The marchers were given two minutes to retreat and then came the order: troopers advance." The reporter stopped talking as the newsreel flashed. Then he spoke again quietly. "You can see them with their pistols drawn and their nightsticks flailing."

Ruby Jean screamed as one loud popping sound followed another. A gray cloud rose from the streets.

"Tear gas bombs," Jerry explained. "I figured that when I saw those two troopers at the end put on gas masks."

The scene ended with noise and confusion and no sense of

what happened. They all breathed with relief when Mr. Cronkite spoke again. "As of this live broadcast, all the marchers are safely off the streets and back in their homes or churches. A makeshift hospital has been set up in the basement of the Methodist church." The relief was short-lived, though, when Mr. Cronkite said at least a dozen marchers were injured seriously enough to be taken to the local hospital. "We have new footage coming in as we speak, and more news from Selma after the break."

Jerry switched back to the local news. A reporter stood on an empty street at dusk. "Watch the difference," he said.

"...and then one of the troopers announced over an amplifying system that this was an unlawful assembly and a march not conducive to the safety of the public. Given a chance to retreat, not one Negro budged, remaining in columns. After the troopers had advanced, they broke up and ran. The Dallas County Sheriff and *volunteer* possemen met them with bricks, bottles, and other debris being thrown by the Negros. They were finally herded back into their homes and churches."

How degrading," Vivian said. "He makes them sound like cattle."

"Here's the scene earlier today."

Again, they saw the troopers advance as marchers ran. Many of them were knocked down. One tear gas bomb exploded. Then the footage stopped.

"Look at that," Jerry said. "That'll change when everybody around the world sees the national news. They'll have to show it then."

"They're making it look like a riot," Miles said. "Turn it back to Cronkite."

Ruby Jean knew the question on her mind was the one none of them wanted to ask yet. *Did anybody die?* She felt better when Mr. Cronkite announced the official count taken to the hospital at seventeen. "They suffered bone fractures, concussions, cuts, and bruises. No life-threatening injuries."

"That's it," Jerry said. "We'll hear from him. Even if it's not until his friend comes in the morning. Sammy set him up to take his place. I forget what his name is, but Sammy says they always leave a few of them behind to take care of business or bail them out of jail. Sammy says since we give him room and board that's business."

"Meanwhile, more disturbing footage has come over the wires," Mr. Cronkite said. The ugly pictures flickered on as the room grew a darker purple. Men rode through on horseback. White people stood on the sidelines and cheered. Ruby Jean was sure someone would get trampled. Jerry said they were the sheriff's possemen. They reminded her of a film she saw in school once about the Ku Klux Klan. But these guys didn't wear clothes made of bedsheets. Two women lay on the median in the highway, their skirts hiked up too far. Stuff was scattered everywhere, and an ambulance was loading someone on a stretcher.

The phone on the wall in the kitchen rang. They all shot straight up

Vivian turned on the light and answered. "Hello." She paused and looked at Jerry. "Yes, it is. Jerry Robinson is my husband."

They watched Vivian's face for the answer. She shook her head okay and gave a thumbs up.

Okay. Yes, ma'am, got it." She hung up the phone and smiled. "We can pick him up. He has a mild concussion, but an x-ray showed no skull fracture. They said he could go home with next of kin. I guess we're next of kin."

Like Sammy, Vivian and Jerry drove a Volkswagen bug, so they all rode to Good Samaritan Hospital in the big Impala.

"Grandma don't care," Trudy declared. "I told her about Sammy and what's going on. And I've got plenty of gas since..."

Trudy glanced at her, and Callie knew she didn't want to lead to any conversation about going off the property to call from a payphone. She glanced out the window as they drove through the now quiet streets, her thoughts drifting to the article she had read in the newspaper from New York about her grandfather, the senator from North Carolina who wanted to become president, and her own father, a lawyer running for Congress. President of the United States. Congress. *What if? And where the hell was Della?*

On the way, they argued about who should be the one to talk to whoever in charge of releasing Sammy. Trudy thought it should be her. "After all, I'm the only one that's the right color. Well, I guess Nellie could be. Do you want to do it, Nellie?"

She didn't, but Vivian spoke first.

"So what if he's the wrong color? He's Jerry Robinson, and he's got an ID that says so if they ask. By the way that reminds me. Did you ever get your stolen ID replaced, Nellie?"

"My cousin Clarence said he'd take care of it." It was the only thing she could think of to say. "I—I told him to just wait until he can get Della's address and send it there."

"Can they do that?" Jerry asked? "You might have to go to the Department of Motor Vehicles."

"Nah, not in Frogmoor. It's a small town. Everybody knows everybody." Thankfully, they seemed to accept her answer. RJ and Trudy said nothing.

In the end, they agreed it would be better if Jerry went into the emergency room alone.

"With all that's going on, we don't need to cause a spectacle," Vivian said.

The rest of them waited in the car. Time seemed to stand still. Vivian chewed her lip, Trudy picked at a fingernail, Miles popped his knuckles, RJ sat trance-like staring straight ahead, and Callie was dying for a smoke. She was about to grab one out of her jacket and hop out and light up when she saw them. Jerry walked slowly beside him. He limped, and his head was bandaged. But when they all jumped out of the car to greet him, he broke into the familiar smile Callie had grown so fond of. He hugged them each one by one, Callie last, and holding her a few seconds longer than he did the others. It's because we worked together and talked a lot, she thought. Or was there more?

He was dirty, his shirttail torn, and he smelled of antiseptic.

Jerry and Vivian sat upfront with Trudy again, and Callie's heart pounded while Sammy waited for a chance to slide into the back and sit beside her.

"Today was the darkest day of my life, guys," he said, eyes downward, his smile gone.

"I'll bet," Miles said. "We heard about it on the radio first, then we saw a bunch of terrible scenes on TV. Not just the local news but the CBS Evening News with Walter Cronkite."

Sammy nodded. "Yep. My big brother was a Freedom Rider back in '61. They were met with a lot of violence but ended up drawing international attention." Sammy took Callie's hand first, and then RJ's and sat back to give them his version of the events they had seen on TV first hand.

"Did you get gassed?" Jerry asked.

"No, I escaped the tear gas. After getting clubbed in the head with a nightstick, I hauled ass into the parking lot of a tractor company. The medical team set up a station in the church basement to treat minor wounds and help with the effects of tear gas. The doctor in charge decided I should go to the hospital for a possible skull fracture, and here I am."

Vivian asked him about what had been on the local news— the violence erupting from the marchers toward the sheriff and his possemen.

"A bunch on horseback charged at them. They were terrified. The men were flailing nightsticks, even whips. So they threw bricks, bottles, whatever they could get their hands on. I don't think any of them were really hurt. They retreated and waited for another backup. Selma's Commissioner of Public Safety, one of the more decent among them, made them back off and convinced the group to go back to the church where they'd be safe."

"We're glad you're okay," RJ said. "I wish you would just not march anymore."

"Thank you, sweet girl, but who would I be to back out now? My brother didn't. It's a family tradition," he said chuckling. "Anthony left with a group of Freedom Riders traveling from Montgomery to Jackson, Mississippi. He and some others were arrested for trespassing when they tried to use whites-only facilities. A judge had them locked up in a maximum-security prison for sixty days. Sixty days! Attorneys from the NAACP appealed to the Supreme Court and got them out. Finally, a few months later, the Interstate Commerce Commission agreed to prohibit segregation on interstate buses and in terminals. That means, my dear Ruby Jean when you and Nellie head out to go be famous singers, you can ride together." He smiled at Callie and squeezed her hand.

"Wow," RJ said. "Where's your brother now?"

"Fighting in Vietnam. For freedom, again."

Everyone fell silent. "I say we liven this group up," Trudy said. She turned on the Impala's radio and found a station still playing music rather than reporting any horrible news. They hummed along with Sam Cooke. Callie and RJ picked up on the lyrics and sang. *It's been a long time, a long time coming, but I know a change gonna come. Oh, yes it will.*

"You both have beautiful voices," Sammy said. The others agreed.

"Thanks," they said in unison.

"I wish there was a place to all go sit down together and have a nice quiet supper."

"There's not. Not yet," Jerry said.

"Well there is one place," Vivian said, "Our own. We'll toss some burgers on the grill and heat up some of Sammy's chili. We'll have chili burgers."

"We've got beer at the house, too," Jerry said. "I bet Sammy could use one."

"No kidding man. Amen to that," Sammy said. "Maybe it will ease this dull headache."

"Gosh, maybe you shouldn't," Vivian said.

"Oh, a couple won't hurt," Jerry said.

"I totally agree," Sammy said. "And I'm starved."

"It's a plan then," Vivian said. "We'll hide in the back and get over this horrible day."

Chapter 14

The neon crescent moon on the sign at the motel flickered in the night sky. The day had been the longest in her life, Ruby Jean decided. Between Snake and school that was saying a lot.

Jerry told Trudy to park in front of room seven. "We have to let the café look closed, or else customers will come pouring in. I can't handle that tonight. But I *will* go check for cards."

The Robinsons always left a sign on the office door with their phone number for any motel emergencies. If both had to leave, they placed cards in a holder on the door with instructions for the name, time, room number, and problem. The sign instructed them to slide the cards under the door.

Miles had to get his Dad's car back home, but Trudy's grandma said she could spend the night. She and Vivian walked to the cottage to get the beer. Ruby Jean and Callie helped Sammy to the kitchen in the back of the café and eased him into a chair.

"We'll take care of everything," Callie assured him. "You rest. What happened to your leg, anyway? Looks like your head's not all there is to worry about."

"Well, Miss Nellie, it just so happens after I got smacked in the head, I fell. I busted my knee cap up pretty good. They dressed it at the hospital. A hug would make it all better."

Callie laughed. "I'll bet. And elevation will make it even better." She grabbed an empty five-gallon bucket and turned it over for him to prop up his leg.

"Thanks, but I still say a hug would be better."

Ruby Jean could always tell when Callie was embarrassed and at a loss for words. One day at Wesley High the student council president, a football player, and a hunk had stopped her in the hall to welcome her to Wesley. He told her she looked real pretty. She had stammered and stuttered something like thanks, glad to be here and ducked behind her locker door. She could see Callie's relief when Trudy and Vivian came in loaded down, with Jerry following.

Vivian pulled out a can of Charlie's Chips. "Don't fire up the fryer, too much mess to clean."

"I say, Jerry, who's the man around here?" Trudy quipped.

"Sorry Trudy," Jerry said. "Stop ya'll and listen. I met up with a couple of our guests. One is a journalist from New York, and the other is a photographer from Atlanta. They're starved. They said virtually every place to eat in Selma and Coosa Springs is closed because of all the trouble today. No one is up to a sit-in tonight. No offense, Sammy. How do you feel? Should I invite them in or fix to-go boxes?"

"I say bring them in. It's okay with me if it's okay with everybody else."

"It might be interesting," Vivian said. She brushed her fingers through her white-blond pixie cut.

The others shrugged. "Okay by me," Trudy said. "Come on girls, let's get the burgers on the grill."

"Are we—gonna sit with them?" Ruby Jean asked.

"I'd like to meet them. You don't have to. You sound nervous." Vivian put white tapers in her mother's glass candlesticks and lit them. "This way we can sit out front."

"Me? I'm not nervous." Yes, she was. But she wouldn't miss it for the world. New York. Atlanta. She just didn't want to sound like a dummy. Maybe she wouldn't say anything. But then she would seem like a dummy.

But Dennis Hopkins, a photographer from Atlanta, and Philip Murray, a newsman from New York didn't make her feel dumb as they woofed hamburgers and bragged about Sammy's chili. Dennis, tall and sandy-haired, reminded her of Roy. Phillip was a smart-looking redhead with black-rimmed glasses who described what happened using words like appalling and outrageous.

"Thanks so much, guys for fixing this," Dennis said.

Phillip nodded with his mouth full and swallowed. "You may have saved our lives."

They said they had eaten at the Blue Moon twice and declared the food fabulous. They told Sammy they were impressed with Snick and admired him for his work. Philip asked how in the world a young college guy had learned to cook so well.

"My grandmother taught me. She was a Southern lady who ended up in Brooklyn. Her name was Lucy. Lucy Lucas," he said winking at Callie.

They smiled at each other, and Ruby Jean knew why. His grandmother had the same name as Callie's. She must have told him about Lucy. More and more, Ruby Jean sensed something going on between Callie and Sammy. She deserved someone nice like Sammy. She wondered how that left things as far as finding Della. They hadn't intended to end up here, and they were really off track. But she didn't care, and it was looking like Callie didn't either. She decided to forget about the dream. There was no Dale and Babs here. She probably had the nightmare because of getting robbed. Her eyes drooped as they all talked.

"They restrained the press about as much as anybody," Dennis said. "It was like they wanted to hide what was going on."

"I reached Brown's Chapel ahead of the other journalists," Phillip said. "After they finally let us through, I saw the sheriff lead a charge of a half-dozen posse men. By the time the other newsmen arrived, gosh, what must have been at least a hundred packed into Sylvan Street a block away from the church."

Dennis Hopkins, the photographer from Atlanta, said he stayed on the other side of the bridge. "I'm glad I did. I saw at least four carloads of posse men overtake the marchers as they came back over the bridge. They jumped out and beat them with nightsticks. And I interviewed two other witnesses that saw them using whips."

"I heard one of the march leaders say he had fought in World War II and was captured by the Germans," Phillip said. "The Alabama state troopers were more inhuman than they were."

"And all because these people down here want the right to vote," Sammy said. "It's unfair representation plain and simple. For example, over in Lowndes County blacks outnumber whites four to one, but not one black person is registered to vote. We're asking to do away with literacy testing and Federal voting registrars. People should only have to sign their name and provide biographical information."

"You're on your way to getting what you want. What happened here today will cause national—no, international outrage," Philip said. "It's just a shame it's taking all this violence. Look what happened to Medgar Evers. Shot hours after Kennedy passed the civil rights law. It's been two years, and his killer hasn't been convicted yet."

∞∞∞

The candles had grown short, wax dripping down onto Vivian's antique glass candle holders. She blew them out and said it was so late now they could turn on the lights. Outside the big glass windows, the motel parking lot was full but silent. Callie laughed to herself when she saw RJ nodding. Poor kid. She had gone through a lot today.

Trudy cleared the table, Jerry passed everyone another beer, and the conversations continued. Vivian talked about being in school and discussed Boston with Phillip. She told them about meeting Sammy and working at Freedom Summer in Mississippi last summer. Sammy had grown quiet but still caught Callie's eye every so often and smiled.

Vivian called it a night. "God, I wish tomorrow was Sunday

again. A normal one."

Callie loaned Trudy a big t-shirt to sleep in, and they giggled like school girls as they pushed the two double beds together to make one. "Hey, I liked that radio station we were listening to in the car. Can you find it again? I sure as hell don't want to watch TV."

Trudy turned the dial on the old radio Jerry had salvaged for them.

Ruby Jean went out like a light on the edge of her bed. Trudy and Callie propped up on double pillows listening to music and talking. "You know, I think Sammy likes you."

"Think so?"

"Yeah."

"I don't know. Sometimes I think so too, but then I think it's just Sammy being Sammy.

The words of a hit song were fading, *Nowhere to run.*

Trudy leaned forward, big eyes shining. "Hey, that's Martha and the Vandellas."

"Yep, it is."

"Wonder if that's your mother singing in the background?"

"Probably."

"That's pretty cool. What're you gonna do about finding her and getting a singing career for yourself going?"

Callie shrugged. "Just wait a while, I guess. I can't leave now with this mess going on. The Robinsons need us. I need to go call Clarence again. I don't want to, but I need to find out what's going on."

"Aren't you sorry at all about your husband dying?"

"Humph. Reggie was no husband. He was somebody my grandmother found to keep me black."

"Don't you want to be black? Or do you want to be white?"

Callie looked at Trudy a few seconds before she spoke. "I just want to be me." She scrunched down into the butter-colored blanket. "You know what, Trudy? I've been thinking. I'd like to get involved while I'm here."

"Like how?"

"I mean I'd like to march, to protest—whatever, to see Negros around here get the justice they deserve."

Trudy laughed. "What if you get caught on camera, and that policeman sees you?"

"You're right. I've thought about that before, but I really and truly would like to get involved while I'm here."

"Well, you could get that nappy red ponytail cut into an afro and dyed black. My cousin's got a hair salon."

"That's not a bad idea, Trudy. I'd match Sammy. That is when all his hair grows back from having stitches."

They giggled and talked more about Callie being a fugitive and having to disguise herself.

"I'll call Rhonda tomorrow."

Callie clicked off the dim lamp and turned down the radio. Once again Sam Cooke crooned about a change going to come, and they both drifted off to sleep alongside RJ in the beds they had pushed together.

Chapter 15

The girls were up and dressed by six the next morning. After strict orders by all of them to stay in his room and rest, Sammy skipped breakfast. Vivian introduced them to Sammy's friend from Snick, a quiet guy named Thomas the same shade of milk chocolate as Sammy. Callie helped Vivian prepare a breakfast-to-go box for Sammy with a heaping pile of Thomas's fluffy scrambled eggs and steamy grits.

Callie and Trudy made their rounds, first turning on the TV in each room, listening as they worked. Every morning news channel reported telegrams and statements from priests and political leaders pouring in.

"… a sickeningly brutal attack."

"… more like Hitler's storm troops."

"… some call for Federal intervention."

Trudy turned the volume down on the TV in room ten. "Maybe they should."

Send Federal troops down here? Do you think they will?"

"It may be the only way this will end."

"What about the fight? The cause? Voting rights for Negros?" The word tasted bad on her tongue now.

Trudy fluffed up the pillows on the bed they had just made and sat down. "We'll win. The Voting Rights Act will pass. I just hope nobody else has to die. Are you still wanting to get involved?"

"Yeah. Yeah, I do. I'm stuck here, anyway."

"So you want to march?"

"Maybe. But I think—what I'd really like to do is test that provision for prohibition."

"Prohibition of discrimination in public accommodations?"

"Yeah, that."

"Why had you rather do that?"

"I think the reason is that with so much Jim Crow laws going on around here, I'd have a hard time. I mean, look at me. Do I use colored facilities or white? Colored, I guess, but I don't think the black people around here would accept me."

Trudy gave her a pretend hurt look.

"Oh, I don't mean all. I mean, it was like that at home, but around here, it would be worse. Back home, everyone knows I'm Moses Gibbs' granddaughter, and they respected him. They knew the story of Della getting knocked up by a white man. They just didn't know who," Callie sighed.

"Humph. Well, I'll get serious about that hair appointment." She reached over and yanked Callie's ponytail with the pink scarf, the one they called her Jackie scarf, tied around it. "Girl, let's finish up. I got to get home and see what's going on. My mother babysat for the Duncans last night."

"The people she does housekeeping for?"

"Yeah, they have little kids. Rotten little suckers, but the Duncans are good to Mama. I'll bet they were involved last night. We do have our white folks on our side here. They work at a college. Professors, or something. Drive all the way to Montgomery every day." Trudy handed her the vacuum cleaner. "Here. You vacuum and take the trash out. I'll go do the bathrooms."

Callie took the vacuum cleaner and shooed Trudy away. "Go home now. I've got this."

"Nonsense. I just got here."

"No, really. There aren't that many checkouts since the Press is still hanging around. Go. Before your grandmother kills us for keeping her car so long."

"Oh, she wouldn't do that. I'd like for you to meet her sometime. And RJ, too," she added.

They looked at each other for a little moment and then

Trudy jangled her car keys and waved goodbye.

Callie used the time alone cleaning to muster up the courage to talk to Sammy. Could his organization use her? What if they didn't want her because she wasn't all the way black or all the way white? She doubted it mattered to Sammy, but it might to some others.

Lost in thought, she finished up the last checkout. Better spray a rag with Windex and dust. She had been in a hurry and didn't want to get sloppy. She saved giving the TV screen a good swipe for last. With the volume low, she had become oblivious to the droning voices. But the words fell on her ears like a load of bricks.

"... and we caught up with 1968 Presidential candidate hopeful Fred Whitfield today in Raleigh, North Carolina." On the screen was the same photo she had tucked away in her nightstand. The senator says he supports George Wallace. Quote: 'George is a good man. He says he wants the best for his state, and he's not against anyone voting that qualifies. If the governor feels like these events in Selma are getting out of hand and should be stopped, then they should be'. Senator Whitfield is a long-time advocate for states' rights and has been against every Civil Rights Act presented. He has never denied being against integration. Meanwhile, the senator's son, Grayson Whitfield..."

Callie turned off the TV and sat down on the edge of the bed, forgetting about wiping the TV. Her throat felt tight, her hands, clammy. The names, the photograph, his words, the article. It all jolted her back to her other reality. Leaving Reggie, Reggie getting shot. What she needed was the courage to stay here. And she needed to call Clarence. Damn the phone being out of order. But she couldn't walk to a payphone in this mess, especially with RJ. The rocks and jeers they had endured before would be downright dangerous now. And she didn't know when Trudy would get her grandmother's car again.

∞∞∞

The breakfast shift was steady but not rushed. Ruby Jean still had to try extra hard to concentrate. Vivian kept the portable TV in the café blaring. She said the breakfast customers would be Press and out-of-town activist, so they would want it that way. She decided she'd just have to trust God and Jesus to take care of Mama and time to take care of getting her and Callie where they needed to be. So she concentrated.

When breakfast was over, Ruby Jean sat down to a grilled cheese sandwich and fries Thomas fixed for her. That's when she saw them get out of a car in the parking lot. Three nuns went into the motel office. Were they there to register for a room? Maybe they were just inviting the Robinsons to church. Did nuns do that? But then she saw them all get back into a big blue and brown station wagon and drive down to the end of the motel. They were there to stay.

The only time Ruby Jean had seen a real nun was at Christmas one year. Aunt Peggy had come down and taken them all to Raleigh to the movies to see Babes in Toyland. All of them but Snake who preferred spending his Saturday afternoons boozing at Ledford's. They had seen a group of nuns coming from upstairs where the colored people sat. Junior had said they looked like penguins loud enough for them to hear. Aunt Peggy laughed, and Mama pinched Junior. He yelled which made things worse.

Mama and Aunt Peggy had gotten into a discussion about them on the way home. "They say they're married to Jesus," Aunt Peggy said, "and take vows not be with a man. That's why they wear all that garb. Can you imagine?" Mama had kept fussing at Junior and was mad at Aunt Peggy for laughing. "They do important work, God's work, and it was wrong to mock them," Mama said. Laughing, she had added that it would beat the heck out of being married to Raeford Lee Carson.

Like Mama said, nuns did God's work. They were here for the cause of getting Negros the right to vote without all the violence. God would listen to their prayers, too, and Ruby Jean figured they would pray, and pray hard for justice. She wondered if God listened to nuns first before anybody else. Mama always said God would answer prayers as long as you had faith that what you asked for was His will. And you couldn't ask for things like bunches of money. Surely it would be God's will for this to end. It was only fair that people have the same rights, no matter what color they were.

Vivian slid into the booth across from her sipping sweet iced tea through a straw. "You did a good job this morning, Ruby Jean."

"Thanks. Those ladies, they were nuns," she said nodding toward the parking lot.

Vivian smiled. "Yes, they were. Did they—did they check in?"

"Yep, they sure did. They said motel space is getting tight. I rented them our last room, the one we try to save for breakdowns. They drove in from Wilmington, North Carolina. They seem sweet, and an interesting combination. One is about my age from the looks of her face. The other two are older. One is probably about your mother's age, and the oldest one could be your grandmother."

Ruby Jean envisioned three faces to fit Vivian's descriptions.

"Go take a half-hour break. Nellie and Trudy may already have finished. I'll see you back here for your lunch shift."

"Okay." Ruby Jean crammed down the rest of the fries and stood up.

"Oh, Ruby Jean. I meant to ask you about your mother. Have you talked to her?"

Ruby Jean didn't know how to start. There had been no time to talk about the phone call yesterday. "Mama's gone to the hospital. Not to get well, but..."

"I understand. I'm so sorry, Ruby Jean. You call home anytime you want to. Okay? From the room."

"I'm trying to remember Mama like she was the last time I saw her, but, thanks, I will." Her cheeks grew warm like they always did when she told a rare lie.

"But aren't you worried your mother might have a vision you're not at your aunt's house?"

"I think as long as I'm safe she'll know. Snake and the younger boys will be the only ones surprised when I don't show up at the funeral with Aunt Peggy."

The door to room three was ajar. The cart with towels, cleaning supplies, and little soaps and shampoos sat parked outside. Ruby Jean walked into the room with the intention of telling Callie about the nuns. She stopped. Callie sat on the edge of the bed with tears rolling down her cheeks. She sat down beside her, taking her hand. "Callie, what's wrong?"

"Nothing, really. I—I watched a replay of what happened yesterday is all."

The TV was off. Ruby Jean knew it was something more than that. Something personal. She hugged her friend. "That's not all, Callie. What else?"

"I guess I'm worried about not getting in touch with Clarence the other day. Nothing to do with Reggie. I wanted to get Della's number."

"Why don't you call from the room, Callie? Or at least from the phone booth outside."

Callie shook her head no. "It's just not safe." She stood up. "I'll be okay. I'm gonna go get cleaned up and try to talk to Sammy."

"About what you and Trudy talked about last night?"

"Yeah. I thought you were asleep."

"I heard." Ruby Jean offered to take the maid cart back to the room behind the office. She checked the dryer. Sure enough, a load of linens needed folding.

The clock in the laundry room had the shorthand past the eleven and the big hand on the twelve. It was time to go back to the café for the lunch shift. The three nuns sat in the third booth to the left. Her side.

"Your first customers." Vivian nodded toward the trio sitting in the third booth. Oh, my, gosh. She was going to serve lunch to nuns. Jesus, please don't let me mess up, she prayed.

Kenneth Sawyers opened the brown envelope the crime lab sent and pulled out a glossy eight by ten color photo of Callie Gibbs. He had convinced the school secretary to contact the company they hired for yearbook pictures. It hadn't been easy. The nosy bitch wanted to know what for.

"We protect our students, Mr. Sawyers," she said. "They're our number one concern."

"She's missing, Ma'am, and her grandmother doesn't have a recent photo of her."

"Well, that's strange."

"Yes, ma'am, it is. Can I get you to do that?"

The word *missing* changed everything, and they ordered the negative that day.

She wasn't a bad-looking girl. Her hair was a strange color, and her eyes weren't as dark as Negro eyes. He could see how Reggie had been attracted to her. *Reggie.* He had exhausted every possible motive from every possible suspect. Every story he checked out found them with an alibi. And they all gave Reggie a reprieve on owing them money.

"Reggie was Reggie." One of them said. "He'd always get back to you."

"Why the hell kill him," another said. "That sure wouldn't get the money back."

So that was it. Kenneth Sawyers, first order in rank assigned to the case, couldn't find a suspect in the killing of Reggie

Knight. There was no smoking gun. They'd been fighting, the old lady said. Callie Gibbs shot her husband Reggie with his own gun, ditched it, and then split town. He would crack this case and finally be Detective Kenneth Sawyers.

He picked up the phone. It was time. Past time. He had enough going that he wouldn't look like a fool.

"Hey, Chief, I've got some information on Reggie's case. I've followed every possible lead, and, well, I think we have reason to believe it was his wife."

"His wife?"

"Yeah. I think we should drive out to her grandmother's house. Pick me up, and I'll explain everything on the way over."

Chapter 16

The blustery winds the marcher's had to contend with yesterday crossing the bridge over the Alabama River tamed down to a breeze with a hint of early spring warmth. Callie found Sammy sitting behind the Blue Moon at a cracked cement table. He didn't see her. He was pouring over a spiral notebook, pen in hand.

"Hi. How's the noggin and the knee?"

He looked up and grinned. "Hello, Miss Nellie. The noggin is about as good as it ever was, and the knee is sore as hell." He stretched out his right leg. "What brings you back here to the jungle?" He looked around at the tangle of vines and dead vegetation creeping around the ancient, battered picnic table. Elaborate scrolling decorated the edge, and two arced cement benches surrounded it.

"Thomas said you'd be back here. I've got a little time to kill before he needs me."

Sammy laid his pen down and motioned for her to sit down "I'm glad you came to visit."

Callie shifted. "Yeah, well, I got something I want to ask you about. Trudy spent the night last night. We were talking, and well, I'd like to—we'd like to help."

"Help?"

"Yeah. We want to support the cause, this voter's rights campaign, and more." She told him what she'd told Trudy, about wanting to test Jim Crow and public accommodations.

Sammy took in all she was saying, nodding quietly. "One question. What happened to your plan to ride off into the sunset and become a singer? You've got a terrific voice, and a foot in the door. Have you heard from your mother yet?"

"Della? Not yet. She—checks in with Grandma once or twice a month. She'll call. Grandma has a number she can reach her at in an emergency." She assumed that was the truth, she hoped so, anyway. "Besides, we can't leave Vivian and Jerry right now, they need us."

Sammy took a sip of an icy drink in a cup sitting beside an empty bowl encrusted with his chili. "So you want to join the cause while you're here."

"Something like that. Like I told Trudy that could be why we're stuck here."

"We? Does RJ want to protest too?"

"She will. She thinks the same way I do. Trudy, too."

"Well, it's always helpful for whites to join."

"Do you think my, ah, in-between-ness would matter?"

Sammy laughed. "In-between-ness. That's a cute way to put it. No, of course not. Look, it's dangerous right now. Especially trying to break Jim Crow. It would be safer to wait until we get these people by law to stop interfering with our constitutional right to protest and get protection from Federal troops. President Johnson wants a voting act to pass but he needs to start pushing it forward more. Maybe helping Vivian and Jerry is enough."

"They helped us out, too. I wanted to get to Memphis and get a job even if it was just doing something like I'm doing here first. And in Detroit, I'll need more money than ever."

"You can't just call and go home to Mama?"

"I told myself I wouldn't go to Della broke. I want to be on my own first. Plus I've got Ruby Jean to worry about."

"It's too bad you got robbed, but I'm glad you made it here. You've been a godsend. I'd hate to see you get hurt, or arrested. True, they have slacked off on arrests, but who knows."

Stay put, Clarence said. Sawyer's trail is cold right now. Don't do anything funny. "You may be right. It's just that I admire what your organization is doing. I think I've come to see how much things need to change."

Sammy paused for a moment. "I understand." He nodded yes and their eyes locked in understanding. "And thank you. It's all about staying peaceful and working through the legal system. That's Dr. King's way, and we follow those ideals. What happened yesterday is making that harder and harder. Tell you what. I'm having a phone conference with our director later this evening. I should find out some stuff. You'll get classified information." He winked.

There came the flirty side of Sammy back, and her cheeks glowed.

∞ ∞ ∞

Vivian did a good job describing the nuns. To Ruby Jean, they were like a daughter, a mother, and a grandmother. Sister Mary Agatha had deep wrinkles like Mama's mother the time Mama got the vision of her dying and hauled all of them, even Snake, to Tennessee. Sister Mary Eunice had a stern face and seemed to be the one in charge. Sister Mary Clare had the face of a young angel with a quick, quiet smile and dimples. Ruby Jean always loved dimples and wished she had them.

Mama used to talk about being as nervous as a long-tailed cat in a roomful of rocking chairs. That's how Ruby Jean felt at first. But talking to the three nuns came easy. It all started when they told her they were from an abbey in Wilmington, North Carolina. Ruby Jean couldn't help but tell them she was from right outside of Raleigh. They lingered over lunch and talked to Ruby Jean each time she refilled their glasses of iced tea. They wanted dessert. Ruby Jean told them they had apple and pecan pie today.

"We get them from a bakery. They're pretty good."

Sister Mary Agatha asked her to join them. "Let us buy you a piece of pie."

It was the after lunch lull, so maybe she could. "Let me make sure it's okay with Vivian."

She came back and told them about Mama being sick, and a little about Snake, and a little about how her friend Nellie had wanted to get away from home. She was careful not to say too much. Callie might get mad. But it was easy talking to the three sweet nuns.

∞ ∞ ∞

Back at work on the late lunch shift, Callie looked through the order window and saw RJ sitting down chatting with three nuns.

Thomas must have noticed the surprise on her face. "Vivian checked them into the last room. Nuns. Can you believe it? They're here to help us protest."

A pang of guilt sliced through Callie. It was only yesterday that RJ called home hoping to talk to her mother. She vowed to have a long talk with her back in the room. She couldn't wait to hear about her chat with the nuns. Wonder if she had been nervous? It didn't look like it.

The stream of tickets was steady but not overwhelming. Ruby Jean got a couple of orders mixed up, but all in all, she was doing great. Just please don't let her have to count back change again. The stockpile of Sammy's special chili disappeared. It reminded Callie of the day she cut her finger chopping carrots. She was amazed that it was only days ago.

Busy as she was, her mind drifted in and out to the dark place she had gone that morning. This time Senator Winfred Whitfield had been more than a picture in a newspaper. He had more than a face. He moved. He had a voice. "Let those qualified to vote, vote," he said. He wasn't against it; neither was George Wallace. But now Callie knew qualified meant passing a literacy test. Moses Gibbs wouldn't have been able to do it. Ruby Jean probably wouldn't be able to either. For the first time, she wondered if Winfred Whitfield was the reason she wanted to protest.

She missed the easygoing banter between her and Sammy. Thomas didn't say much and always looked serious. "Did anyone take Sammy some supper?" she asked Thomas.

"Nah, he said don't bother. He had some stuff in his room. He's been busy as heck making notes, writing messages, and talking on the phone."

When the after-dinner lull came, Callie pulled carrots, onions, and celery from the cooler and started chopping. The locals had learned to ask for the Blue Moon's homemade chili, and people from out of town were catching on quickly. An arm went around her waist and a hand over her eyes. "Sammy?"

He took his hands away and laughed.

"How did you sneak in here?" She gave him a playful box in the chest.

"Ouch, you're hurting a sick man," Sammy said, pointing to her pile of chopped vegetables. "We ran out of chili?"

"Yep."

"Oh, no." He faked a fainting spell. "Better get busy and make more." He reached for an apron.

Thomas was filling a lone ticket on the carousel for an HB with FF for Ruby Jean. "Woah, take it easy. How are you feeling?"

"I'm good, just lonely and bored." He winked at Callie and tied the apron in the back."

"So what's going on, my man?"

Callie perked up. Would this be the classified information Sammy mentioned?

Sammy turned and leaned against the steel sink where he was rinsing out a huge pot. "Judge Johnson, the Federal District judge, denied the motion for a temporary restraining order against Wallace and his brigade today. The court says it's best for all if we wait until they have a chance to make a decision. They're afraid people will get hurt. They set a court date for Thursday."

Vivian came through the swinging doors with a load of dirty

plates. "Good. I agree. Look at your head."

"Shit, my knee is worse than my head. Anyway, a march is planned for tomorrow. Same thing, trying to get from Selma to Montgomery. Dr. King himself is leading it."

Vivian gasped and almost dropped the tray of plates. "Dr. King? I'd love to see him again."

"But you said no one's allowed to march until after that court date," Callie said.

"It's going to be a symbolic march. We're all confident we'll win in the end because we're within our constitutional rights. Nobody will advance toward any troopers or posse men. We'll turn and go back; they'll get their way. We'll state our purpose and declare we're coming in peace. Kind of like aliens would say to natives. They have enough sense not to attack if we turn around. Not with all this bad publicity."

Vivian sat the tray of plates down. "You're not marching, are you? You're not able."

Sammy looked at his shoes and sighed. "Here's the deal. Some of our people are getting impatient and pissed off. They want something done now. They're drifting toward a Malcolm X mindset. By any means necessary. We've got to show some kind of aggression."

"Well, if you march, I'm marching," Vivian said.

"Me too," Callie said.

"No. No, I don't want you to. There will be state troopers, and they'll have the same gear. You know that. Besides, you've got the motel to take care of."

"But you said no troopers will dare attack. We can close the place and put out the emergency cards. The whole motel is full of those Concerned White Citizens of Alabama folks and news-men, anyway," Vivian argued.

"No, don't go."

"Then don't you go, either. If you go, we all go. Right, Nellie?"

Callie cringed. For more than once, she wished she didn't have to be called Nellie. "Right."

Quiet Thomas in a white apron turned around palms up. "All

right, all right. Sammy's right. It's better if you guys wait until after a court ruling. And Vivian's right, too. Sammy, take your kitchen back over, and I'll march. You need to stay off that knee another day. Save your strength. No doubt you'll need it later."

"That's for sure," Callie said.

So much had happened in the little time they had been there. For her, it all started with the senseless killing of Jimmie Lee Jackson. Callie feared what would happen next, but it was mixed with a different fear, a fear of doing nothing to change things.

Chapter 17

By early Tuesday morning word about the second planned march buzzed around the news channels like rumors running through the halls of a high school. Thomas left to join the march. Sammy was back, and Miles would be in later after a brief bout with a stomach virus.

Callie sensed the tension when they met at breakfast. Sammy served pancakes with sausage and blueberry syrup and asked them all to bow their heads in silent prayer.

"Amen." Sammy signified the silent prayer over.

They all said amen in unison and dug into breakfast eating in silence.

Vivian spoke up. "Sammy, if you think you ought to march, just go. We can handle it."

Sammy swirled a forkful of pancake in a pile of syrup. "No, I'm okay with staying here, Vivian. It's okay. Let's just run the hotel and café today. We can regroup and see what happens. I pray it goes peacefully like it's supposed to. Anyway, you're right, my knee is sore as hell. If they did let us across the bridge to head to Montgomery, I'd be in real trouble."

"What about your head, Sammy?" asked Ruby Jean.

Sammy faked amnesia "My head. My head? Who *are* you? Where *am* I?"

They all laughed, their spirits lifted. But Callie was secretly disappointed they weren't marching with Martin Luther King today. And she thought maybe Sammy and Vivian were too. Even Ruby Jean was fired up. She told her all about the nuns last night before they went to bed. Callie got a little nervous when she told them where they were from. Wilmington was just a few hours from home. "Just what all did ya'll talk about?" Callie had asked.

"We talked about Mama dying, and visions," RJ said.

"Anything about me?"

"Just that you left a mean husband to go live with your mama. Is that bad?"

Callie had told her no, there wasn't any problem.

Vivian twisted her napkin and laid it on her plate. "Well, one thing is for sure. Whatever happens, we'll see the whole thing on television, and so will the whole world."

Callie heard Trudy's voice. *What if you get caught on camera, and that policeman sees you?* She squeezed her frizzy copper ponytail. It had been a long time since she'd been to a beauty parlor. And she had the money. It was time for a visit to Trudy's cousin's salon.

∞ ∞ ∞

Trudy's cousin Rhonda's hair salon was in the heart of one of Selma's Negro neighborhoods not far from the church Sammy said the marchers were to congregate. The houses sat closely together along tree-lined streets, some of them over-painted in colors that made your eyeballs hurt, and others with flaking gray paint. They didn't pass right by Brown's Chapel, but Trudy pointed out the way.

"I personally love your hair. But if change is what you're after, change it is." Rhonda's short, broken off hair was clipped in the back with a long, silver clip, the kind you secured rollers with.

"Girl, I did so much shit to my hair, it all broke off. I've got new weave to put in later. What brings you here so early, Trudy? I thought you had a new job."

"I do. We do. The motel is full of out-of-town folks connected to the marches. No check-outs, so we finished early.

Nellie here is dying for a new 'do."

"Humph. Well, there's a couple of ways we can go here. You getting paid by the hour, Trudy?

Yeah, but I get a good base pay. So what can you do for Nellie?"

"Come on over to the basin for a good washing, and we'll talk." Rhonda draped a big plastic bib around Callie, tying it behind her neck.

Warm water ran through her hair, and Rhonda slathered her up with a coconut smelling liquid. Her deft fingers massaged her temples and the back of her head.

The smell was like the gel the barber used when Granddaddy Moses took her to his barbershop for a haircut. He would wash her head the same way and apply the slick gel. Lots of things reminded her of Granddaddy Moses these days. He was her life support until he died tragically at the crossing of Frogmoor's railroad track. The engine in his little orange truck had stalled. The coroner's report showed that at that very moment, Moses Gibbs had suffered a heart attack.

Rhonda gave her a final cool rinse, lifted her head, and wrapped a towel around her hair. "Okay, as I was saying, we got a couple of different looks we can go with. I can give you a hair relaxer treatment if you want to go straight. The only thing is, you got to repeat treatments pretty soon, and you really need a straightening iron. You may not need as much though since you 're mixed. I think that's cool. If you want to be a blonde, I can do that too."

"What about one of the new afro dos?' Trudy asked. "They're easy to take care of. All you need is shampoo and a pick."

Rhonda snapped her fingers, "Good idea. Trudy said you planned to join your mother in the music business. The 'fro has become a political statement and a fashion statement too. Are your ears pierced?"

"Yeah, but it's been forever since I wore earrings."

"You should get some big hoops. Those, maybe a headband,

and you can walk right into the music industry."

"What about her color? Are you gonna dye it black?" Trudy asked.

Rhonda leaned back and studied Callie's face. "You know, I would go with a dark chestnut. It would go pretty with your eyes and your skin tone. Don't run from being mixed. Be proud of it. And you wouldn't have to have a color job for a while like you would if we dyed it black."

Callie looked through the pictures of afro hairdos in a magazine Rhonda gave her. It was radical all right. Different from any Frogmoor hairdo, and just the disguise she needed. Certainly easy to care for, and she needed that. No coming in for a straightener.

Rhonda snipped and clipped until what looked like her whole head of brassy hair was laying on the floor. She almost passed out from the smell of hair dye. The whole process seemed to take forever. And she was getting anxious to go call Clarence.

Rhonda brought out a pair of gold-tone hoop earrings. "Here, you can wear these until you can get some." She fastened them into Callie's almost overgrown pierced ears.

"Ouch!"

"Don't look yet." Rhonda added a little makeup and swiveled the salon chair around to face the mirror.

She gasped. The girl smiling back at her didn't look like the Callie Gibbs that had trod through the forests of Alabama after being robbed. And her racial identity crisis certainly didn't get solved. She couldn't decide if she was white looking black or black looking white. What would Sammy think? But one thing was for sure, she looked different. And hadn't that been her goal?

∞∞∞

At exactly five minutes past noon, Trudy drove her

grandma's car out of Rhonda's parking lot. Callie would be late for kitchen duty to help Sammy. Not terribly late, but late.

"So, how do you like your new 'do?"

Callie felt her spongy hair. "I guess it's okay. It's just so different. Do I look black or white?"

"You look mixed, silly. Like Rhonda said, don't hide it. You 're gorgeous. Perfect for Detroit."

"I know. It's just going to be hard to get used to." But use to it she would have to get. It was a done deal. She wouldn't have to worry now about getting caught on camera.

"I'm starved. Want to breeze through McDonald's? Vivian wants me to work in the laundry room for a while this afternoon."

"If we hurry. I've just got to call Clarence. And Vivian will be pissed."

"Vivian won't be mad. She's a girl. She'll love what you did. Besides, Miles will be there."

They zipped through the McDonald's drive-through and came out with burgers, fries, cokes, and an apple turnover for Trudy.

"They don't call it fast food for nothing." Trudy pulled over only long enough to get started and then headed on to Coosa Springs Mall. "Aren't you going to eat?"

"Uh, I think I'll wait until after I call Clarence."

"Nervous?"

"No, just not very hungry," she lied. She took little sips of her soda as Trudy pulled in beside the same phone booth she had tried to call Clarence from the last time. "I'll only be a few."

"Take your time." Trudy reached into the McDonald's bag and grinned. "I've still got an apple pie to eat."

The phone at Lettie Smith's residence rang two short bursts on each ring. Aunt Lettie was still on a party line, and that was her ring. Lucy had been able to afford the extra fee for a private line, thanks to her supplemental income from Senator Winfred F. Whitfield. Her ring was one long ring. The short bursts droned on. Please answer, she prayed.

"Hello." *Thank God.*

"Hey, Clarence, it's me."

"Are you okay?"

"Yes, Clarence, I'm fine. Just checking in. What's going on? Did you get a phone number for Della?"

"I'll answer your second question first. Yes, I've got a phone number for Della."

"What? Whoopee, that's great!"

"Yeah. Well, I need to answer your first question. What's going on is this. Sawyers came out the day before yesterday asking about you."

Callie tugged on one of the hoop earrings Rhonda had loaned her. *I'll send them back to you. Don't worry, I've got more.* "So what else is new? You already told me I was a suspect."

"I told you that you might be a suspect. It's a little more serious now, Brown Sugar. He brought Chief Price with him."

"So?"

"So this. I did some snooping after class yesterday. They got the negative of your high school picture and sent it to the FBI listing you as a missing person. But that could get upgraded to a person of interest in Reggie's murder."

Callie reached up and touched the softness of her new afro hairdo. "So how did you get Della's number?"

"Lucy sort of freaked out when Sawyers showed up with the chief. She told them she had heard from you and that you left to go stay with your mother in Memphis but that her record company sent her to Detroit. She said you ran out of money somewhere outside Tupelo and that you got a job where you were staying."

"That's not a lie."

"Yes, but then they wanted to know if Lucy could get in touch with you."

"What did she tell them?"

"She said you didn't leave a number, but you would call back later. Lucy made things sound as normal as possible, and she told them you had been gone for two days when Reggie was found."

"The last time I talked to Lucy she practically accused me of doing it. Why the big change?"

"There's another situation I've got my eye on. Reggie was seeing a girl, and Lucy never could stand a cheating man."

"So Reggie was seeing some girl behind my back. How does that help me? Now they'll think I shot him because of that."

There's more. She has a mean husband. Some badass from Tarboro. Her sister lives out here. She comes to stay with her to get away from him. He's been hanging around out here, and I found out he was in town when Reggie got shot."

"How did you find all this out?"

"It's called chain talking. One person says something to somebody, and they say something to somebody else. In other words, word gets around Brown Sugar. You have to learn to investigate."

"That doesn't make any sense, Clarence. Can't they find the real killer? You know, and I know it wasn't me. I was gone."

"I wish you could prove that. Sawyers is not likely to look too hard until he can eliminate you. Did you find your bus ticket stubs?"

"Yeah, I don't have them."

"The bus company probably has a record."

"Uh, Clarence, we missed that bus. But we got a ride with a trucker."

"So you can't, can you? Prove it, I mean."

"No, I guess I can't."

"Damn, girl. You ought to tell us where you are. You're not caught up in any of that protesting, are you?"

"What protesting?" Thank God Clarence couldn't see her eye roll.

"You know what protesting. Civil rights, Vietnam. The whole world is protesting something these days. You're not in DC, are you?"

"What the hell would I be doing in DC, Clarence? I left for Memphis."

Callie had learned to stuff plenty of change in the pay-phone, but still, the operator interrupted. *"Please deposit…"* She jammed more change into the slot.

"…can't understand why you don't trust us," Clarence was saying.

"Trust? Why should I trust anyone Clarence? My own grand-mother set me up with the likes of Reggie to keep me from wanting to embarrass my father and grandfather, a lawyer and a senator climbing up the political ladder."

"Give Lucy a break. She feels bad because she told Sawyers ya'll had been fighting. She even called Della and told her what was going on."

"She called Della?"

"Yeah. She called the recording company and got a new number for her. Della said to tell you to come to Detroit. She'll do her best to get you an interview singing. And it will sure look better if Sawyers finds out you actually did go to live with your mother. I've got the number right here. Got something to write with?"

Della wanted her. Singing job. The words didn't quite sink in. She had wanted Della's number, and now she could have it. "Hold on." She left the receiver dangling and ran to ask Trudy for a pen and paper.

Trudy dug in her purse. "The closest I can get to something to write with is a lipstick. But I don't have anything to write on."

They searched through the glove box of the Impala for a bill, church bulletin, or anything to write on. They found only a flashlight and a pair of gloves. Callie frantically looked up the road at the nearest store and then down at her dwindling pile of change. She had talked for a long time. Now she would really be late. She'd have to try and memorize Della's number.

Chapter 18

Ruby Jean tried to imagine what Callie's new hairdo would be like. Maybe cut shorter, straightened, and dyed black. She wouldn't have to worry about getting caught, on camera, and with every passing day, more news people poured in.

The clock on the wall in the café was a big plate with a knife and fork for hands and dots for numbers. Vivian said her daddy made it a long time ago. She was proud of it. It was confusing as heck to Ruby Jean, but she was pretty sure Callie was about an hour late getting back. Thank goodness the lunch shift was a light one. The three sisters already left for Selma, and a lot of the other guests too, judging by the few cars parked in front of the Blue Moon.

The kitchen door swung open. Vivian motioned for her. "Take a few minutes to come see Nellie. They just came in through the back."

Ruby Jean glanced back at her customers and followed Vivian.

"Look at her. She looks like she stepped right off one of those album covers in my living room."

"I told you she wouldn't be mad," Trudy said.

"Of course not. We all have stuff we need to do during the week. I keep telling her to take off and go get her driver's license replaced. I'm sure that 'do took a while. She looks gorgeous. Love the color."

Callie had on makeup and some of those big hoop earrings colored girls like to wear. She remembered Mama talking about some Negro women who stopped straightening their hair and wearing it close-cropped. Callie's didn't look close-cropped. It was a poof about as high as her hand. It wasn't at all what Ruby Jean expected.

Sammy was standing by the stove eating an apple and grinning. Miles whistled. Callie glanced at them, then looked back at the girls and smiled. Ruby Jean tried to read her face. She looked kind of like that time when the student council president welcomed her to school and told her she looked pretty, but there was something else. She wondered what she found out from Clarence.

"Well, we'd better get back to the tables," Vivian said. "Trudy, you've got laundry to do, and Sammy, your head sous chef is back."

"And I got to get my Dad's car back to him before his lunch break," Miles said.

Ruby Jean would have to wait until her break to find out.

Callie closed the door to room seven behind her and breathed a heavy sigh. It was four o'clock before she could take a break. She had chopped ingredients for chili, flipped burgers, grilled hot dogs, and helped Sammy fill orders with a vengeance to make up for lost time. Little conversation had passed between them, and Callie was glad for that. When he did mention her hair, he said she must have heard from her mother because she sure looked ready for Detroit.

It was at this point she realized she forgot Della's number. She had repeated it over and over in her head until they got back to the Blue Moon. All the attention to her hairdo must have knocked it right out.

She headed to the nightstand between the beds. She remembered the area code and the first three numbers, but the last four were scrambled in her brain. She reached into the drawer for a notepad and a pencil. Maybe if she wrote them down, she could unscramble them. She pulled the folded section of the New York Times out and glanced at the picture of *them* once again. Tossing it aside, she grabbed the notebook and pencil and sat down at the small round table by the window. An almost a full pack of Salems sat in front of her. She hadn't smoked much lately. Vivian and Sammy kept telling her how bad it was for her. She'd never heard anything like that. She lit one up and jotted down 313-578. That was the area code and first three. What followed? Was it 49 or 94? It was useless. She scratched across the pad so hard the pencil lead broke. *Damn!*

A key clicked in the doorknob outside.

"Ruby Jean?"

"Hey, Callie. I asked Vivian if I could take my break when you did. Is everything okay?" Ruby Jean sat down across from her looking at the angry scribble on the notepad. "Did you get Clarence this time? What did you find out?"

Callie nodded. "Yeah, I talked to Clarence. I got a number, or I thought I got a number, for Della."

"A number for Della? Really? What do you mean you thought you did?

"I didn't have anything to write with, so I tried to memorize it." She picked the notepad back up and stared at it.

The doorknob turned again. Trudy opened the door dangling RJ's key. "Are ya'll trying to get robbed again? I forgot my purse in the laundry room and had to come back. Vivian told me you both were on a break. What's going on?"

"I forgot Della's number."

"Oh, shit. That's okay. We'll go back and call again."

"I have no idea when. I can't go back today, that's for sure, and I'm getting kind of scared to be out at night around here."

"Why don't you call from here?" Trudy asked.

"Once I get Della's number, I'll call from here. But I don't want to take the chance of calling Aunt Lettie's house. If I'm wanted, I sure wouldn't want them dragging me away from here."

"Well, I told you how what I think about that. I think Vivian and Jerry would totally understand everything. But if that's what you want, we'll go. Tomorrow."

"But we were gone today."

"Vivian already said she wants you to go get your driver's license. Besides, I heard Mama complaining that the Duncan brats are going to be home. School's out for some meeting or something. Miles can be there.

"There's only one catch to that Trudy, I don't have my birth certificate with me."

"So? No one knows that."

"Yeah, I guess you're right. Okay then. That's good because there's something I didn't get to tell you in the car. I was too busy muttering Della's number over and over."

She told Trudy and RJ about Lucy's visit from Sawyers and the chief. "Clarence says it'll be better if I'm really with Della. He said Lucy tried to make things sound as normal as possible. She feels bad, Clarence said, about telling them Reggie and me had been fighting. She knows it wasn't me. Clarence told her about taking RJ and me to Charlotte."

"Does Clarence know you missed the bus?" Trudy asked.

"He does now."

"And you have no proof you left when you did except for what Lucy and Della says. Right?"

Callie sighed. "That's right."

RJ's face paled. She wrung her hands as she glanced around their cozy room. "Gosh, Callie, does Della know I'm with you? I kind of thought we'd get a place—sort of like this. On our own. What if she doesn't accept me because of—you know."

"Well, she accepted a white man to be my daddy. She –"

Trudy interrupted. "Wait, wait. You don't know that. Maybe he forced himself on her. That's happened to a bunch of black women. They say Thomas Jefferson banged one of his slaves all the time and even fathered a few kids by her."

Callie thought about the times she walked the streets of Raleigh studying white men. "I guess it's something I'll never find out."

$$\infty\infty\infty$$

It was so warm Sammy had the back door of the café propped open. The smell of deep-fried potatoes reminded Callie she had skipped lunch.

It looked like business slowed again, probably because of the big march. Good. She had a lot to the think about. Sammy sat perched on a stool in front of the little portable TV he set up. Callie could hear the TV in the front blaring at the same time.

"Hey, how's the march going?"

Sammy turned at the sound of her voice. "Impressive. Peaceful. No violence, just liked I hoped. I'm kind of wishing I was there."

"Me too. It would have been neat to see Dr. King in person."

Sammy pulled up a stool beside him and motioned for Callie to sit down. "Have you eaten?"

"No, I'm glad you asked."

"You'd better grab something. I predict a very busy evening."

Callie fixed herself a hotdog with their special chili and a big plate of the hot fries that made her salivate on the way in. Sammy got a fountain drink for her, reminding her once again of his sweet manners. She would miss him. But she couldn't work in a café the rest of her life and neither could he.

"I miss yanking on your ponytail, but I must say you look nice, and it's a great career move if you want to be a singer in Motown. He traced a big circle around his ear. What happened to the earrings?"

Callie laughed. "I took them off at break time. I figured they didn't quite fit in with this job."

"You're probably right. I might have checked for tickets

hanging from them."

Callie punched him.

"Ouch. Get busy. Chop some chili stuff."

They did their prep cooking and watched a recap of the march. The news anchorman said around fifteen hundred people participated in the attempt to cross the bridge and head for Montgomery. The young and the old, Negros and whites marched. They came from all walks of life: clergymen, grandparents, teenagers, and even senators' wives. Callie saw blondes in polo coats, young white hip guys with beards wearing turtlenecks, and grandmothers in dressy coats, hats, and beads. She looked carefully for RJ's new friends, but she didn't see any nuns. A sea of black and white faces marched and sang, some of them holding up signs. *Police intimidation enslaves us all*, Callie read. Reggie and Sawyers. She had to decide what to do about going to Della's in Detroit.

They watched the marchers halted by a court order read aloud. Callie tensed as they continued marching toward a wall of troopers. Then they stopped. The leaders prayed as the marchers dropped to their knees. They rose and turned back.

Sammy turned off the little set and sighed. "I like the way it ended. As I said, it was planned that way, but I'm afraid it's going to cause some contention among some of our Snick members. They're tending to lean toward radicalism."

"You mean like Malcolm X? By any means necessary?"

"Something like that. They want their views respected. But I don't think militancy is necessary. Not yet, anyway. Johnson's on our side. Most of the sane world is."

Callie cut potatoes into wedges dropping them into a big bowl of icy water to chill. Sammy claimed they fried better that way. Sammy stirred some wedges and other vegetables she diced earlier into oil for a big pot of his beef stew. While they worked, he talked about school and how he planned on getting a degree in constitutional law. Callie was glad for the distraction.

"This is great field experience," he explained. "It all goes back to the case of Plessy versus Ferguson. Way back in 1892, an African-American refused to sit in a car designated for—Negros—God, I hate that word, on a train. It happened in Louisiana where it was against the law. Four years later, the Supreme Court ruled that simply distinguishing between blacks and whites didn't go against the Constitution. Things didn't start turning around until after Brown versus the Board of Education in 1954. I'm sure you're familiar with that case being one of the first blacks to integrate schools in North Carolina."

Callie jerked two new tickets from the carousel. "Sure," she replied. The truth was, she didn't know that much. Sammy's knowledge impressed her. She toyed with the idea of telling Sammy about Winfred Fitzgerald Whitfield. That would be a twist. Wonder what he would think about who she really was? But then again, even she wasn't so sure anymore. She had gone on a journey to find out, and the path was becoming murkier rather than clearer.

Business picked up leaving no time for talking. It wasn't until around eight-thirty when the orders coming through dwindled to a trickle. Miles would be coming in a few minutes to help them close up. Callie grabbed a soda and snuck outside for a break and a smoke.

The night was clear and starry. She spotted Venus again, remembering the night in the bungalow when she had pointed it out to RJ. She had to make a decision. The decision wasn't about whether to go, it was about when. She didn't want to wait too long. But then again, she hated cow-towing to a crime she didn't commit. She shouldn't have to. She threw the half-smoked Salem on the ground and stomped it out. By God, she said she wasn't going to Della's broke. She would get enough money together to get her own place and some kind of job. Something like she had here. That way, RJ wouldn't have to worry. Besides, it was only decent to give an employer notice before leaving. She went back in and helped get the café in apple-pie order for the next day.

∞ ∞ ∞

Ruby Jean crawled into faded cotton pajamas, emptied the change from her apron onto the table, and made stacks of quarters, dimes, nickels, and pennies. She could count money that way. She just had a hard time counting back change. That's because you had to take away and take away was harder than adding. This was the best night so far, making tips, and she hadn't gotten one order wrong. She even had one whole paper dollar.

She had put going to Detroit out of her mind. Now it all came rushing back. The truth was, she was scared to go to Detroit. Tennessee was only a state away from North Carolina, and if worse came to worse in Memphis, she could always get back to Carl or even Aunt Peggy, God forbid. She knew this day would come. She'd hoped it would be later. She picked up the piles of change to add to the pillowcase under her mattress. Callie flew in closing and locking the door behind her.

"I've got things figured out. Grab your bag of money."

She obeyed, and Callie got out her own stash of money.

Ruby Jean watched in fascination as Callie first counted her own pile and then hers and added them together on the same notepad she scribbled on earlier.

"Here's how I figure it," she began. "By putting our money together and working about ten more days, we'll have enough for bus tickets and for a room for at least a month. We'll get jobs. We've got experience now, and references. I'll get Clarence to mail my real driver's license, and you can get Roy to send your birth certificate. We'll have our own place, and Della nearby to help us get auditions." Callie cupped her new hairdo with both hands. "If we have to wait until we're twenty-one, then so be it. We'll have jobs."

Ruby Jean propped her elbows on the table resting her chin on her hands. "You'll get a job singing in no time, Callie, but I'm not that good."

"RJ, I know it's scary, but Della will like you, and if singing doesn't work out for you, we'll find some kind of training program for you. Remember? I told you, you can do something like being a nurse's aide."

"I believe you, Callie, it's just that Detroit is so—so far away. I'm so comfortable here. I was hoping Vivian might want to hire me on."

Callie stared at her, mouth open. She reached out and took Ruby Jean by the hand. "Look, if you need time to think about it, I understand. We don't have to leave like tomorrow. I've still got to call Della, which means I have to go call Clarence again."

"What about those FBI men?"

Callie tapped her nails on the table. Rhonda had done them while waiting for the hair dye to set. "I'll figure something out. After I call Della, she can tell them I'm on the way. Hopefully, they'll find the real killer by then. Clarence is working on some stuff."

"I don't know which is worse. Going all the way to Detroit or staying here without you. But if I stay, Callie, you can have all my money."

"That's nonsense, Ruby Jean."

"No, it isn't. You'll need it worse than me. I can make more. After all, you're the one that got robbed getting me here. Away from Snake."

"Well, I—"

The knock on the door wasn't loud but insistent. Both girls froze. Callie slipped the night chain into its lock and cracked open the door. "Sisters? Come on in." She turned to Ruby Jean looking relieved but confused.

Sister Mary Eunice stepped into the room. Sister Mary Agatha and Sister Mary Clare stood behind her. All three were in flannel gowns, black shoes, coats, and hairnets. "We're so sorry, girls, but we thought you might help. Our TV isn't working, and we wanted to see if perhaps you were watching the eleven o'clock news. You see, we had a flat tire on our way to the march, so we didn't make it. A carload of young white ministers stopped to help us. I got a call from one of the parishioners sponsoring us. Three of the young men who helped us were beaten by locals tonight while leaving a Negro restaurant. One of them, badly."

Nuns wanted to come into their room. Nuns from North Carolina. They offered them their chairs at the table, but Sisters Mary Agatha, Mary Eunice, and Mary Clare politely declined and sat on the edge of the bed. RJ had done a perfect job describing them.

They watched the eleven o'clock news. After an overview of demonstrations in Washington and other places, they found out a few details about the beatings of the ministers who helped the sisters. It was eerie to think about. Two of them were okay, but one had been transported to a hospital in Birmingham with a serious head injury. His name was James Reeb, and he was a Unitarian minister from Boston.

They chatted easily with the nuns. Callie had been afraid they would ask nosy questions, but they didn't. Sister Mary Agatha only asked if Ruby Jean still felt that her mother was comfortable, and she said yes. They talked about how shocked they were to see the way the Negro protesters, and others were being treated. Now three white ministers had been attacked, and one was in serious condition.

Callie insisted that the two older nuns take her and RJ's chairs, so they did. They perched on the edge of the bed beside Sister Mary Clare. She was petite and pretty, and she couldn't be much older than her and RJ.

Sister Mary Eunice took the lead and told them about themselves. "We're actually sisters, not nuns. The difference is nuns stay more or less secluded to pray, and sisters go out to serve in the community. All three of us worked at an orphanage in New York City before going to Wilmington, and Mary Clare herself is a grown-up orphan from the same home."

"The racial discrimination here in the south is terrible and hard for us to understand." Sister Mary Agatha took off her glasses and polished them on the sleeve of her nightgown. "Many of these people are decedents of slaves brought against their will. Many of them have enriched our nation, and we are compelled to help."

The other sisters nodded in unison.

"It's horrifying that blood has to be shed over this. Our Jesus bled for us, and these victims, Jimmie Lee and James, and others have become saints. We must honor them by continuing their cause. Things must change." She put her rimless glasses back on and peered over them at Callie. "It's even illegal in many states for blacks and whites to marry each other."

The comment was the closest one of them came to hint at having questions. But the sisters gave Callie a warm feeling. A feeling that she could open up to them without consequences that would be hurtful.

"I'm mixed. I guess that's obvious," she said with a little laugh. "My dad is a white man. But I don't know him."

Sister Mary Agatha blinked and nodded. "And you are lovely. You both are."

The three sisters thanked them and said goodnight.

Callie closed the door behind them and locked it. It seemed to have no end. Somebody else may have been killed. Once again they were in the middle of a horror story, suspended in time in Coosa Springs, Alabama.

Chapter 19

allie used to turn on the radio and sing her way through her morning routine; now she turned on the news. The entire world was reacting to the beatings of three white ministers. Even the schools in Selma closed until things died down. Miles would have been able to work, anyway.

She skipped breakfast and bought cheese crackers and a Coke from the vending machine out front. Today was the day. Trudy was taking her to the payphone. She wanted to get an early start and finish up the rooms well before lunch.

RJ cried for a while after they showed a picture of Reeb with his wife and four little kids and then got ready for her breakfast shift. Callie watched her, thinking. It would break her heart if she decided to stay here, and she would worry about her. She couldn't make her come, but still, the truth was, she was like a sister now like they lied about in the beginning. She heard once that if you told a lie enough you would believe it yourself. It must be true.

"RJ, don't you want to go with us to the phones later? Take an early break. It would give you a chance to call Roy."

"No, it's not necessary," she said. "Besides, what would I tell Vivian?"

"That you wanted to go to the drugstore and buy some personal stuff."

She thought for a minute. "No, I don't want to."

When Trudy got there, both girls clocked in on their time cards in the laundry room. Today they had two checkouts to clean and get ready for check-ins. They finished cleaning by midmorning and slipped in the back door of the café.

"Good morning, Sammy," Callie said. "I sure was sorry to hear about James Reeb.

Sammy nodded. "Me, too. I hate it like hell. Did Vivian talk to you?"

"No. I didn't come up to breakfast. I'm starved. Talk about what?"

Sammy handed her something wrapped in waxed paper.

"What's this?

"A breakfast biscuit. It's Jerry's idea. Breakfast to go for those on the go. Even McDonalds doesn't have this yet. Want one, Trudy?"

"Nope. No, thanks."

"Vivian and Jerry closed the café until Monday so they can join in on some of the marches. All of us. I told her you wanted to do something."

Callie opened the biscuit. "Sausage and egg in a biscuit. Clever. What about the motel and the café?"

Sister Mary Agatha offered to mind the office and sell these." He nodded at the huge batch of biscuits. Her knee is still messed up, and she can help like this, she said. She and Jerry will stop in to check on things."

Trudy grabbed a soda and went to hang around outside. "Let me know."

"What's going on?" Sammy asked.

"Gosh, I was going to ask her about doing some stuff before lunch. With Trudy."

Sammy wiped flour on his apron. "Vivian won't mind."

Vivian brought back a tray of dirty dishes to the sink. "Mind what?"

"Well, Trudy has her grandmother's car, and, uh... we planned to do some running around before lunch."

"Running around?"

"Yeah, go check about getting my driver's license replaced, go to the drug store, things like that."

"Clarence isn't going to mail it?"

"Maybe, who knows? I thought—well, you know," she stammered. "Sammy told me about ya'll closing to march. That's awesome. I guess I should wait until tomorrow to go."

"No, that's fine. Go. I told the sisters you might want to go to Selma with them in the morning. Trudy, too. Ruby Jean seems excited. She said you'd want to go."

"I do. I *do* want to go."

"Good. Come on back and help when you finish. Business is slow, anyway. Where is Trudy?"

Callie called Trudy inside.

Hey, Trudy, can you work in the laundry room when you get back with Nellie? I'd like to get a double batch of clean linens in each room before we take off. We're all going to be in Selma tomorrow. Involved. You too, Trudy?"

Trudy saluted. "I'll be reporting for duty."

Good," Vivian said. "Now off, you two. Get things done and get back. We'll get the sisters over tonight and make plans."

Trudy pulled the Impala out of the parking lot and headed for Coosa Springs Mall. They decided the Jackie scarf and sunglasses weren't necessary now after Callie's new hairdo.

"Wonder why Ruby Jean didn't want to come?" Trudy asked.

"She wants to remember her mother as she was. She says Ida Carson is at peace. The sisters have helped her feel better, especially Mary Agatha."

"But isn't that kind of running away from stuff?"

"For other people but not RJ. Everything she feels is real and honest."

Callie told Trudy about RJ's reluctance to go to Detroit. "She wants to stay here, but I can tell she doesn't want to be separated from me at the same time".

"She wants to stay here? And work at the café?"

"Yeah, she's hoping Vivian will let her stay in the room and work. And she's also afraid she'll end up living with that aunt she hates.

"Well, if she stays, I'll watch out for her."

"Thanks, that makes me feel better. I'll miss you."

Callie smiled. "We'll stay in touch."

"No matter how famous you get?"

"Always."

They were both quiet until Trudy pulled into the Coosa Springs Mall.

"I'll drop you off at the payphone and hit McDonald's. Want something?"

"No, I had that breakfast biscuit. You should've grabbed one."

Trudy shrugged. "I'll bring you some fries as a surprise. Got plenty of change?"

"Plenty." Callie hoped Clarence was home, but it was okay if he wasn't. She could call Lucy. She went nowhere during the week, she would miss her stories. She ventured out on Saturdays to the beauty parlor and the grocery store. On Sundays, she went to church. She would tell Lucy she was still working and call Della from the motel. Would they bug Della's phone? No, she was a missing person. Not even that, now. Lucy had covered for her. She was just a girl that ran away to find her mother.

Clarence answered on the first ring. "Hey, Brown Sugar, I was hoping this was you. You want to reverse the charges this time?"

"No. Quit trying to trick me."

"What did Della say? Are you on your way?"

"That's why I called. I lost her number."

Clarence sighed. "That's a blessing."

"Why?"

"It got you to call back. You need to know. I went to hang out at the station the other day, field experience for school. You're not a missing person anymore."

"Isn't that supposed to be good? You don't sound good."

"I'll just tell you like it is. You're wanted as a person of interest now."

Callie clutched the receiver. "A person of interest? How is that different? "

"Brace yourself, Brown Sugar. A person of interest in connection with Reggie Knight's murder."

Callie tugged on the phone cord, a silver snake. Clarence

seemed to sense her tension.

"Look. It doesn't mean you're wanted for murder. They want to question you, find out what you know."

She pulled the silver snake tight.

"You're still our princess who took off to find her queen mother. I just wish you could...

"Could what" Callie moved closer to the phone. The silver snake coiled again. "Prove where I've been?"

"Something like that. Anyway, you need to get to Della's. Soon. It's your best defense."

"I get it, Clarence. So give me the number."

"Got something to write with this time?"

"What?"

"I know you. That's what happened last time.

Asshole. "Yeah, I got something to write with. She reached into her pocket and pulled out the bottom half of the notepaper she had scrawled madly on, and a pen.

Leaving the pen behind—maybe it would help somebody out—she walked out of the phone booth and lit a Salem. Wanted for questioning. How bad was that? She would answer their questions—when they came to her. She still refused to act guilty. But Clarence said she'd better get to Della's. Maybe she'd better call from here instead of the Blue Moon. She counted her change. Would she even be able to get her on the phone? She dropped in the change needed. Five rings. Time to give up. A click.

"Hello?"

"Mama? Hey, Mama."

"Hey, Callie."

"I got your number from Lucy."

"I know. They told me what was going on."

"I didn't shoot him, Mama."

"I know you didn't, baby. Lucy said he'd been hitting you."

"He was." She couldn't keep the quiver from her voice.

"Oh, my poor girl. I didn't know all of this."

How could she? She rarely called.

"Baby, I've got a cab honking outside. I've got to get to the studio. Call me back and tell me where to send a bus ticket. Clarence said you won't tell them where you are. Heck, I might even get you on a plane. Let me check. Wouldn't that be fun? Call me."

The line went dead, a handful of change clinking into the coin return. *Damn!* Callie slammed down the receiver. Just like always. She had needed to talk to Della. To tell her about working a little longer and getting a place of her own.

They got back in plenty of time for what was a normal lunch shift. RJ and Vivian scampered between tables and the lunch counter about half full from what they usually were. Trudy left to get the laundry ahead. Miles left. Callie and Sammy were alone as they pulled tickets and filled orders.

Sammy had calculated how much food to cook. "When the food runs out, the closed sign goes up. We don't want to leave leftovers." He scraped the last of the beef stew into two bowls.

"Come on, Miss Nellie. Are you hungry?"

"Yep." She was. Very. She had eaten nothing since the French fries Trudy bought for her.

They both took a bowl and sat at the card table in the back of the kitchen. The beef stew was lukewarm but tasty.

"So did you get stuff done?" Sammy asked.

"Actually, I used most of the time to talk to Della."

"You got hold of her?"

"I did."

"You're leaving soon, I'll bet."

"Well—I'm not really sure when. But yeah, soon." She sipped on the watered-down Pepsi she had been nursing all afternoon. Sammy waited for her to say more. She swallowed another bite of stew, stalling for what to say next. He kept looking at her, waiting for her to speak. "I didn't get to talk to her as long as

I wanted to. A taxi was honking for her. She had to get to the studio."

"Wow! That's pretty impressive. Do you think she'll be famous someday?"

"Maybe. She's really good. And that's how you get your foot in the door—being a great backup singer."

"And you will do the same thing."

She shrugged. "Got to try."

"I must say, from what I heard the other night, you sing well. I'll bet you're excited."

"A little." She broke into a big grin. "A lot."

Sammy leaned back in his chair. "Wouldn't it be great if you came to sing at my college? We've had some good headliners: Smokey Robinson, Little Anthony and the Imperials…He opened his arms wide. "I can just see it. Nellie Wilson, homecoming dance, Boston University."

Callie giggled. "It might take a while. Della's got to agree to sign a contract for me until I'm twenty-one." A vision of Nellie Watson's driver's license with the ink smudge flashed in her mind.

Sammy scoffed. "At the rate I'm getting through school, no worries there."

Callie picked at her beef stew. "I was kind of hoping all this stuff would die down before I leave. What will happen now that James Reeb and those ministers were attacked?"

"It means a pouring in of even more support, especially from the clergy, and that's a good thing. It overshadows the militant types out there, all those crazy kids. It also means Johnson and Congress are more and more likely to be shamed into getting a bill passed.

"That's what I don't want to be: one of those crazy kids."

"You won't be. Stick with the nuns."

"Will I see you?"

"Possibly. I'll be working with the crazies convincing them violence will not work, so I'm not sure."

Callie gave him a warm look. "That's awesome."

"Thanks, Miss Nellie." He winked.

She melted.

He leaned forward. "It also puts pressure on everybody from President Johnson and George Wallace on down the ladder. And as much as I hate it, at least James Reeb won't have died in vain. Jimmie Lee too, and others, for that matter. The ones we don't hear much about that just end up mysteriously murdered."

Callie thought about Trudy's daddy and shivered.

"And yesterday, the Department of Justice asked for a court order to block Alabama officials from interfering with a peaceful demonstration. Not only that, the FBI is investigating several things. The beatings of Reeb and his friends, the assault on newsmen, and other stuff."

Callie wondered if the FBI being busy might help her out. She didn't know how many there were, but probably a lot.

Sammy continued. "They'll have a hearing in a day or two at the federal district court in Montgomery. Judge Johnson pretty much has his hands tied now to lift the temporary restraint he imposed on the big march Dr. King is planning." Sammy closed his eyes. "I can just see it. Dr. King and his aides leading the way, Snick members behind them, followed by all kinds of people. No signs, arm-in-arm instead, singing freedom songs loud and clear." He opened his eyes. "Lots of pretty girls. I hope you're here for that, Nellie."

She sighed. "Yeah, me too. Sort of," she added quickly. "How long do you think all this will take?"

Sammy picked up their supper dishes and put them in the sink to soak. "Got to keep with the dishes. I don't leave dirty kitchens." He sat back down and crossed his arms. "The march should take place any day now. It won't be a quick change, but a voting rights bill is a big, big step. That could take a few months. Other changes, like booting out Jim Crow from every corner in the south will be slower."

"Hmm. We need to get that guy out of here. Hey ho, hey ho."

They both laughed.

"Hey, I've got an idea," Sammy said. "Why don't you hang

around until the end of summer until I have to hang it up and go back to school? You'll see plenty of progress by then. Can you wait a few months to be a famous singer?"

"That's an interesting thought." Shocking was more like it. What would she say now?

She didn't have the freedom to decide that. "But… I guess I'd better talk to Della again first. See what she has planned."

They filled a few more late supper orders, and finally, Sammy gave Vivian and RJ the cutoff sign. Callie wished she could do just that. Stay until the end of the summer. It would give her time to get up plenty of money for a place of her own, and maybe RJ would change her mind. The more she thought about it, the more she didn't want to leave her behind. But she had to get to Della's because Reggie got blown away by some enemy. And she was wanted for questioning in his murder. She guessed she wasn't free from Reggie after all.

Chapter 20

Callie woke up before the clanging the alarm clock pulled her out of a dream as it usually did. She opened her eyes, wide awake. The only light was the sliver that shone through the bathroom door they left ajar each night so some light would shine through. The pitch-black scared RJ.

She had to sit up and lean forward to make out the time: four thirty-five. Going to demonstrate today is what did it. She used to wake up the same way when she was a kid, and Granddaddy Moses had planned a trip to the mountains or the beach. She would pack clothes and comic books in a brown paper grocery bag. Lucy would pack a bunch of picnic lunches and drinks in a cooler, and Granddaddy would stop at the ice plant on the way out. Many years ago, Della went with them.

She got up quietly and opened the bathroom door to let in more light. She ran water in the percolator from the bathroom sink and put on the coffee, hoping the rich aroma wouldn't wake RJ. It sure would wake her; she knew because Reggie used to do that for her at the beginning before the insults, accusations, and slaps started. Shivering, she put on her jacket, feeling in the pocket to see if her cigarettes and matches were there.

Last night's rain had left a fog so thick she could only see the glow of the Blue Moon's neon light, its flickering l, and M recently replaced by a sign company Jerry hired. She sat down in the once rusty metal chair—Jerry had repainted them all a fresh blue—and lit up.

Della. She had talked to Della yesterday and called her Mama.

Jesus. When was the last time she had talked to her on the phone? Probably a couple of Christmases ago. She used to call and ask what Lucy had bought her with the money she sent. Then one year, there were no stuffed animals, sweaters, and diaries, only money Lucy put in a card for her.

In the beginning, Della would take a bus from Memphis and come home for Thanksgiving, Christmas, and once in the summer. But the last time she had set foot in Frogmoor was for Granddaddy's funeral when Callie was fourteen.

She put the stub of a cigarette out and lit another. So much for quitting. One week. She needed one week at least. Two days off wouldn't help her money situation any, especially if RJ decided not to go. She would tell Della she needed to give notice at her job. If RJ didn't go, she supposed she would just stay with Della, and then find a job and get a place. The thought occurred to her that Della might even like that. She might live a fast life in Detroit. Parties, men.

She finished her cigarette and went inside. The perks had slowed enough to pour a cup of coffee. The phone rang, startling her. Ruby Jean sat up and turned on the lamp. Callie answered. It was Sister Mary Eunice.

"Hi. Are you girls up? We're leaving at daylight."

Callie hung up and sat staring at the phone. On second thought, if she woke Della up, she might not be at her senses. And she didn't want anything hanging over her head today.

The next phone call to Della would have to wait.

Ruby Jean fumbled around getting dressed, changing blouses three times before putting the first back on, a plain white one with a Peter Pan collar. She had slept later than the others. Callie and the sisters went to the café to get some to-go biscuits. Sister Mary Agatha had promised that would be all they needed because the basements of two churches in downtown Selma had tables of food yards long packed with food yesterday. She said people brought in pans of fried chicken and potato salad.

They hated that the older sister wasn't going. Ruby Jean asked her yesterday how her knee was. "Worse, child, worse," she had said. "But I'll be fine. I can help out here. In the meantime, you young folks go." She had pulled down her glasses, squinted, and said: "give 'em hell."

Ruby Jean chuckled. Sister Mary Agatha was sweet, and funny, too. She brushed her hair and stopped to think. Ruby Jean Carson from Frogmoor was going to be in a famous march with nuns. They were still nuns to her even though she called them sisters. Probably because of Junior and what happened at the movie theater that time. She dug into the bottom of her duffle bag for a pair of bobby socks. She pulled the socks apart and the necklace she kept hidden fell out. She picked it up, inspecting it. The chain had turned because it wasn't real, but the cross was shiny as ever. It was made of silver just like a dime. Mama bought it for her on her sixteenth birthday. Should she wear it? She saved it for special occasions, and this day was pretty special. She fastened the dangling cross around her neck and grabbed her jacket.

Ruby Jean and Callie crawled into the backseat of Sister Mary Eunice's roomy station wagon. Sister Mary Clare sat upfront. They were going to meet Trudy at her cousin's beauty shop, the one where Callie got her new hairdo.

Sister Mary Eunice pulled out of the parking lot and headed for Selma.

Ruby Jean hadn't been to Selma, but Callie had, and the sisters, of course. "How long will it be before we're there?"

"Oh, it's not far," Sister Mary Eunice said. "Fifteen minutes, maybe."

Callie looked at Ruby Jean and nodded. "We're about to go help make history, RJ."

She hugged herself and reached for the silver cross tucked

under the buttons of her blouse.

In a few minutes, they parked in front of a small pink house. Ruby Jean read the sign: Rhonda's Beauty Shop. Signs were so much easier than reading a whole page. Trudy and her cousin Rhonda came out to meet them.

"Hey, girl!" Callie and Rhonda gave a high-five. "Your hair is still looking good."

"Yours too. I love the new weave. Rhonda, this is my friend Ruby Jean."

She liked Rhonda right away. When Callie introduced the sisters—Trudy already knew them, a little—she was polite, welcoming them to Selma, shaking their hands.

"What a blessing it is for you to let us park at your place of business, Rhonda," Sister Mary Eunice said. "I much prefer walking a few blocks than searching for parking. It's good to see you again, Trudy. I hear you're joining us."

Trudy broke into a smile. "I'm honored. We thank you all a lot for coming to Selma. I'm sorry about Sister Mary Agatha's knee."

"She'll be fine," Sister Mary Clare said. "She always trusts God to use her as He wants, and she's happy watching the motel."

Sister Mary Eunice agreed. "How about you, Rhonda? Will you join us?"

"No, Ma'am, I can't today. I got young'uns to watch. No school. But park here anytime, Sister."

The two sisters took the lead, and the three girls followed.

They walked along, talking. Sister Mary Eunice told them about what had been going on. "A good number of the demonstrators have spent the last couple of nights camping out in the streets, refusing to leave until they take down the barrier and let them go to the Dallas County Courthouse. Dr. King's assistant is leading that group."

"Have you seen Dr. King?" Callie asked.

"He was in seclusion in an office in the back of the church the other night. He sent his blessings. He may be back from Montgomery today." Sister Mary Eunice turned to face them.

"The biggest hindrance has been the mayor's decision to use his executive power to ban marching."

"Won't we get arrested or something?" asked Ruby Jean.

Sister Mary Eunice stopped walking, so they all stopped. "That's highly unlikely. They've stopped all that. But there are rebel rousers you should stay away from. Stick with us and the clergy. There is power in numbers, but we must go forward in peace."

She motioned for them to join arms, and they walked on. The sound of singing grew closer. People carried signs. A whole group of men, Negro and white, held up signs saying I Am A Man and others saying Segregation Has To Go. She'd heard enough to know what the long word starting with an s was.

They marched into the crowded street towards the church. Brown's Chapel, the sisters, called it. Ruby Jean's chest felt like it would burst as they joined in the singing. They sang to the tune of *This Little Light of Mine*, a song she knew well. The group had new words for each verse: *I'm so glad I'm fighting for my rights*, then *I'm so glad integration's on its way. Singing glory hallelujah, I'm so glad.*

The church came in sight. It was huge like a castle with arches and towers. Walking up the steps, she felt as much as a princess or an important person as she ever would. She held hands with Sister Mary Clare, smiling with her deep dimples. Ruby Jean could tell she was about her age. What if she became a sister herself? Boy that would keep Aunt Peggy away.

The sisters led them downstairs where people were walking around and talking to each other, shaking hands, and embracing.

Sister Mary Eunice waved to a group of men standing with three other nuns. Some men wore church suits, and some dressed as priests. "Come girls, and I'll introduce you to some clergy and activists we've met this week."

After Sister Mary Eunice had introduced them all, they all walked as a group downstairs for refreshments, Ruby Jean holding on tight to Callie's hand.

The church's kitchen was about a hundred times bigger than the one at the Blue Moon Cafe. The refreshments sat on long tables covered in white paper. Ruby Jean counted about a dozen different kinds of cookies. There were chips, loaves of bread, and sandwich stuff. Stacks of plastic cups surrounded big bottles of Dr. Pepper, Pepsi, and Sun Drop.

They all filled a paper plate with snacks. Ruby Jean decided on Dr. Pepper, barbeque chips, and two chocolate chip cookies. The group sat at the end of the long row of tables, the sisters talking with the others. Ruby Jean felt a little out of place. She could tell Callie and Trudy did too. It was like they couldn't think of anything to say. Sister Mary Eunice must have sensed it. She started talking about the Blue Moon and how they all worked there. She told them about Jerry's to-go biscuit idea.

"In fact, that's where Sister Agatha is today. Her knee has been giving her a fit, so she's selling biscuits and minding the office so the owners can get out and march."

"That's fascinating. About the biscuits, I mean," the priest said. "And where are the Robinsons?"

"The Robinsons are coming with their own church group. I hope we see them."

One of the other nuns spoke up. "This kitchen has been like the Story of the Multitudes all week."

Trudy munched on a Lorna Doone. "I remember that story from Bible School. Jesus fed five thousand people with two fish and five loaves of bread. Do you think he really did that?"

The priest answered. "We must interpret that story to mean something, dear. When we work together, we get things done. Then thousands of people can be saved by grace."

Trudy swallowed. "Makes sense."

One of the ministers looked at his watch. "The speakers are starting in ten minutes. Shall we go?"

They walked up the wide staircase. Ruby Jean decided it looked kind of childish for her to hold Callie's hand, so she didn't.

Callie looked at her funny. "Are you okay, Ruby Jean?"

"Yeah, sure, Nellie."

Callie smiled at her. "You stay close."

"I will."

They entered the big part of the church. The sisters called it the sanctuary. Ruby Jean stared at the big windows. They were so beautiful they took her breath away. They glowed with all the colors of the rainbow, and with pictures of Mary and the Baby Jesus in the middle.

Rows and rows of people sat in pews, not benches. Before Aunt Peggy moved back to Tennessee to take care of Grandma, she used to take them all to the big church in Raleigh sometimes. That's where she learned about pews. But the church she and the boys went to with Mama when she wasn't too tired to walk there had benches and a few folding chairs for the old people.

A young man not much older than Sammy named John Lewis stood at the microphone to introduce the first speaker, James Bevel. Callie elbowed Ruby Jean. "That's the chairman of Sammy's organization," she whispered.

"Do you think he's here?"

"Who, Sammy? Probably." Callie glanced around at the crowd.

James Bevel talked about how he had known and worked alongside Martin Luther King for a long time. Ruby Jean swelled with pride at what he said. "You have succeeded in showing the country that blacks in Alabama were being denied the right to vote."

They prayed and sang hymns like *Onward Christian Soldiers.* They sang another song Ruby Jean hadn't heard before. The name of it had to be *We Shall Overcome.* The verses went on and on, the voices strong and happy. More preachers and priests spoke. Then they got organized into groups for marching.

The group joined the crowd and started the walk. Sister Mary Clare said she couldn't believe how the number of marchers had swelled just since yesterday.

"People have been pouring in," said one of the ministers. "I heard sixty to eighty new civil rights leaders and around four hundred ministers of all faiths."

Sister Mary Eunice said they would march as far as the barricade. "We'll see what happens then."

Reporters with big cameras and little cameras walked along both sides. Ruby Jean knew the big cameras were TV cameras, and the others were for taking newspaper pictures. Callie was trying not to look face-to-face at them. Maybe she should do the same. Her hair didn't look all different like Callie's did. What if one of them at home turned on the news? The twins and Junior wouldn't, but Roy might. Mama used to watch it if Snake was asleep when wrestling was on.

A bunch of white people watched them pass yelling things that weren't nice. "White niggers," shouted one. "Asshole commies," shouted another.

They reached the barricade and stopped. Ruby could see the big green courthouse ahead. The girls stood back as the nuns and priests argued with a big man in a hat smoking a cigar. A rowdy group pushed through the crowd trying to get past. It scared Ruby Jean. She had learned to hate any kind of fussing. She reached for her silver cross, but the only thing there was the dull chain. *My cross*. Her real silver cross was gone. It must have fallen off. She looked all around on the street where they had stopped.

The crowd was spinning around her. She had to find it. Had to. It was real silver. Mama gave it to her, and Mama was on her journey to heaven. She remembered touching it going down the church steps that lead to the street.

She tiptoed around the crowd, eyes down, searching frantically. No, it couldn't be. She would find it. The cross was shiny, and the sun had just broken between dark clouds. A picture of the church windows flashed through her mind. Okay, she would go back to the top of the church stairs. She still had the necklace on then. It would be okay. She would find it and go right back. Sister Mary Eunice had said they weren't going past the police barricade.

The steps up to the church were empty now. Halfway up, a gleam caught her eye. The cross. Thank God. She picked it up, kissed it, and tucked it firmly in the pocket of her jeans. She ran down the steps and headed back to the barricade. All of a sudden a boy grabbed her by the hand.

"Come on, white girl. We're going through no matter what they say. Having you is gonna help us. Let's go."

Ruby Jean froze. "I can't. I—I've got to get back to my friends."

"Where are they?"

"At the barricade."

"We'll get you back there. Let's go." He pulled her out of the crowd into a group of about a dozen Negros, young ones, about the same age as the twins. They ran around buildings, between stores, and into the parking lot of a place with lots of apartments. By then, Ruby Jean was so off-track, she didn't know what else to do but run with them. They said they would get her back to the barricade. Surely they would help her find Callie.

The next thing she knew they were on the other side of the barricade. This wasn't good. What if she got arrested? What if she never saw Callie again? Suddenly more policemen than she had ever seen in one place charged at them. They started jabbing with their clubs. One jabbed her in the stomach like Snake used to do to Mama, except he used his fist, not a club. It hurt, but it didn't knock her down. What if the next one was worse?

She turned and ran back. She had to get back to the barricade. She stopped for a second to check and make sure the cross was still in her pocket. It was. But before she could take off again, the running youngsters knocked her to the ground.

She was stunned, the breath knocked out of her. Then someone stopped to help her. She looked up and saw a familiar face: a man with curly black hair. She stared, he stared.

"I've seen you before, haven't I?" he asked.

It was the trucker that was a preacher with two little girls at home. He was dressed in his preacher clothes, the stubble of beard gone from his face. "Your name's Nellie, right? One of the girls hitchhiking to, ah—Memphis, I believe." He held out his hand. "Matthew. Matthew Prescott. Good to see you again. How in the world did you end up here?"

Ruby Jean trembled like the last leaf of winter in the wind. "No. I'm Ruby Jean. It's kind of a long story, Mr. Prescott. But right now, I need to find Nellie."

She told him about trying to find the silver cross and getting pulled into the crowd that wanted to break through. "I guess it was a dumb thing to do, but..."

"I can understand. And it's easy to get lost in a big crowd."

Ruby Jean brushed the dirt from her jacket. "It sure is. Anyway, we were at the barricade standing with nuns. A whole group of them."

"They shouldn't be too hard to spot. But you're way off course. Let me help you get back to where they are."

It started raining. Not hard, but enough to plaster Ruby Jean's hair to her head. Matthew Prescott took her by the hand, and they wound their way through the crowd. People had broken up into groups, some arguing with the men on the other side of the barricade, and others carrying signs, singing.

"There she is!" Callie was standing with Sister Mary Eunice, looking around. Looking worried.

She yelled. "Callie!" she yelled. Oh, heck. "I mean Nellie!"

Callie hugged her hard.

"There you are. Oh, thank heavens. Child, what happened?" Sister Mary Eunice asked.

"I'm sorry. My necklace broke. I had to go look for my silver cross."

"Silver cross?" Callie looked at Matthew Prescott, her face a big question.

"I'll tell you about it later. Look, Nellie, look who helped me. Remember him?"

Callie looked at Matthew Prescott. She started to say something but stopped.

The rain came harder; Sister Mary Eunice guided them back to the church. "We need to tell Mary Clare and Trudy. We sent them to wait there in case you showed up."

"Oh, sister, I'm so sorry," Ruby Jean said.

"It's okay, dear. Let's get out of this weather and have something to eat. We've served our Father well today."

Matthew Prescott joined them for cookies and coffee. Ruby Jean and Sister Mary Clare sipped hot cocoa, the warm chocolate milk calming the trembles in Ruby Jean's tummy.

"Reverend Prescott, I can't tell you how grateful we are to you for helping Ruby Jean find her way back to us," Sister Mary Eunice said.

He shrugged. "I was at the right place at the right time. She got sucked into a rowdy crowd, and I was working with some other ministers and Snick members to get them under control before they got hurt."

"Snick? That's our friend Sammy's organization. Sammy Lucas," Callie said. "Do you know him?"

"Ah, Sammy. Indeed I do. Just saw him earlier."

Preacher Prescott told them about his church, his trucking job, and his family. "The church is good to me, but you see, I have two little twin girls, and they're handicapped."

Ruby Jean's heart broke while he told them about Hannah Faith and Anna Grace Prescott. They were twins, both born with something called muscular dystrophy.

"They're six years old now and in wheelchairs. Bethany, their mother, can't work, of course. It's a little harder for her now that they're getting bigger."

"God bless you for coming, Reverend Prescott." Sister Mary Eunice said.

"Well, I wanted to come and join the march for a bit. Some of my fellow deacons are here with me. I hope I can find them," he laughed. "I might be the next one lost." He took a sip of his coffee. "Enough about me. I'm still waiting for the story about how you two girls ended up here. Ruby Jean said it was a long story."

Callie looked at Trudy. Trudy looked at Ruby Jean. Ruby Jean looked at Callie. Callie began. She told them about the robbery, and that they were friends, not sisters. She told the sisters and Matthew Prescott everything except her real name, stealing Miss Wilson's ID, and that men from the FBI wanted to talk to her about Reggie getting shot.

Chapter 21

That night, after the march, Callie and Ruby Jean sat on the bed together counting money.

"You know what, Callie?"

"What?"

"Counting money is a lot easier when it's your money."

Callie laughed and blew her nose. "I guess you're right." She didn't know if it was because Ruby Jean got lost today or what, but she made a firm decision to go with her to Detroit. Good. She didn't want to leave her friend behind. She would never forget her panic this afternoon when she turned around, and RJ was nowhere in sight. Then a pounding rain came. A case of sniffles she already had turned into a full-blown cold.

"It was weird running into the preacher trucker guy, wasn't it?"

"Reverend Prescott? It sure was." Callie had been a little spooked. Even crazier, he knew Sammy. Well, maybe not crazy. They both worked with the same organizations. She had a pang of disappointment when she didn't see him today.

Callie plopped two Alka-Seltzer Plus tablets in a glass of water. Sister Mary Eunice had insisted on going to the drugstore for her. She had been sweeter than ever after she told them how Reggie treated her, and how they missed the bus, hitchhiked, and ended up getting robbed. he still couldn't bring herself to tell anyone other than Trudy about being wanted for questioning in his murder. It might somehow lead to the fact she wasn't Nellie Wilson. For the hundredth time, she wished she hadn't taken Miss Wilson's driver's license.

"RJ, have you had that dream anymore? The one about me and Babs sitting in jail?"

"No. I've been concentrating on Mama. You said it was just a bad dream."

"Right. Do you still feel like your mother is okay?"

"You mean is she here or in heaven?"

"Well, yeah."

"I know she's okay. She knows I'm okay. I see her face, and she looks peaceful."

"I'm glad." Callie folded all the bills and scraped up the change into one pillowcase. She did some quick calculating. "We've probably got enough for a cheap motel for two weeks. I figure Detroit prices will be higher than they are here."

"Are you going to tell Della about me when you call?"

"No, I thought about it, but I think we'll do it this way. We're adults. And if I do that, it will be like I'm a little kid asking Mommy if I can bring home a friend "Mommy," she said in a sing-song voice. "Can I bring my friend?"

RJ nodded without saying anything.

"Don't be nervous. We'll get jobs. I'm determined. And if worse comes to worst, we've got Della. She'll like you. I prom-ise."

She leaned over and squeezed RJ's forearm. "I'm sure Della would never put you out on the street."

RJ nodded. "Okay."

"What helped you make up your mind to go, anyway?"

"For one, you're my best friend. I can trust you. And I'd really miss you."

Callie felt tears swelling and turned to look away.

"And, I figure the further away I am from Aunt Peggy, the bet-ter off I'll be."

Callie blinked. "Boy, you don't like that Aunt Peggy, do you?"

"No, I hate her. I know it's wrong to hate, but I do."

"Well, Granddaddy Moses used to say when you hate somebody, it's really the things they do that you hate, not them."

"That makes sense. Like the sisters love everybody but hate the mean things people do."

The phone rang. "Grab that RJ. It's probably one of the sisters. I've got to pee."

"It's Vivian. She wants to talk to you."

After talking to Vivian a few minutes, Callie hung up the phone with a big smile. "Yes!"

"What was that all about?"

"We're staying here and working tomorrow." Callie drew a dollar sign in the air. "The sisters told Mary Agatha about what happened."

"Oh no. Am I in trouble? Are you?"

"No, silly. Mary Agatha is hankering to go marching. Her knee's all better. Plus she and Jerry planned to do some work around here tomorrow. But Sammy wants them to go to Montgomery with him to a protest at the capitol. She said you and Trudy could work in the laundry room and check on all the rooms, take out trash and stuff."

RJ bounced on the bed. "Yay! That's good. I've had enough marching for a while."

"Tell me about it. And she said since I have a cold, they'll put a sign on the office window to call room seven for any problems."

The two girls dressed in the big sweat-shirts from Framington State College that Vivian gave them. They both admitted they felt good in a college shirt, and these were warm and cozy.

"Put something funny on the TV. No news, please."

RJ flipped through the five channels they got.

"How about—"

"Wait, wait. Stop there." It was Mary Wells belting out the lyrics to *My Guy.* "Look. I think Mama sings with them sometimes." There she went again. Mama, not Della.

"Do you see her?"

Did she? She hadn't seen Della in five years. One almost could be. She took a double-take, and another, inching up to the screen. "I don't think so." Surely she would recognize her own mother. "But she works with lots of groups."

A few more groups played, and the show ended. They ended up watching the eleven o'clock news after all.

James Reeb succumbed to his injuries and passed away.

Chapter 22

Last night's news of the death of James Reeb sent a new wave of shock and rage throughout the nation. Callie flipped through the morning news channels to see serious demonstrations in New York, Washington, and other cities. It seemed no end was in sight and she would be leaving Coosa Springs long before the trouble was over.

Between no guest turn over and the café being closed, the Blue Moon was a dead zone. Callie sat cross-legged on the bed surrounded by wads of Kleenex. She didn't really feel all that bad, but she didn't want to get sicker either. And today gave her a perfect chance to call Della. RJ and Trudy were taking care of rooms, and she was alone.

This had to be it. No going to the payphone with Trudy anytime soon, and she didn't have the luxury of putting this call off any longer. She stared at the phone a few seconds and glanced at the clock. Just after nine. Probably early for her. Was she even in town? Lucy once said she mostly worked in a recording studio but traveled with different singers sometimes too.

Taking a deep breath, she picked up the receiver and dialed.

Della answered on the third ring.

"Hey, Mama,"

"Hey, Callie. I hoped this would be you. Are you ready to come to Detroit?"

"Almost."

"What do you mean, almost? Where are you?"

"On my way. Like I told Clarence and Grandma, I got a place to stay and a job. And I really need to give my boss at least a week's notice."

"What kind of job?"

"I'm a sous chef at a restaurant. They would need to replace me."

"They could do that in no time. Just hop on a bus and come on. No excuses."

Della knocked down any pride she had in her job. "Mama, this is different. These people are my friends, and—well, they've been through a lot lately. And I need to save up a little more money."

"Mother said you took three hundred dollars from her. You spent that much in two weeks?"

A hundred images popped into Callie's head. Had it only been two weeks?

She's not mad, I told her I'd pay her back."

"No, I'll pay her back, Mama. I'm an adult."

"I'll wire you money for a bus ticket. I checked the airlines. The last-minute ticket is outrageous. So you don't need any money."

"I've got more than enough for a bus ticket. I'd need money for a place to stay."

"No, you don't, silly. I've got two bedrooms. One is full of junk right now, but the couch makes into a bed. We'll do that for now."

Thank goodness she had called while RJ was working. This conversation was about to take a turn. "Mama, I've got somebody traveling with me."

"What? Did you run off with some boy? That's not going to look good."

"No, Mama, a girl. A girl from school."

"Is she a runaway? I can't harbor a runaway."

"No, Mama. She's nineteen." Callie paused, thinking. "Do you remember old man Carson? That old mean white man with the big tobacco farm? The one they called Snake?"

Della took a moment to answer. "Yeah, seems like I do."

It's Ruby Jean Carson. He treated her terribly. He abused her.

In a lot of ways."

"So things were so bad ya'll dropped out of school. I know your story, Callie. What about her? What kind of problem does she have that she's still in high school at nineteen?"

"She's had some trouble with reading." *Math too, but why push it?* "She's not dumb, and she sings real pretty, too. It's just a problem some kids have. She's been working here at the restaurant as a waitress. She's done really good."

"Listen, Callie, Mother said the cops had been on her like vultures. She told them you were on your way here. Don't make her out to be a liar. You need to get on up here, soon. I can't have any trouble. We can get a room for you nearby if that's what you want. Just get here. By next week at the latest."

Callie barely heard RJ and Trudy come in at lunchtime. She sat staring straight ahead.

"Earth to Callie," Trudy said. "What's got you all caught up into stares?"

"Hey, ya'll," she said, still gazing at nothing.

"I bet she got through to Della," RJ said.

They both sat down on the bed beside her. Trudy looked disgusted while picking up used Kleenex with her fingertips and putting them in a plastic trash can beside the bed.

"Talk to us, girl."

"Oh no, I bet you told her about me, and she don't want me."

Callie shook her head. "No, I told her about you, RJ. She's okay with it."

"What is it? Trudy asked.

"We've got to get up there in a few days."

"A few days?" Trudy jumped back bumped her head on the headboard. "Ouch! Why only two days?"

Callie sighed. "She thinks I need to do what Lucy told the

cops I was doing. Going to Detroit. The thing is, she's right. It'll look funny when the cops in Detroit find Della, and I'm not with her. She said she don't want any trouble. I figure we should leave by Thursday at the latest. We'd be getting there on the weekend."

"Couldn't you ask Della to stall for you? Like, tell them you were working a notice on a job and are on your way?" Trudy asked.

Callie swung around and dangled her legs off the bed. "I thought about that. But they already wonder why Lucy didn't know exactly where I was. I can't keep getting by with that. It'll look like I've been hiding."

"I see your point."

"Me too," RJ said. "When are you going to tell Vivian?"

"Tonight if I see them come in. I don't want to just call her. If not, in the morning, at breakfast. The café opens back up tomorrow."

She told RJ about the second bedroom and that they might have to sleep on the sleeper sofa a night or two.

"That's okay, Callie."

"But don't worry. She said she had no problem with us getting our own place. She wants it to be close by. The thing is, I didn't tell her about the robbery. It won't be too long. We'll get jobs and put it with what we've got left after getting the bus tickets.

"That's probably a good thing," Trudy said. "It is Detroit."

"Yeah, but I didn't plan on going into it like this. I wanted to be on my own."

"Sometimes we have to change our plans," Trudy said.

Callie stood up and paced around the room. "Seems like Reggie Knight is still in charge of my plans, and he's dead."

Chapter 23

On Monday morning, Callie sat at the round table by the window watching the darkness turn to dawn on one of her last few days at the Blue Moon. RJ was still fast asleep and snoring softly.

Vivian and Jerry must have gotten in really late last night, but the café would be open at six-thirty. They'd be there. She had to tell them. But the question wasn't so much when to tell them, but what? Why on such short notice?

Callie couldn't figure out why she wasn't more excited to be going to Detroit. Della had the connections to help her with a singing career. Only a few weeks ago, she would have been ecstatic. *I still want that.* She touched her new hairdo. She had turned a few heads belting out tunes during the march the other day. *I know I have what it takes.* What else was there for her besides free tuition at some school she didn't want to attend?

She thought she knew what the problem was. It might be silly, but she hated to miss the big march Sammy had described. Sammy. That was another story. She had to figure out what to tell them all. No, it couldn't be the truth.

The thumps in the percolator sped up and slowed down again. She poured a cup of the scalding coffee and waited for it to cool down thinking of what to say. An answer came. She would tell them Della thought she might have an interview set up for her already. She didn't want to miss it. Vivian and Jerry would be happy for her; Sammy too. She took a sip of coffee and scalded her tongue. Mother always says lies beget lies, RJ had said.

Ida Carson was so right.

On the walk to the café, she told RJ about what she decided to tell them.

"Mama always said—"

"I know, RJ. You don't need to remind me." Her tongue felt like hot sandpaper.

The smell of sausage and bacon sizzling perked up any loss of appetite Callie's cold had robbed her of. Jerry and Vivian were back at the helm. Miles was in, Sammy wasn't. Vivian announced at breakfast that although back open, the café would close after lunch. James Reeb's memorial service would be held at two in the afternoon. They'd all want to go. Dr. King himself was to deliver the eulogy. She said they would have a closed supper before opening the café back up to customers.

"Sammy will be back from all that crusading he's been doing with Snick. Meanwhile, Callie, you can help Miles in the kitchen until we close. We've got a few checkouts. I think people are planning on leaving and coming back when the big march gets approved. Ruby Jean can go help Trudy with rooms when breakfast slows down. We're going to be really busy for the next couple of weeks."

Callie cringed. That made telling them worse.

Jerry opened the doors, and the breakfast shift began. After a few questioning looks from RJ, she got a chance to talk to her.

"I think after our closed supper would be the best time," she whispered.

RJ nodded. "Okay."

Jerry rang out the last of the lunch customers. They locked up and left to go to pay respects to James Reeb at Brown's Chapel in Selma. Callie, Trudy, and RJ rode with the sisters in their clunky station wagon. Vivian and Jerry followed in their Doodlebug. They arrived just before two and sat in the balcony.

Callie looked down at a sea of people of all kinds. Some looked like important dignitaries, other ordinary people like them. Priests in collars and nuns in black and white swarmed like God's own patrol.

The air grew stuffy. People pulled out church fans batting the warm air around their faces. Callie sensed a restlessness growing among the crowd.

Sister Mary Agatha leaned over and whispered. "I have found here in the south everything starts later than they say it will."

"It's politeness," Sister Mary Eunice added. "They want to give everyone time to get here and get in without being rushed."

Vivian and Jerry nodded, smiling.

The waiting continued. All around, people were glancing at their wrist watches.

"All these people from out of town? I bet they've got planes to catch," Trudy said.

A rustling rose from the crowd below nearest the doors. They heard loud cheering outside. The audience stood and applauded as Dr. Martin Luther King, Jr. and his closest aides advanced to the podium waving and shaking hands along the way.

The service began, people looking relieved to stand and join in prayer and song.

Dr. King walked to the podium and began his speech. "Who killed James Reeb?" The crowd grew dead silent as Dr. King answered his own question. "A few ignorant men. What killed James Reeb?" He paused, hundreds of ears hanging on for his next words. Dr. King cited reasons from a corrupt political system to an uninvolved clergy to uncommitted citizens. Heads nodded in agreement and shame.

It was a short speech, a powerful one. He left them all with an urge to continue his work, and for the white south to come to terms with its conscience. The speech stirred her soul. But Callie wouldn't be there, she would be in Detroit. If only she could stay a few more weeks.

Dr. King led them in prayer and stepped aside. The choir led them in song. They joined hands singing verse after verse of *We*

Shall Overcome. Callie got goosebumps when the words changed to *Black and White Together.*

Someone touched her on the arm. Still singing, she turned as Sammy scooted in beside her, smiling, taking her hand.

After the service, Sammy walked with them back to their cars.

"Are you going back to the Blue Moon?" Callie asked.

"I sure am. And I'm working after we eat."

"Good. Me too."

Sammy gave her one of those looks again. But now that she was down to a few days here, it was unnerving. Hadn't he mentioned inviting her to visit at his college? Or was he kidding about her getting a singing gig there?

Sammy opened the car door for them, and waited, waving as Sister Mary Eunice pulled into the line of traffic.

The time was close. Time to tell another lie.

∞ ∞ ∞

Vivian gasped. "Thursday! You're leaving Thursday?"

Everyone at the table grew quiet. Callie's heart dropped to her feet.

"Well, by Friday morning at the latest. I think the audition Della was talking about is over the weekend." She glanced over at RJ who was busily studying her plate. "I'm sorry, Vivian. And Jerry." She couldn't look at Sammy.

"You needn't be sorry, Nellie," Vivian said.

Silence.

"Hey, that was your goal, right? We knew that from the beginning," Jerry said.

"Well, we'll miss you girls," Sister Mary Eunice said, "but you must follow your dreams."

"I know. I just hate leaving on such short notice, leaving our jobs like this. Ruby Jean does too."

"We'll get by. Right, Sammy?"

"We will, Vivian."

Callie still couldn't look at Sammy.

"I can probably come back after picking up Dad at school," Miles offered, "if he doesn't need the car."

Vivian snapped her fingers. "That reminds me. Guess who called the other day interested in getting his job back? Ricky Cooper. Seems he's dying to get back into the student work release program. And we've still got you, Trudy, right?"

Trudy pointed to herself. "I ain't going nowhere."

"And we'll be here for a while longer," Sister Mary Agatha said. "We're here until things pan out for the big march. And…" She propped on an elbow and slid her rimless glasses down her nose. "I hear the dear mayor, and the sheriff have decided to revert to mass arrests rather than allowing anyone their right to a peaceful protest."

Sammy spoke up. "That's right, Sister,"

She had to look at him now. It was too awkward not to.

"They can arrest people under an old city ordinance banning parades without a permit, and there you go. Like Dr. King said today, a corrupt political system. And that's just one thing wrong."

Sister Mary Agatha sighed. "Well, back to the problem. Use us as you like, Vivian. I'm not sure if they'd arrest a nun, but we're going to wait things out. Who says a nun can't clean rooms? And Sister Mary Clare is still a postulate. She can take that little mantilla off and take a worldly job as a waitress for a bit."

Sister Mary Clare giggled.

Sister Mary Eunice clicked her tongue. "Honestly, Agatha."

They laughed and talked some more about what might happen in the days ahead.

Whew. That was over. Now to deal with Sammy

At four-thirty Jerry unlocked the café doors and flipped on the neon open sign.

Back in the kitchen, Sammy gave Callie a hug. "Congratulations. I'll miss my sous chef." He pretended to cry and wipe tears with the bottom of his apron.

Callie laughed. "I'm sorry for the short notice."

"We'll get by. Like Jerry said, that was your plan. I'm proud of you."

"Thanks. I—I'm proud of you, too. As heartbreaking as all this has been, it must be rewarding to be a part of all this."

"Just remember what Snick stands for. Student Nonviolent Coordinating Committee."

By five o'clock they were slammed. It was all they could do to keep up with the flow of orders, and there was no time for conversation. That was a good thing for now. She wasn't up to elaborating on her audition lie.

Vivian brought a tray stacked high with dirty dishes to the kitchen. "Miles, we'll need you busing tables out front. Thank goodness and school being out you're still here."

Looking beyond the order window, Callie noticed the crowd looked like a cross-section of the crowd at Brown's Chapel. The sisters perched like partridges on bar stools with coffee and desserts, greeting guests. Then the extraordinary happened.

"Sammy, come see this!"

He turned from flipping burgers and looked to where she pointed. Vivian was seating four patrons. Four men who looked like ministers. And all four of them were Negros.

Sammy gave her a high five. "I'm glad to see that times are changing."

"Oh, I hope Trudy stops by before they leave." She usually stopped by and came in the back door of the kitchen when she finished in the laundry room for a free fountain soda before heading home.

It wasn't until almost closing time when she and Sammy got to talk.

"So you're leaving Wednesday or Thursday?"

"Yeah, I think Thursday morning. Early. That will at least give Vivian and Jerry a little time to get things situated. And

Trudy can give us a ride to the bus station before they need her."

"Are you and Ruby Jean going to work Wednesday?"

"Sure are. We need every cent we can get." She told him about wanting to get a place of their own and jobs something like they'd had here. "Until we can—do something different."

"Does Ruby Jean want to sing too?"

"She does, but she doesn't have much confidence. And I don't know what she would do about getting a parent to sign a contract for her. I'd like to get her into some sort of school or training."

Sammy filled a couple of stray orders. "Listen, I won't be in tomorrow. Snick stuff. Thomas is coming in to cover for me. Remember him?"

She nodded.

"But after we close Wednesday, I'd like to do something for you."

"How sweet. What?"

"Ah, well, actually, more like something *with* you."

"With me?"

"Yeah, uh—oh, heck. I'll just come out with it. I'd like to take you out. Just us two. Like on a date."

"A date?"

"Yeah. There's a drive-in movie over off the highway on the way to Montgomery. Wouldn't that be a great get-a-away after all this? What d'ya say?"

"A drive-in? That sounds a little racy, Sammy Lucas."

He held up both hands. "I promise to be a gentleman. It'll be hands on a big bucket of popcorn."

She laughed. "I accept."

A date with Sammy on her last night here. Was this a beginning to an end? Or an end to a beginning?

Chapter 24

Tuesday afternoon on their between lunch and dinner break, Callie helped Ruby Jean sort her tips into piles. Trudy had brought them a cigar box full of coin wrappers from when her grandmother was the church treasurer.

"One, two, three." Callie counted the orange rolls of quarters. "Damn, girl. You did good in tips." Four rolls of dimes and five rolls of nickels added up to sixty bucks, and there was a smattering of change. "Together with our daily pay we have over four hundred dollars."

Ruby Jean counted on her fingers. "If we hadn't gotten robbed, we'd have seven hundred."

"Don't remind me." Jobs first. They'd make up the difference and get a place of their own. They had experience. And references, too.

"Jerry said he'd be glad to swap dollars for all this. He said it would save him at least two trips to the bank."

"I'll bet. Well, I'll call Della again and let her know we'll head for the Trailways bus station Thursday morning and that we'll call when we get to Detroit."

They looked at each other.

"Are you ready for this?" Callie asked.

"I'm a little nervous, but I'm glad you told your mama about me."

"Don't be nervous. We've got money, and we'll get a place to stay. And jobs." Callie sighed. "I sure wish that audition story was true."

"It *will* come true. In no time. Just you watch, Callie."

Before Callie picked up the phone, a knock came at the door. They scrambled, hiding money.

"I guess this is what it does to you when you've been robbed," Callie said.

But their caller was far from a thief.

"Sister Mary Eunice! What a surprise." Callie opened the door wider.

"Nellie, Ruby Jean. Hello, girls. I'm sorry to interrupt your afternoon break, but I—the sisters and I wanted to tell you about something you might be interested in. May I?"

"Of course. Come in and sit down, Sister." Callie pulled out a chair for her. What in the world, she wondered.

"Well, since we've sworn off marching until the court order goes through, we've been checking into other ways to be useful."

"Other ways?"

"Yes." She pulled at her stiff collar. "We're focusing on restaurants. One in particular. It's called the Edgefield Inn, and it's on the outskirts of town next door to the Selma Country Club." The sister cleared her throat. "I've spoken to Vivian about this, and she is okay with it. You see, Vivian says our presence in the café helped attract those black patrons yesterday. She's grateful the ice has been broken and expects more."

"I'm happy about that."

"Me, too," RJ added.

"She said it was a subject close to your heart, Nellie. Anyway, I'm rambling. Let me get to the point. This Edgefield Inn has a history of turning folks away. Even white folks if they don't look like they are of a certain class. They do it in many roundabout ways. If we all go in together, we can make quite a statement. We've already talked to Trudy, and she has agreed to go." She held up a hand. "Don't answer now. You're on break. But think about it, and we'll see you at dinner. Vivian is willing to let you go for an hour or so early. She says it's the least she can do for integrating restaurants."

Sister Mary Eunice got up to go. "Oh, one more thing. Of course, you'll get a free fancy meal, too."

Callie opened the door for the sister and closed it behind her. "Wow! Can you believe that? Should we?" They couldn't very well march again with the threat of arrest looming. It would be one more thing to do before leaving. But she wouldn't unless RJ did. "What do you say, RJ?"

"I say it sounds like fun. Shoot. I never had a free fancy dinner. Come to think of it, I've never had a paid one neither."

"Then it's settled. We'll do it."

Just as Sister Mary Eunice and Vivian predicted, a scattering of people of color came and went during the early supper hour. Callie noticed several shades of skin, some as dark as Trudy and some almost as light as herself. She and the ever quiet Thomas worked side by side filling a steady stream of orders. School was back open today, so Miles had to leave to get his dad. Vivian said they could leave a little after six. Jerry would help her wait tables, she said, and Thomas had cooked food ahead.

Callie glanced at the clock. Two more hours. And this time tomorrow she would be working her last day alongside Sammy with a date planned for later. She was already getting a case of the jitters, but like RJ told her, whatever happens, will happen. RJ and her innocent wisdom.

Everything was set. She'd called Della at the end of the break. No detectives had come around asking questions. *Yet,* she emphasized. Della seemed excited for them to come. So far, smooth sailing. She could concentrate on her date with Sammy and the sisters' mission. Being a part of making change happen would feel good. Vivian and Jerry had been beaming all afternoon, but it occurred to Callie that all restaurant owners might not be as accepting as the Robinsons. Namely, the ones at the

Edgefield Inn.

∞∞∞

Sunset colors streaked the western sky. Sister Mary Eunice drove past the city limits of Selma into the flat, open countryside. The modest city dwellings turned into larger country homes.

"There it is ahead. The Edgefield Inn." Sister Mary Eunice pulled into a spacious parking lot.

The Edgefield Inn had picture windows all around. Just enough daylight was left to see a sprawling golf course beyond. No doubt the tail end of the Selma Country Club.

An older gentleman with a bad toupee led them to sit at a long velvet-covered bench along one wall. "I'll let you know when tables are ready."

"We're all together," Sister Mary Agatha said. "One will do."

He nodded, unsmiling.

"Interesting wallpaper," Callie said looking around. The whole wall was like a mural of a cotton plantation. Ladies in pastel hoopskirts carrying parasols strolled the lawn in front of a big white house with columns. Rolling green hills outlined the distance where Negro slaves with straw hats bent over picking cotton.

The restaurant was not overly busy, and Callie watched as the tables were cleared. Still, they were left to sit. The gentleman host brought four more customers to wait on the velvet bench. A few minutes later, he returned, smiled, and led the group that had come after them to a table.

"Wait a minute," Trudy said loud enough to be heard. "We were here first."

Sister Mary Eunice silenced her with a look that said *let me handle this*. "Let's just bide our time until it's blatantly clear we are being ignored," she whispered.

More customers came in and were led straight to empty tables. Sister Mary Agatha excused herself to the bathroom and came back. "I found a table with eight chairs at the back. Let's assume we've been forgotten by the gentleman with the animal on his head and go seat ourselves."

Trudy looked at her as if to say *no, she didn't say that.* Sister Mary Clare giggled.

They settled in, expecting to be brought menus. Instead, the host approached empty-handed.

"I'm sorry, ladies, but this table is reserved for a large group coming in later. I have a table for you, sisters, if you will please come with me?"

"Is it not possible to move those two small tables over there together?" Sister Mary Eunice asked. "We prefer to dine with our friends."

He paused. "Let me get my manager."

The host returned with a younger version of himself. Probably his son, Callie decided. "Excuse me, ladies. The three girls here will need to show their club membership."

"What about the sisters," Callie asked. "They don't have to show theirs?"

"We don't require anyone with the clergy to show membership."

"Obviously, you don't require a lot of people to show membership." Trudy raised her voice. "Like the people the host led in front of us when we were first."

The manager hesitated. "I'm afraid I'm going have to ask you, three ladies, to leave. Sisters, you're welcome to dine here."

"That's against the law, sir," Callie said. "You're violating our Constitutional rights."

"She's right," Sister Mary Agatha said. "Section 201 of the Civil Rights Act of 1964, public accommodations. That includes restaurants like this one."

"And this is 1965, sir." Sister Mary Eunice added.

The manager huffed, his face grim. "I just explained our

policy. We serve clergy and club members."

Anger washed over Callie ten times worse than she had ever felt at Wesley High School. "Do you have a sign saying so out front? I don't think so. We were escorted to that bench where we sat waiting for a table while other people got seated ahead of us." She looked around and saw they already had nearby customers' attention. *Why not ask them?* "Hey, raise your hand if you're a club member."

No one raised their hand.

"So go check their cards," Trudy said.

"Ladies, again, I am asking you to leave the premises."

Callie checked the expressions on the sisters' faces. They looked nervous but determined.

Sister Mary Agatha spoke up. "If you turn them away, you turn us away. That will make quite a story for my journalist friend. Which will likely bring an investigation of your restaurant's compliance with the Public Accommodations Act."

The manager turned beet red.

"Girls," Sister Mary Eunice began, "go back and wait for a table. Perhaps this gentleman will change his mind."

Callie, Trudy, and RJ stood to go back to the bench, prepared to wait. Callie decided they would sit there until the sisters were ready to leave. That would de-escalate the situation. What more could be done? As Sister Mary Agatha said, a story and an investigation would follow. They had made their statement.

Callie saw heads turning to the front of the restaurant. The grouchy host was leading two cops. He'd called the cops? This couldn't be real. A fat white cop smoking a cigar and his skinny white sidekick approached them.

"These three girls here?" asked the fat cop.

"Nah, not the white girl. She was quiet." The gentleman host had ditched his polite host voice. "These two, ah, colored girls here was making all the racket."

The manager spoke up "I asked them to leave. Twice. They refused."

The fat cop turned to his counterpart. "Trespassing, or DC?"

The skinny cop shrugged.

"Were they loud? Argumentative?"

"Very." The manager said.

"We'll go with a disorderly then. If we do trespassing, we gotta arrest the white girl, too."

"Arrested? You can't be serious," Trudy said.

"Yes ma'am, we're serious. Got an ID?"

"No," Trudy said. "I didn't drive."

"No," Callie said, panicking.

"That's okay. You can give us your name in a statement down at the station. It better be your real name. Cuff 'em, Hendricks."

They both looked at the sisters in desperation as the officers handcuffed them and read them their rights. The sisters still held a determined expression. RJ started crying.

"Come here, dear," Sister Mary Agatha held and comforted her.

"Don't worry, girls." Sister Mary Eunice said. "We'll take care of this. You'll be out in no time. Stay brave."

The last trace of daylight was slipping away. Callie and Trudy sat side by side in the back seat of the fat cop's squad car. The cop rolled the window down to talk to Hendricks, who had arrived in his own car for backup. As they chatted about what they were going to do when their shift ended, the fat cop lit his stub of a cigar.

Trudy began coughing and gagging. "Hey, officer, I'm asthmatic. Please put that out."

He puffed, blowing a plume of smoke. "I'm up here, you're back there. Plus the window's down."

She coughed harder. "Seriously, sir, asthma attacks can kill you. You'd have a potential murder case on your hands. And there's a witness." She coughed again and nodded toward Callie.

"It's nigras like you causing all the trouble around here." He got out of the car and slammed the door.

They watched as he got in the car with Hendricks to finish his chat and cigar.

"Are you all right? Was that real?" Callie whispered.

"No, I did it to get him out of the car, so we could talk. Listen, don't be too scared. This has become routine around here. The sisters can get in touch with groups that help bail protesters out. And disorderly conduct isn't that serious. Rhonda's husband got one once. He was out in no time. Went to court and paid a twenty-five dollar fine. Anyway, a good civil rights lawyer can probably get the charge dropped."

"That's comforting. For you. Did you hear what he said? We'd better give our *real name*."

"Oh, yeah. What are you gonna do?"

Callie shrugged and winced from the pressure of the handcuffs. "Damn, these things hurt. I don't know. If I tell them, I'm Callie Gibbs, and they bail out Trudy Marshall and Nellie Wilson, what then? And Callie Gibbs is wanted for questioning in a murder case."

"They won't have any information on Callie Gibbs down here," Trudy said. "You're not an escaped convict. It's a good thing you didn't tell anybody exactly where you are."

"I guess it'll depend on what RJ says," Callie said.

"Do you think she'll tell the sisters your real name?"

The fat cop opened the door and slid in. "No talking ladies. Anything you say can and will be held against you. I don't want to know you're even back there."

The squad car wound through the streets of Selma as the radio crackled and the cop, who turned out to be Officer Lewis mumbled something into the speaker every few minutes. Callie and Trudy talked with their eyes. It was clear that Officer Lewis was working his beat, killing time, looking forward to the end of his shift.

At least it gave Callie time to think. What would RJ say? Knowing RJ, she'd be scared and tell the sisters the truth, about her name, anyway. She wouldn't say anything about Reggie.

Finally, Offer Lewis pulled into the station and led them

inside. He pulled out a book of tickets. "State your name and place of residence."

She took a deep breath. "I'm Callie Gibbs, and I reside at the Blue Moon Motel in Coosa Springs."

Chapter 25

The sisters calmed Ruby Jean to where at least she wasn't sobbing hysterically. After the buzz died down, a waitress, a sweet-looking redhead with freckles asked the four if they were ready to order.

"I thought you said this table was reserved," Sister Mary Agatha said.

"Oh. Well, they canceled, and the manager said to treat ya'll well. He said he was sorry they had to do that."

"Humph. We'll just have something to drink. Thank you."

Ruby Jean wouldn't get a free fancy meal after all, but neither would Callie. What would they feed her in jail? Bread and water? Her eyes brimmed with fresh tears at the thought. She fought hard not to go back to sobbing out loud.

Sister Mary Eunice pulled a small spiral notebook from her purse. "Now, don't you worry, Ruby Jean. This little book has all the phone numbers and addresses we need to get help. What we need to do now is get back to the Blue Moon and start making calls. And Vivian and Jerry have to be told." She put the notebook back in her purse, took out a few dollars, and laid them on the table. "I hope the waitress keeps this as a tip. Let's go."

It wasn't until the ride back to the Blue Moon was almost over when it hit Ruby Jean. Something else to fear, and a big problem. That cop said they'd better give their real name. Would Callie do that? Clarence said the FBI had a picture of her. Well, her new hairdo would take care of that. No, Callie would tell them she was Nellie Wilson. And Ruby Jean would have to stand by her best friend in the world.

Sister Mary Eunice parked in front of the office door at the motel. Vivian and Jerry were both inside despite the no vacancy sign. Ruby Jean knew by now they usually had put up their bungalow phone number and left.

Vivian unlocked the office door. "Hi, sisters, come in."

The two older sisters stepped in first. Ruby Jean and Sister Mary Clare went in last holding hands.

"We're just trying to catch up on some record keeping. How did it go?" She glanced toward the parking lot. "Where's Trudy and Nellie?"

Sister Mary Agatha cleared her throat. "I'm afraid they're why we're here, dear. Things aren't good."

Vivian's face paled. Jerry stopped what he was doing and looked up.

Sister Mary Eunice told them what happened. "I feel responsible for talking the girls into going on our mission."

The others defended Trudy and Callie.

"They didn't do anything to get locked up for. They weren't disorderly," Sister Mary Clare added.

"But the good news is," Sister Mary Eunice began as she pulled out her little notebook, "we have the numbers of people who have been collecting funds to bail out protesters for months. It's what they do."

Vivian turned to Jerry. "We can help, too, right?"

"Of course. A disorderly conduct charge won't be too bad."

"Vivian," said Sister Mary Eunice, "I promised the girls dinner. They're probably starved. Can you whip up something for them in the kitchen? Add it to our charges, and I'll go take care of this from the phone in our room."

"Sure I can Sister, and I certainly will *not* add to the price of your room. I'll have a plate for you, too."

"Bless you, Vivian. I should only be a few minutes."

Ruby Jean hadn't even thought about being hungry, but the smells coming from the kitchen caused her tummy to growl. Callie would be hungry, but they'd get Trudy and Callie out of jail. Tonight. Callie would work tomorrow and go on her date with Sammy. Only one thing nagged at her: Callie's lie about her name. Mama always said lies beget lies, and she also said one day the truth would come crashing in on you.

Trudy and Callie both sat on the cell's only narrow cot, a cot with a thin mattress. The jail cell made the bungalow back in Frogmoor look almost luxurious. Only enough light passed through the bars to see three dingy walls and a metal toilet in the back corner. The floors were concrete; at least the bungalow had tile floors. And windows. Windows with pretty new checkered curtains Reggie let her buy when they first moved in. Reggie had sheets hanging over the windows, and she laughed at him.

Callie had been excited about her first home in the beginning and planned to fix it up cute. That was before Reggie started getting home late and being mad over stupid stuff. She walked over to peek out the bars. She stood and stared for a while, seeing nothing but an empty cell across from them. "I wonder why they put us both in here with just one bed. That cell across from us is empty." She looked from left to right. "I can't see anything, but it's awfully quiet."

Trudy walked over to look through the bars with her. "Well, for one thing, they're probably saving space. Remember, they said they were going to start arresting protesters again. And for another, they know we'll get bailed out pretty quick. We were with the sisters. I can't believe they locked us up. We'd done hushed and was going to sit down."

"I know. Disorderly conduct sounds so bad. Why didn't they just call it trespassing?"

"Those cops knew they wouldn't get by with it. It's hard to arrest somebody for trespassing in a public place. Now if Ruby Jean had been *black,* it might have been a different story."

The two of them sat back down on the cot.

"I'm glad they put us together, even if it means we both have to sleep on this cot. I hope we can fit without one of us falling off," Callie said.

"Want to practice?" Trudy laid her head on one end. Callie squeezed in beside her with her head on the other end.

They laughed and joked some more about being in jail, laughter numbing the tension Callie felt coursing through her. "I guess we missed the dinner hour." "Yeah, they eat early around here. Lights out at eight, and all that."

They had nothing to do but talk and wait. Trudy talked about what her life was like in Birmingham before her daddy's murder.

"We lived in a brick house beside the church. They called it the parsonage. The cutest little house you ever saw. Mama fixed us all up so pretty for church. We had Christmas parties, Easter egg hunts. Then one day they found daddy behind the church. Murdered. Shot in the head. We had no choice but to leave and come down here to Grandma's."

"That's so sad, Trudy. I'm sorry."

Callie told her about the fights she and Reggie had. "It all started one night not long after we were married. He threw a plate of cold spaghetti all over me. From then on, I set supper inside a warm oven." She told her about the other times, and the time he slapped her to the floor after accusing her of having Ruby Jean's brother to come over while he was at work.

"What about your mother, Della? I brag all the time about knowing somebody whose mother sings with Martha and the Vandellas."

"Well, she's not one of them; she mostly works in a recording studio. She hasn't gotten famous yet, but she's done all right for herself. Della left high school to work as a maid for some rich people close to Raleigh." Callie closed her eyes. She couldn't bring herself to say *the Whitfields* as in Senator Winfred Whitfield. "She rode the bus in from Frogmoor every day. Then one day she never went back." She raised her head and opened her eyes. "She never went back again because was going to have a child. Me. Granddaddy gave up farming and got a job in the mill. The sweet old landowner he had worked for as a sharecropper died and left Granddaddy the house he had worked and paid rent on for years. He got Della a job, too, and I stayed with Lucy while she worked. Then Della got discovered and left when I was twelve. Granddaddy Moses said it would be a great opportunity for her."

"He was right," Trudy said.

Both girls dozed off despite the uncomfortable sleeping arrangements. They both woke up to a jingling at the jail door. The bars slid open.

"You Trudy Marshall?" an officer asked.

"Yes."

"Your bail's paid. You can go."

"What about Callie? Callie Gibbs?" Trudy asked.

"Ain't nobody posted any bail for nobody by that name, Miss."

Callie's heart pounded. RJ went with Nellie Watson. Probably the first lie in her life.

"Don't worry," Trudy whispered. "I'll figure something out."

Chapter 26

Ruby Jean sat staring towards the front of the Dallas County jail praying hard. Praying for the big glass doors to open wide and for Trudy and Callie to come out under the lights hand in hand, smiling.

After Sister Mary Eunice had arranged a bond, the Robinsons closed the motel office and drove all of them except Mary Agatha and Mary Clare in the station wagon to pick up Trudy and Callie. The other two sisters offered to stay at the bungalow and answer any emergency calls from the motel guests.

They all waited, hardly saying a word until Jerry came out. Alone.

Vivian spoke first. "There's Jerry. Wonder where they are?"

Ruby Jean trembled inside. Something was wrong.

Jerry slid into the driver's seat and turned to Mary Eunice. "They have to be processed out. It might take a bit. The best thing we can do is wait right here and wait for them to walk out the doors. Then I'll go get them."

The night air grew chilly. Jerry turned on the car engine, and the heat from the heater was like a warm hug. Ruby Jean stopped trembling and started praying again. They watched people come and go. Ruby Jean cringed each time someone came out that wasn't Trudy or Callie.

Finally, they saw Trudy walk out the doors and look around. Jerry got out of the car and walked toward her, waving. She broke into a fast walk toward Jerry.

Ruby Jean closed her eyes and crossed her fingers. She opened her eyes a few seconds later hoping to see her, but Callie wasn't there. She didn't come out. Instead, Trudy and Jerry walked back to the car with their heads down. It looked like they only said a few words to each other.

Ruby Jean knew then. She might not be good at school work, but she had what Mama called horse sense. Callie wasn't getting out. Not yet. She had told the truth, and Ruby Jean had lied.

Jerry opened the door for Trudy, and she got in the back with Ruby Jean and Vivian.

Vivian reached across and took her hand. "Trudy! Thank Goodness. But what about Nellie? Is she still being processed?"

Ruby Jean held her breath. Maybe that was it. Oh please, let that be it.

Trudy hung her head in her hands. "Oh, Sister. Vivian and Jerry. There's something about Nellie she didn't tell you. Or anyone except me, and Ruby Jean, of course. Her name isn't Nellie Watson, it's Callie. Callie—"

Ruby Jean watched as jaws dropped. "Gibbs. Callie Gibbs." Ruby Jean had to save face for her friend. "She is who she says she is. I mean, everything else she said about herself is the gospel truth. About how her mother was gone so much, and how Reggie always beat on her and made her feel bad about herself."

"She's right," Trudy added. "It's just that—well, for a few reasons, she stuck with that name."

Vivian and Sister Eunice looked the way Ruby Jean felt once when she fell from the barn loft and got the breath knocked out of her.

Jerry grabbed the steering wheel and sighed. "Well, it's a story that needs telling but it's a story that will have to wait. We can't very well go back in and say, oh, we're sorry, we meant Callie Gibbs, not Nellie Wilson. The only thing we can do is set a new bond for Callie Gibbs and hope they don't think something fishy is going on. They've been busy and eager to get people out, so we've got a good chance. I've got money in the safe. I haven't had time to make a deposit in a couple of days." He cranked the station wagon. "Let's go back to the Blue Moon and get this mess straightened out."

Jerry allowed no one to talk about why Nellie was really Callie until they got back to the Blue Moon with the other two sisters. Now they all crowded around the back table in the empty café.

Ruby Jean cried fresh tears as Trudy wolfed down a hamburger and gulped coffee with loads of cream and sugar. She worried Callie would be hungry.

Trudy was explaining why she stole Nellie Wilson's driver's license. "Things with Reggie went from bad to worse. He kept slapping her around. She thought if she could pass for over twenty-one she'd have a better chance of making it on her own. She couldn't get any sympathy from her grandmother."

"Dear heavens, that poor child," Sister Mary Agatha said..

Jerry stood up. "I've heard enough. I'm going to bail Callie Gibbs out of jail. Sit tight, ladies. It may take a while."

Ruby Jean spoke first after Jerry left. "She had wanted to wait until she finished high school before she left. Then I had that vision after I knocked Snake out with the frying pan."

"But I don't understand why Nel… or Callie didn't trust us enough to tell us her real name," Vivian said.

"She was afraid you and Jerry would be mad and kick us out."

"Oh, for heaven's sake," Vivian said.

"I told her that was nonsense," Trudy said, "but the thing is, she found a chance to take her English teacher's driver's license. By putting a smudge of ink on the picture, she could pass it for her own. That way if she didn't find Della, she'd be old enough to sign a contract if she got a singing job. I guess she decided to stick with that name."

"She wasn't going to do anything bad with it," Ruby Jean added. "Then the couple that robbed us took the driver's license too. The girl's boyfriend said she could pass using it and they'd go buy liquor with it."

"Oh, my," Mary Eunice said. "Did she report any of this to the police?"

"No, and it gets more complicated." Trudy paused and took a deep breath. "One day when she called her cousin Clarence to see what was going on, she found out somebody shot and killed Reggie. Right after her and Ruby Jean took off."

"What?" they all said at once.

"Apparently she's wanted up in North Carolina where she's from for questioning," Trudy said. "They got her high school picture and sent it to the FBI. That's why she changed her hair. In case someone came around asking about Callie Gibbs. Then you and Jerry wouldn't have to lie, Vivian."

"I wonder if that will cause her problems getting out of jail?" Vivian asked.

"We got a chance to talk about it." Trudy told them about the cop's cigar and her fake asthma attack. "I told her they probably didn't know anything about her around here. And they've been all tied up with everything going on in Selma. She thought Ruby Jean would be afraid to lie, so she decided she'd go with Callie Gibbs."

"Well, we can't judge her," Sister Mary Agatha said. "She needs our help. All we can do is pray Jerry can bond Callie Gibbs out of jail tonight."

Chapter 27

Callie paced back and forth in the jail cell, clenched fists holding the sides of her head like a vise. The clanging of the closing bars still rang in her ears. Trudy Marshall got bailed out to freedom. She was here alone.

Ruby Jean went with the name Nellie Wilson. Callie guessed it had been a fifty-fifty chance, and she lost the call. With more time to get inside RJ's head, she would have remembered her friend's deep loyalty. Probably one of the few lies she'd ever told, she had done it for her.

Trudy said she'd figure something out. She had to believe her; she pulled the clever asthma trick. What might she try next?

Maybe she would think of a code name. Something Callie would recognize, like Carrie Dibbs. Or she would use her initials for something like Connie Gaston. Then she would say *yes that's me*. Like Trudy did when they asked if she was Trudy Marshall.

She grew tired of pacing like a caged leopard and sat down on the cot's thin mattress. She'd almost gotten comfortable there laying with Trudy. Now the low light cast shadows of the bars on the concrete floor—shadows that curved over the cot and crawled up the wall. She watched a cockroach scurry across the floor. The jail food crumbs that attracted it were gone, and now it couldn't find its way out. She didn't have the heart to stomp on it.

But there were no cracks or crevices for Callie to escape. All she could do was wait. She would get out. Trudy wouldn't let her down. Neither would the others. Even if it meant telling the truth about her name, and everything else. And that would be the best thing. She should have told the truth in the first place. Why hadn't she? She had wanted out of the trap of being with Reggie, and instead, she landed into the rut of a deep canyon of lies.

Trudy seemed to think a DC, as the cops called it was no big deal. But she had stolen someone's ID. That was probably worse. And how long would she have to wait to go to court? She was supposed to be leaving for Detroit in less than forty-eight hours.

So far, Trudy had been right about the Selma Police. They must not know of any all-points bulletin out for a Callie Gibbs, wanted for questioning in the murder of her husband. No, her deepest worry was the name, Nellie Wilson. The name she had been using in Coosa Springs. And even if Trudy didn't, she intended to set things straight.

The voices in the distance were like echoes in a tunnel. Callie opened her eyes long enough to remember where she was. She had no idea for how long, but she managed to fall asleep even in jail with a cockroach for a cellmate. What time was it?

Keys clanged. She sat up. Without speaking an armed guard sat a tray on the floor and slammed the door shut. Callie remembered someone saying once that the hardest part of being in jail is not knowing what time it is. But when she picked up the tray of runny eggs, soupy grits, one slice of dry toast, and a plastic glass of something purple, she realized it was Wednesday morning. The Wednesday that was supposed to be her last day working at the Blue Moon, her last night in Coosa Springs, and her first date with Sammy.

She began pacing again. She'd been in jail all night. What happened? She mentally counted the time frame from when they left the Blue Moon for the Edgefield Inn. It couldn't have been much after eight when they got checked into jail. Or it could have been later. The fat officer took his time getting them there. And how long had they been in before Trudy got out? *Think.* They talked for a while and then dozed off. She wasn't sure for how long. It must have gotten too late for them to do anything last night. That had to be it. She felt better.

She took the tray over and sat on the cot inspecting the eggs and grits. She decided she would have to be at the point of starvation to eat the eggs. She took one bite of the grits and gagged. No butter, no salt. She ate the toast and drank half the purple stuff. It tasted like watered-down Kool-Aid with a drop of sugar. She peed in the toilet for the first time, the cold steel making her shiver.

Maybe if she slept the time would pass. Surely something would happen by late morning. She laid back down and forced her eyes shut. If she could just pretend to be back in room seven in the last few minutes of the night's sleep. The minutes when you were still dreaming but knew it was a dream, and it was time to wake up. She waited for images to come like in one of her crazy morning dreams. It started working. Her mind clouded over, and her breathing slowed. But then the jangling keys jarred her wide awake. Oh, it was the guard coming back to get the rest of the delicious breakfast before that roach bug finished it.

But instead, he asked, "Callie Gibbs?"

"Yes." Answering to her real name felt good.

"Come with me."

The guard led Callie down a long narrow hall. Why did he say *come with me* instead *of your bail is paid* as he did with Trudy? You can go, he'd said almost cheerfully.

After the darkness of the cell, the overhead lights were a blinding white. They turned right. This didn't look like the way they came in. The guard led her into a room with an officer sitting behind a battered wooden desk. Maybe she had to get processed. She wanted nothing more than to get out and explain her lie. She hoped everyone would trust her again. What would Sammy say?

"Sit down, Miss Gibbs." The officer pointed to a rickety chair that matched the desk. "I'm detective Stephens with the Dallas County Police. Miss Gibbs, your bail was paid last night."

Thank God, they came through. They came for Callie Gibbs. But why was she here with a detective?

"I'm sure you're anxious to get out, and we want you to. But there's something we need to clear up." The detective looked across the desk at her with piercing blue eyes. He was a handsome guy, the kind white women would give up their brains for.

"The officer working the desk last night left me a note. I got it when I came in early this morning. He had papers for a Nellie Wilson's bail, and it never went through. He couldn't locate anyone by that name. He noticed that the young lady you came in with got bailed out right away, but you didn't."

"I—"

Detective Stephens held up a hand. "Now I realize you two could have been bailed out by different people, but that's not usually the case in these civil rights protests. And between you and me, I'm not quite sure why you were brought in. I read the police report, and things are sketchy. That's another matter. However, we have a problem." He sighed. "A few weeks ago a couple of youngsters about your age went on a robbery spree. They hit a string of liquor stores around Birmingham. One clerk got lucky when Bonnie—we call 'em Bonnie and Clyde— dropped the ID she was using to prove she was old enough to buy liquor. The name on the ID was Nellie Wilson. We need to know if you know Nellie Wilson, *and* we need to make sure you *aren't* Nellie Wilson.

RJ and her dream. When would she learn to trust RJ's visions? "Officer, 'er Detective Stephens, I can explain. I'm Callie Gibbs, and Nellie Wilson is a teacher at my high school. I took it from her. The ID I mean."

Callie spent the next ten minutes explaining how she had been in a situation she needed to get away from. An abusive, dangerous situation, she called it. She told him about leaving to go to her mother for work as a singer, about missing the bus, hitchhiking, and getting robbed.

"I wasn't going to do anything wrong with Miss Wilson's ID, I promise. I like her too much. I was afraid I might need it for work if I didn't find my mother in time. Mother has a way of forgetting to keep in touch, you see. I mean, she does, but she gets busy and sometimes long stretches go by before—we hear from her."

The detective hesitated and then spoke. "Where are you staying, Miss Gibbs, and where are you from?"

"I've been at the Blue Moon Motel and Café in Coosa Springs since the end of February. I'm from Frogmoor, North Carolina. It's a little town in Wake County on the east end outside Raleigh."

"Describe the people who robbed you. Do you know their names?

"Just their first names. Dale and Babs. That's what they called each other. Babs had dark curly hair. Dale had short blond hair and was wearing a ball cap. It was after Malcolm X got shot, and they kept laughing really loud about it."

The detective shuffled through some papers and opened a folder. He handed her a mug shot. "Is this Babs?"

Callie clutched the picture of Babs. "Yes, that's her."

Detective Stephens picked up a ballpoint and popped the top up and down. "That collaborates with what we have. A copy of the ID was made and the original sent to Nellie Wilson's address in Frogmoor."

Callie's hope soared. They had proof she was telling the truth. With any luck, she would be back at the Blue Moon for her last day in Coosa Springs. She just hoped Sammy wouldn't hate her. He had said, sometimes the truth can set you free, Miss Nellie. She hoped this was one of those times.

"Okay, Callie. We need help to get this Babs. They caught Babs Delano with Dale when he went down. But she denies any involvement, and he's sticking up for his gal."

Good ol' Dale. He did have one redeeming quality. He was loyal to his girl.

"I'm asking you to make a statement for a recording. Is that okay?"

"Sure."

Detective Stephens flipped a button on the side of the recorder. "Just describe the robbery as you told me. And describe Babs and Dale." He nodded go.

Beads of sweat popped out on Callie's forehead as she related once again the details of the robbery. She described Babs, Dale, and their van in great detail. "Again, I'm sorry for taking Miss Wilson's driver's license," she added.

Detective Stephens clicked off the recorder and smiled. "Thanks, Callie. This will help a lot. Taking an ID is not too big of a charge if you haven't used it for a crime, especially if Nellie Wilson doesn't want to press charges. And from what you've told me, she probably won't. Let me tie up some loose ends, and we'll call your friends to come get you. You've had nuns and preachers calling about you. You must not be too bad." He flashed a pearly white smile.

"Do I have to go back in that cell?"

"No, of course not. Wait right here."

The handsome Detective Stephens left the room. Only then did she grow aware of the clock on the wall. It was twelve minutes after eight. Thinking nothing, she watched the big hand tick off seconds. She told the truth, and the truth was about to set her free.

At twenty-one minutes past eight, the cute detective came back with the guard. "Stand up, Miss Gibbs."

The guard handcuffed her.

"What's going on?"

Detective Stephens excused the guard. "I'll take her back. Miss Gibbs, I decided to call the sheriff's office in Frogmoor just to make sure Nellie Wilson didn't want to press charges. I felt it was in your best interest. I wanted to put in a good word for you. You helped us nail Babs Delano. Unfortunately, they said you're wanted for questioning in a murder. They want to come pick you up, so we have to detain you. You're being extradited back to Frogmoor."

The room started to spin like when she drank a beer too fast. Extradited. She'd only heard that word when Reggie talked about it. Someone would come from Frogmoor and take her to jail "What about the people that paid my bail?"

"I'll get their information and let them know."

Detective Stephens folded his arms on the desk. "Do you want to talk about it, Callie?"

Callie shrugged. "It's about my husband. He is—was a rookie cop."

"In Frogmoor?"

"Yes."

"Is that who you were running from?"

She nodded. "Somebody shot and killed him, but it happened after I left."

"They *found* him after you left."

"Well, yes, but I didn't do it. I was already gone, I swear."

"What you need is a lawyer, Callie. If you can, I would suggest hiring your own instead of asking for a court-appointed one. Those attorneys are overworked and underpaid. A lawyer you hire will pay your case more attention and get you a preliminary hearing. Then he can present evidence in your favor."

Like Matt Prescott, the preacher–trucker they had ridden with. And getting robbed. And turning in Babs Delano.

"In any case Callie, they can only hold you for twenty-four hours, or in some states, it may be forty-eight. After that, they have to let you go if they don't have enough evidence to formally charge you." He leaned forward. "A good lawyer is important. But for now, I'll have to lock you back up to wait for your, uh ride back to Frogmoor."

She choked back a sob. RJ would be so scared and worried. She had to catch herself before panic took her over the brink. What would Trudy do? She had said save their phone calls in case they really needed them.

"Wait. Don't I get a phone call?"

"I told you we'd call your friends that paid your bail."

"I mean to my family back in Frogmoor. I need to call them."

Detective Stephens unlocked the handcuffs so that her right arm was free. "Here. You can go ahead and make your call."

Clarence drove the bread truck on Wednesdays. She prayed he hadn't left yet. She was on her way to Frogmoor, and no one could do anything to stop that. But they could only hold her for twenty-four hours or something like that. She hadn't killed Reggie. They'd have to let her go. Then she would beg, borrow, or steal to get a bus ticket back to Coosa Springs.

She needed a lawyer. A good one and quick. She knew what she had to do. Clarence had to call the Blue Moon Motel in Coosa Springs and ask for Ruby Jean Carson.

Chapter 28

Ruby Jean washed her face, brushed her teeth, combed her limp hair, and dressed faster than she ever had before in her whole life. Surely it wouldn't be long before Callie got here. Maybe they had already called Jerry to come to get her. They both had a job to do. It was their last day, and she had that date with Sammy. Oh gosh, what would Sammy say?

They had all waited and waited last night, and then Jerry came home without Callie. A detective needed to come in and ask her some questions about a robbery but he wouldn't be in until early the next morning. They had known right away it had something to do with the stolen driver's license. She must have told them about it. Her dream about Babs and Callie in jail had hit Ruby Jean like a slap in the face, She decided not to say anything about the dream to the others, but she knew Callie would think of it too.

She had been a slobbering mess last night when they found out Callie wouldn't be getting out right away, and the youngest sister offered to stay with her in room seven. She kept her mind off of things by telling Ruby Jean about the orphanage where she grew up. Then they played in some makeup Vivian had given Callie and her, the sister even putting on some herself and making them both laugh. Before going to bed, they prayed and prayed for Callie to get out, but it hadn't worked yet. She would have been the first person Callie wanted to see.

The sisters perched on stools at the counter with coffee, elbows propped, and head in hands. Vivian quietly folded silverware into napkins. Long-faced, mama used to say. Ruby Jean, why are you so long-faced?

Sister Mary Agatha motioned with one arm. "Come here, child." She embraced Ruby Jean. "Did you get any sleep?"

Ruby Jean hugged the other two sisters. "A little. Thank you for letting Sister Mary Clare stay with me."

Vivian looked up. "I don't think any of us got much sleep. Trudy called in. She overslept. Poor thing. I wish I could give her the day off. Are you okay, Ruby Jean?"

"I think so, Vivian. I have to be. I've got a job to do. Callie, too."

Vivian sighed. "God, I hope she gets here soon." She glanced at the clock. "We've got a little less than an hour before opening. Sammy's back there cooking. He'll be bringing out breakfast." She glanced back and lowered her voice. "I haven't told him anything yet. I know him and Nellie, or Callie rather, had a little something going on."

"She's supposed to be leaving tomorrow," Sister Mary Agatha said. "I feel totally responsible, and I'll do anything I can to help."

Ruby Jean shook her head. "It's not your fault, Sister. Callie wanted to do that. Go to the restaurant, I mean. To show them they weren't doing the right thing. And it's not your fault Callie lied about her name. I mean, she didn't mean to lie, it just happened."

Sister Mary Eunice pat her on the cheek. "Bless you, child, you are so wise. Wise beyond your years. Under the circumstances, she will be forgiven."

The café door rattled. Ruby Jean held her breath as Jerry walked in. He must have gotten the call. He walked closer. Ruby Jean's heart fell into her stomach. It sat there pounding away. He just looked at them, and they looked back.

"Callie got cleared from the robbery and the ID problem."

Ruby Jean crossed her fingers and held her breath.

"But you don't look happy," Vivian said.

Jerry sighed. "They can't let her go. This detective Stephens guy called Frogmoor to help clear up the stolen ID. She's wanted for questioning up there. For her husband's murder. They're holding her until Frogmoor comes for her. In other words, she's being extradited."

Ruby Jean broke down. She wailed louder than ever. She couldn't help it.

"Oh no, oh my God," Vivian said. Then she sobbed too.

The sisters and Jerry were bent over them both when Sammy came through the door balancing trays of grits and eggs.

"What the heck's going on?" he asked.

∞∞∞

Ruby Jean's wails had turned to quiet sobbing. Plates of breakfast lined the counter and sat growing cold as the café's regular opening time approached. Vivian decided to keep the café closed for now.

"I'm putting a sign on the door. We have to have time to get ourselves together."

Trudy pushed Ruby Jean's damp bangs out of her eyes and handed her a clean napkin. "Ruby Jean, get ahold of yourself. We'll get through this. She's wanted for questioning, that's all, so far."

Ruby Jean hiccupped. Trudy was right. Callie was innocent. Surely they'd figure it out.

"I must admit I was a little mad and hurt a few minutes ago when I learned she lied about her name. I don't understand why she didn't trust us enough to tell us the truth."

"I thought the same thing, Sammy," Vivian said. "Who knows why we do the things we do? I think she just got caught up in things. But she's in a bad spot right now. I wish we could help her. I know the girl we know is incapable of murder."

"She wasn't even there when it happened," Ruby Jean said quietly. "We left on Monday, and Callie said they found him dead Wednesday."

Sister Mary Eunice snapped her fingers. "Matthew Prescott!"

They all looked confused, but Ruby Jean knew what she meant.

"Matthew Prescott, the preacher-trucker?" Sammy asked.

Sister Eunice told them how he had been the one to rescue Ruby Jean when she got lost at the march. "Turns out he was the one who picked them up hitchhiking, and they recognized each other"

"That could be good if they believe Matthew Prescott," Sammy said.

"Believe him? He's a preacher," Trudy said.

"The law puts no one above the law. Sorry, Sisters."

"That's quite all right," Sister Mary Eunice said. "We know what you mean, Sammy. I'll get in touch with Matt and tell him what's going on. I think two or three of us should go up there."

Vivian started scraping the breakfast plates. They had picked at them a little, all except Ruby Jean. "Ruby Jean, you'd better eat something. I do too, but we've got a business to run. We could close the café and say we're renovating, but we can't leave the motel. We have guests."

The sisters looked at each other.

"Okay, it's time," Sister Mary Clare said. She took off her mantilla and shook out blond curls.

The others gasped.

Sammy stared. "Holy, moly!"

They all laughed.

Jerry came in taking in the scene. "At least you sound happier. Listen. Nellie—I mean Callie's cousin Clarence is on the phone in the office. I can't get used to calling her, Callie. He wants to talk to you, Ruby Jean."

"Clarence? Clarence called?"

"Yes, girl, go. Come on, I'll go with you." Trudy pulled her off the stool.

She picked up the receiver Jerry had left on the desk. "Clarence?"

"Hey, Ruby Jean. Yes, it's me, Clarence. Look, don't be upset.

I'll be sure to help Callie. But she wants you to do something. Something important."

"What?"

"She wants you to look in the drawer beside the bed for a letter and a newspaper article. Give it to the sisters. Callie needs a good lawyer."

"Did they arrest her for killing Reggie? She couldn't have."

"She hasn't been arrested yet, but she might be. Just give it to the sisters. Callie says they'll know what to do."

Ruby Jean had seen her reading a letter and looking at a picture in the newspaper when Callie didn't see watching. It had something to do with those people that Callie said was her daddy's family. "I will Clarence. I'll do that. Will you be able to see Callie?"

"I will."

"Tell her I love her." She hung up. "We've got to get some stuff out of the night table drawer, Trudy."

Trudy read the letter and looked at the picture in the newspaper. "Whew! This is crazy stuff here. Let's go."

Jerry hadn't been able to tear himself away to go back to the motel office. Vivian and Sammy were pacing, and the sisters were wringing their hands.

Trudy handed the letter and the folded newspaper to Sister Mary Eunice. She read the letter silently and then looked at the photograph on the front of the folded newspaper. "Senator Winfred Whitfield." Her voice was a loud whisper. "This could totally destroy him." She cleared her throat and read the letter aloud.

Sammy grabbed the newspaper and inspected the article. "It's him. Senator Winfred Whitfield. Nellie, I mean Callie asked me about him one day. Holy cow! That bigot is her grandfather."

Jerry pounded his fist on the counter. "What a lousy guy."

"Poor Callie, Vivian said. "I'm getting used to calling her that. What a terrible thing to find out. Her family just bartered her back and forth like a piece of furniture. But what good does the letter and article do Callie now?"

"Don't you see?" Jerry asked. "She needs a good lawyer. She needs the family she is a rightful part of. This lawyer, and not to mention the senator."

Sister Mary Eunice waved the letter. "Tomorrow, we go. Callie won't be getting to Frogmoor until sometime late tonight or early tomorrow morning. I'll call Matt Prescott." She looked at Ruby Jean. "Of course you'll go, honey. Clare will be here, and Agatha can stay if you need her."

"Hey, nothing says an old nun can't work a cash register. I'm afraid I don't cook, though."

"Then it's settled. We leave for North Carolina tomorrow." Sister Mary Eunice waved the letter again. "And we're going straight to the senator's office. I'll call today and try to get an appointment to speak to the senator himself as a representative of the Cape Fear Religious Order. Luckily, tomorrow is Thursday. I heard once that senators fly to Washington on Tuesday mornings and come back to their districts on Thursdays. If Callie needs a lawyer, we'll make sure she gets one."

Ruby Jean felt like honey had been poured over her soul. Tomorrow they would go back home and help Callie.

Frogmoor, North Carolina

March 17, 1965

He knew she'd mess up. They usually did. Now he was on his way to get her. Kenneth Sawyers gassed up the squad car and headed out of town to Alabama, to Selma, where all that nigger trouble was going on.

The detective he'd spoken to had been tight-lipped. But the chief called and found out. Arrested for disorderly conduct trying to get served in a white restaurant. It was almost funny.

His work would soon pay off. While the chief ran a wild goose chase after some unknown enemy of Reggie's, he put facts together. Like the coroner's report. The final report showed the time of death to be possibly forty-eight hours before the body was found. Reggie reported his wife missing on Tuesday morning. She wasn't in school on Monday. Lucy Gibbs said they'd been fighting, another fact. They didn't get along. That would plant motivation in the court's mind. Then her grandmother claimed she left first for Memphis and started working to follow her mother to Detroit. In fact, she had been headed in the opposite direction. And now he had absolute proof she was the one who stole Nellie Wilson's ID. Clearly, she intended to change her identity, just what a murderer would do. Oh, he had her all right.

He couldn't wait to make detective. He'd have more power to find his own wife. The time had come to track that bitch down. With this out of the way, he could. He'd have her begging to come home when she found out about his promotion. He'd do her lowlife vacuum cleaner salesman boyfriend over good and get by with it because he was a detective.

He cruised down the interstate planning. Places to look, numbers to call. He saw a car broken down ahead. He slowed. A woman was tying a handkerchief to the antenna. My God. Shirley?

He flashed his light and pulled in behind her. It wasn't Shirley, but it could have been from a distance.

"What's the trouble, ma'am?"

"Flat tire."

Her mousy but curly hair blew in the chilly wind. She wore a sleeveless white blouse despite the cold day, her upper arms covered in chill bumps.

She's probably left her husband, he thought. He looked for a ring but didn't see one. Not that it mattered to women these days.

He changed her left front tire easily.

She thanked him. "Thank God you stopped by, officer."

"You're welcome, ma'am." *For helping a tramp on the run.* He let her pull into traffic first and then followed behind her for a bit. He passed her and blew. She waved. He couldn't help feeling good about helping the woman no matter what she had done wrong. Love thine enemies; turn the other cheek. He needed to be a better Christian. Maybe he'd try to do something kind for Callie Gibbs Knight. Like a stop at a burger joint and get her something to eat. That would be nice of him. He smiled.

Darkness fell when he saw the sign: Welcome to Alabama. He dreaded the tiresome drive back, but he'd be leading Reggie's killer on the way to justice. And it would be the last time he had to do a job like this. Detectives didn't have to.

Chapter 29

Callie had guessed correctly that Sawyers would be the one they sent for her. It was something they would have put on Reggie, and Reggie was gone. But despite making a long haul to Alabama, Kenneth Sawyers seemed to be in the best of spirits.

"Sooo... you came off down here and tried to get lost amongst a bunch of protesters. Good idea 'til you got caught trying to eat in a white restaurant. They don't go for that around here, do they? I guess you found *that* out"

She said nothing. She had decided to keep her mouth totally shut. Anything you say can and will be held against you became a mantra that she repeated over and over in her head. But what about the questioning? Would they lock her up if she refused? Wait. She was innocent. She'd tell the truth. She left, got robbed, and got a job.

By now Clarence would have gotten to talk to RJ, and the sisters would have the letter and the newspaper article. She worried about the extortion part. *As you know, Mrs. Gibbs, extortion is against the law.* But the sisters weren't Lucy Gibbs. Would they somehow be able to use it to help her?

The back of the squad car was a jail in itself, a cage-like partition separating the back seat from the front. She didn't see why she had to be in cuffs. Where the hell could she go and how? Sawyers did it to be a prick.

Sawyers slowed down. "Burger Chef. Next exit. I could go for coffee and a burger. How about you? Oh yeah, you're handcuffed. Tell you what. I'll take 'em off and leave 'em off 'til we get to the station."

"No, not hungry," she mumbled.

The smell of charbroiled hamburgers danced through the car like a cobra to a flute, but she wasn't about to let Kenneth Sawyers worm his way into her brain.

She dozed off and on as the hours on the dark interstate passed. Finally, the headlights lit up the green and white reflective sign welcoming them to Frogmoor. Sawyers slowed down to obey the thirty-five miles an hour speed limit.

Callie glanced at the clock on the wall when they went into the station. Three thirty in the morning.

Only one half-asleep officer sat behind the desk. "You finally got back?"

"Long trip. Been on the road since early this morning. Lock her up. I'm going home and get some sleep."

The officer stood.

"Wait, a minute. You can't hold me for more than twenty-four hours."

"Me and the chief will be back in the morning. Go get some sleep."

Callie had napped in the car long enough to be awake. She paced around the cell stretching her arms and massaging her wrists. At least she was out of the pinching handcuffs. She laid down, but sleep wouldn't come. The one good thing about the small Frogmoor jailhouse, she could see into the office and tell the time. She watched as the clock hands moved ever so slowly as sleep finally took over.

At a little past six in the morning, Sawyers opened the cell door and called her out. He didn't cuff her this time as he led her back to the front. Chief Price had taken the sleepy officer's place behind the desk.

"Sit down, Mrs. Knight." He began by asking her to state her name.

She looked at him, confused.

It's the way we start. Standard procedure.

"I'm Callie Gibbs. I go by Gibbs, still."

"But you were married to Reggie Knight. Right?"

"I was."

"When was the last time you saw Reggie?"

Callie knew exactly when she had last seen Reggie. It had been late Sunday night before she left on Monday. He had the next two days off and came home drunk as a skunk. She had pretended to be asleep. He knocked her out of bed and made her fix him grits and eggs. But she pretended to think. "On Monday morning before I left. He was still asleep because it was his day off."

"You were aware he'd been shot and killed, right? Before we picked you up?"

"Yes, I found out when I called to check in with my grandmother."

"Is it true you two weren't getting along?"

That was obvious, and Lucy had told him as much. She might as well say yes. "That's right."

"Why did you leave town?"

Be careful. "I left town to go stay with my mother and start a new career."

"Just a few months before graduating from high school? That seems strange."

"I decided I didn't need high school. Mother was going to help me get a job singing. She's almost famous. Look. Reggie was killed on Sunday. I'd been gone two days."

"Correction Mrs.—ah, Miss Gibbs. Reggie was *found* on Sunday. According to the coroner's report, he could have been dead for up to forty-eight hours."

Callie decided she had said enough without the presence of a lawyer.

Sawyers brought a tape recorder over and sat it down. Price leaned forward and clicked it on. He spoke slowly and deliberately. "Miss Gibbs, you shot your husband with his own gun and ran off with a stolen ID. You hid the gun somewhere. Didn't you, Miss Gibbs? He pounded on the desk, raised his voice and glared at her. Didn't you?"

It was like a scene from Dragnet, she thought and would have been funny if not happening to her. "No!" she yelled back. "I didn't! I have the right to a lawyer, or at the least, a family member. I'm not saying anything else."

Sawyers leaned over and clicked off the recorder.

The chief sighed. "Miss Gibbs. You steal somebody else's driver's license *before* Reggie gets shot. You weren't in school on Monday before the murder. You leave town, the driver's license, your own teacher's, ends up around Birmingham, and then so do you. And your grandmother tells us you're on your way to Detroit. The prosecutor can use all that to establish premeditated murder." Chief Price leaned back and scratched his head. "Look, I know Reggie. I *knew* Reggie, and he had his issues. I'm not going to say you have to talk without an attorney present. But keep this in mind. A confession would get you a chance to plea bargain at least to second-degree murder, maybe manslaughter." He shook his head. "You'd better think about it."

Callie looked at Sawyers and then turned to the chief. "I didn't do it, and I'm not confessing to anything."

Chief Price turned to Sawyers. "Okay, cuff her. Read her the Miranda and lock her up."

"Wait, a minute. Lock me up for what?"

Sawyers pulled cuffs from his belt. "We've got probable cause to arrest you for the murder of Reggie Knight."

Icy water flowed through Callie's veins "Wait! I get a phone call. I can call my lawyer—or somebody."

Sawyers cuffed her and recited her Miranda rights. "I'll come get you in a little while. I got stuff to do."

He was being a prick again. The jailhouse was dead as a doornail. She had only passed by one inmate who looked like he was sleeping one off.

"Let her call before they take her to the county," Chief Price said.

Callie turned from one man to the other. "The county?"

"Yeah, the county jail," the chief answered. "This here's pretty much just a holding tank. You'll get fed there."

Back in the cell, the tears came. She was innocent, locked up for a murder she didn't commit. If she could get out, she bet she and Clarence together would figure everything out. But God only knew where bail money for murder would come from. There were no civil rights groups around here to help her out. Unless... Would the sisters be able to get the money from the Whitfields with the letter? It was her only chance. Okay, so say she didn't get bailed out. Worst case scenario: They would have to get her a lawyer. What was that Detective Stephens said? A preliminary hearing. A chance to present evidence. What evidence did she have? God, how she wished they hadn't missed the bus that day.

Matt Prescott. He was her only alibi, along with her own testimony and turning in Babs. That and whatever the sisters could do with the letter was all she had going for her. And whatever Clarence could do.

She got her phone call twenty minutes later. Thank God Clarence was home. "Clarence, they arrested me. They're taking me to the county jail. Arrested—for — probable cause. For murder."

"Try not to worry, Brown Sugar. I got your message, and I told RJ to get that out of your drawer and give it to the sisters. So Ruby Jean knows about the letter?"

"Yeah, roughly."

"Sisters? Is that like in nuns?"

"Yes."

"Nuns resorting to bribery? Where the hell have you been?"

"I'll tell you later. For now, they're nuns, not saints. They have a passion for civil rights, and Whitfield is a well-known bigot. I'm counting on them to use the letter to my advantage. Somehow."

Chapter 30

The sisters' station wagon lumbered up the interstate toward North Carolina. Ruby Jean stretched out in the roomy back seat with a pillow and a blanket, eyes, still puffy from crying, half-closed. As badly as she needed to catch up on the sleep she had lost, she fought to stay awake and had since last night. She left both lamps and the TV on, only drifting off a little while before the Star-Spangled Banner came on with the flag waving on the screen.

She fought sleep because she kept feeling like she would have a bad dream or a vision, and she didn't want that right now. She wanted to hang on to Trudy's words. *Get ahold of yourself. She's just wanted for questioning so far.* Ruby Jean had asked why they couldn't just ask her questions over the phone, but Trudy said it didn't work that way. She pictured Callie out of jail by the time they got there. Sister Mary Eunice had gotten Clarence's number before they left. They would call him after talking to the senator, and he would tell them. They would go pick her up, maybe meet Clarence somewhere, she hoped. She didn't want to go out to Frogmoor. They'd go back to Coosa Springs, and Callie would think of an excuse why they would be late getting to Della's in Detroit. Callie was good at thinking of excuses.

Ruby Jean's thoughts turned to Mama again. She fought off the sad ones with good memories. Memories like watching Alfred Hitchcock on Saturday nights with Mama and the boys. Snake, after an early afternoon at Ledford's, would have already had his rant and passed out on the four-poster bed Mama's mother had given them. They would eat popcorn Mama popped on the stove and drink Pepsis. They stayed up late, late, and

Junior would wet his bed. But Mama would get up, change him, leave Snake's breakfast on the stove, and take them to church.

The lull of the road rocked her like a baby. She listened to the sister and the preacher talk back and forth about the big march. It helped keep her awake.

"It's looking like it will happen." Sister Mary Eunice said. "Judge Johnson handed down his ruling in Federal Court in Montgomery yesterday. The marchers are within their rights. He said the law clearly states people have the right to petition grievances to the government, and they can do so in large groups. I heard they're trying for this Sunday the twenty-first."

"Yeah, but we've still got to get around Wallace," the preacher said. "He's expected to go to the state legislature to fight it. Claims Alabama can't afford to call up the state's National Guard."

Ruby Jean caught herself nodding off and watched out the window as the sun came up, glad for the light. Vivian had given her a stack of magazines for the trip, and Sister Mary Clare handed her a little brown bag of licorice before they left. She found them both, flipped through the magazines and chewed on a licorice stick.

Sister Mary Clare and the preacher talked on about the march and how wrong it was to deny anyone the right to vote. Ruby Jean focused on the pictures of pretty girls in dresses and ads for shoes and makeup. She perked up when Sister Mary Eunice asked the preacher about his wife and children, remembering her fantasy about how perfect their life would be.

He explained that they had the kind of muscular dystrophy that struck early. "Bethany handles the girls well, but it's getting harder as they get older. We may be able to get them into a school soon. The same law that's responsible for integration, you know, is now applying to children with disabilities."

Ruby Jean thought about the special school Aunt Peggy had wanted to put her in.

"I read about that," the sister replied. "Congress passed a bill to create a Bureau of Education for the handicapped."

"Yes, they did. Nothing has been mandated by law yet, but it's coming. In the meantime, I'm planning on getting some help for Bethany, a sort of caretaker. The church has promised to help with expenses, and with help for Bethany, I can make more long hauls."

They started talking politics as Mama called it. Ruby Jean turned back to her magazines and licorice. They talked about Callie's grandpa, the senator.

"You know, he was a Democrat until recently," Sister Mary Agnes said.

"Right. After the Civil Rights Act passed last year, he switched parties because of his opposition to it. He's all for states' rights and wants to run for president? It would be a disaster for several states if he won."

For some reason, the preacher and Sister Mary Eunice lowered their voices. She tried to hear what they were saying. Something about bail and extortion.

She flipped through the last of the magazines and grew tired of the licorice, putting the slimy black stump back in the brown bag. They rode in silence, Ruby Jean fighting sleep. Sleep and a picture that kept trying to creep up on her. But it wasn't about Callie. Her Mama's face was forming from the swirly things on the back of her eyelids.

Preacher Prescott parallel-parked on a busy street in downtown Raleigh. He had taken over driving for the sister after they had lunch at Shoney's. Ruby Jean straightened her rumpled skirt and blouse and glanced up at the tall buildings reflecting the afternoon sun. Some of them were so tall they seemed to touch the sky. She'd never been to the top of a building as tall as these.

Sister Mary Eunice said the senator's office was a block away, and they were lucky to get a parking space as close as they did.

When they got to the senator's building, Ruby Jean was glad to count only ten rows of windows. Ten floors up shouldn't be too scary. She tried to guess which one would be Senator Winfred Whitfield's office. She pulled her sweater tightly even though the day was warm. She was about to meet not only the state's senator, but her best friend's grandfather who had sent money all those years, and the letter Sister Mary Eunice now had. Callie hadn't wanted to tell even her who her daddy and grandfather was, but this is what she wanted now, or else she wouldn't have told her and Trudy to give the letter to the sisters. Callie's daddy was a lawyer, and she really needed one. But the sisters said her grandfather wanted to run for president and would be very interested in the letter.

The elevator stopped on the fifth floor. They walked down a long carpeted hallway to the last door on the end, the door with Senator Winfred Whitfield on a plaque in gold letters. Inside, several people were sitting at desks looking busy — some typing, some going through mail, and others talking on the phones on their desks.

A pretty young receptionist approached them, her blonde hair up in a French twist. "How may I help you?"

Sister Mary Eunice answered. "We have an appointment to speak with the senator at two o'clock."

The receptionist smiled. "Sister Mary Eunice of the Cape Fear Religious Order, I presume."

The sister smiled back. "Right."

The receptionist offered her hand to the sister. "It's good to meet you, Sister. I'm sorry, but the senator just got in from Washington, and he has several urgent phone calls to return. We've had to change his schedule. He *may* be able to speak with you briefly before he heads home at six. But if you can come back first thing in the morning, say around eight, I can pretty much guarantee you an early appointment."

Sister Mary Eunice looked at the preacher. He nodded. She opened her purse and took out the letter. She handed it to the receptionist. "My dear, could you be as kind as to deliver this to the senator immediately? You see, the matter is urgent and time-sensitive."

The receptionist hesitated. "Well, I—okay, I suppose I can do that for you."

"Thank you so much, dear."

"Yes, thank you," the preacher added.

"You're welcome, have a seat."

The three of them sat down in black and gold striped adjoining chairs. The receptionist returned a few minutes later and led them back to Senator Winfred Whitfield's office.

A tall man stood staring out the window, his back to them. Ruby Jean hadn't even stopped to think about what Callie's grandfather might look like.

"Senator, your appointment is here."

He turned from the window. He had gray hair like any grandfather would. He wore a dark blue suit with a white shirt and a red tie. "Yes, come in. Have a seat, please," he said.

He sat across from them. His eyebrows were thick and almost grown together in the middle. He looked from one to the other of them with eyes like Callie's. The way he looked at her made Ruby Jean think he was trying to decide if she was Callie.

He had the letter spread out in front of him. "So how are things down on the coast, Sister?"

"I haven't been there for a while, Senator. I've been in Alabama. In Selma, joining the voter's rights movement and the fight against segregation. Allow me to introduce my friends, Reverend Matt Prescott and Ruby Jean Carson."

The senator nodded at them. "So you're here to speak for the Negros in Alabama." He picked up the letter. "What has that got to do with this?"

"I'm not here for the Negros in Alabama, Senator. I'm here for your granddaughter, Callie. Callie Gibbs."

The senator listened as Sister Mary Eunice told Callie and Ruby Jean's story from missing the bus, to getting picked up by the preacher, to getting arrested at the Edgefield Inn. "Your granddaughter has been in an identity crisis for most of her life,

Senator," Sister Mary Eunice explained. "She was coerced into marrying a black police officer, and tantalized into denying her white heritage, her questions silenced for years."

Preacher Prescott spoke. "Now that her lowlife husband was killed around the same time she left, she could face a murder charge."

"What do you want from me?"

"Your help," the sister answered. "That is a copy of the letter. I have the original, signed in blue ink."

The senator's dark eyes flashed fire. "You're here to blackmail me," he stormed. "You, a nun. You're asking me for money?" He leaned across his desk like he was about to stand up. "That's extortion."

Sister Mary Eunice shook her head. "I'm not asking for money, and I would say it's more like fighting evil than blackmail. Callie needs her people's help, and we're prepared to do whatever it takes to get it. Politically, I have several journalist connections."

The senator looked at them with hooded eyes and glanced at his watch. "Okay, Sister, you win. I'll get in touch with my son. He'll contact Mrs. Gibbs and make arrangements."

Sister Mary Eunice handed him a slip of paper. "This is her cousin's number. Clarence Truelove. It's better to go through him."

"I'll see that it gets done. My son will make the arrangements." He nodded toward the door.

"It needs to be immediate, Senator. If Callie is formally charged, she will need a preliminary hearing."

The senator nodded without standing. "I'll make the call as soon as you leave."

∞ ∞ ∞

Ruby Jean took her time eating the chocolate fudge sundae.

First the cherry, then the whipped cream. She was down to the ice cream and chocolate sauce, Preacher Prescott was on his second cup of coffee, and Sister Mary Eunice was on her third try calling Clarence. She still held on to the hope that Callie hadn't been arrested after all. She wanted so much to hug her and take her back to Coosa Springs. They could sit in the back of the roomy station wagon and look at magazines. This time Callie could read some things she'd been looking at to her. She had brought her last two nights tips with her to buy her a burger or something. Sister Mary Eunice or Preacher Prescott would have too, but just in case.

Sister Mary Clarence slid into the booth beside her. "Okay, I got Clarence on the phone. A bail hearing is set for three o'clock this afternoon. He's been working on finding out something about the bail. I told him to listen out for a call from Grayson Whitfield's office. He hasn't gotten it yet, but then he and his aunt have been out."

Ruby Jean laid the long plastic spoon down. "That means she got arrested, doesn't it?"

"Yes, it does, Ruby Jean," Sister Mary Eunice said, "But don't lose it. I can assure you that Senator Winfred Whitfield is already in action. He has a lot at stake."

"Yeah, like voters for a future presidency," Preacher Prescott added.

Her lower lip quivered. But she had decided not to be a big baby about things anymore. She knew Callie would want her to be strong, and Trudy would too. "So what happens now?"

Sister Mary Eunice glanced at her watch. "It's almost two-thirty now. We just go."

The swirly patterns were back, and this time, she didn't even have her eyes closed. She couldn't decide if it was about Callie or Mama, but she didn't want to have a vision. Not now.

Chapter 31

The county jail was an improvement — the long, light-brick building ultra-modern compared to the dinky jail in Frogmoor. Lunch was almost decent: watery beef stew with four saltines, something akin to mashed potatoes, and canned peaches. She ate every bite and washed it down with weak Kool-aide, the standard jailhouse drink, she decided.

The early lunch had been a good diversion, she had been starved. Getting booked, fingerprinted, and photographed had been humiliating. The female officer that did her fingerprinting seemed a little kinder than anyone else. Callie managed to ask her in a weak voice what would happen next. She said the next step was a bail hearing. She knew what that meant. They had to give her the opportunity for a judge to set a reasonable bail.

But murder? What would reasonable bail be, and would a judge even consider bail for her? She saw a Dragnet episode once where the bail was $25,000 and another where bail was denied. And if she didn't get out, she had the right to a trial, and the right to a lawyer. If she couldn't afford a lawyer, the court would appoint one.

Time became irrelevant, a concept Callie wasn't familiar with anymore. It could have been hours, or it could have been minutes when she was led from the holding cell into an empty courtroom. The guard seated her beside a slender man in a pinstriped suit. He introduced himself and started talking. Duty lawyer, something about duty lawyer. She stared at the pinstripes on his suit. She needed to concentrate and listen.

"Now, Miss Gibbs, under the circumstances, the judge is

likely to find probable cause for second-degree murder. That means the murder wasn't premeditated, but rather you were urged on in some way. If you plead guilty, the judge would have the option to reduce the charge to voluntary manslaughter. Your bail would be cheaper and the sentence lighter." He placed his hand on her arm. "And, you could still retain counsel and have a jury trial. Meanwhile, you would be out of prison and under the supervision of a probation officer."

Callie stared around at all the polished wood with the judge's bench taking center stage. She was in the principal's office for slapping a boy that kept pushing her down and calling her a half-breed. Granddaddy Moses had come to meet with Mr. Smith all dressed up in a pinstriped suit. He'd had plenty to say and threatened Mr. Smith's job. She didn't get bullied again. Not that year.

"Miss Gibbs, did you hear me? Do you understand?"

No words would come. She nodded. All she could do now was pray. *Granddaddy, please tell God not to let me go to prison for something I didn't do.* What if she got a life sentence? She would never be free from Reggie Knight after all.

A voice from the corner shouted, "All rise!"

The judge entered, a stout white man with a balding head. "Please be seated." He peered over wire rims at the papers in front of him and called the duty lawyer and another man, the prosecutor, to the bench.

They were whispering. What was going on? If her life was on the line, she needed to know what they were saying.

The judge spoke. "Mrs. Knight, or Miss Gibbs, same case, approach the bench please."

She heard the judge read the charge, an ugly sound. Murder. Second-degree murder. "Miss Gibbs, how do you plead to this charge?"

Lesser sentence, manslaughter, lower bail. The words swarmed in her head. Her voice was a murmur. "Not guilty."

"Miss Gibbs, please speak up."

"Not guilty. I'm not guilty. I didn't kill Reggie."

"The court will enter a plea of not guilty."

Silence echoed from the walls. The judge bent over papers. Callie's legs were like rubber.

The judge slammed his gavel once. "Bail is set for $25,000."

That was it, just as she had feared. What next? Were they going to drag her off in handcuffs?

More whispering. More shuffling papers.

"Mrs. Gibbs, and Mr. Truelove? Step forward, please."

Callie turned and saw Clarence and Lucy step forward. Her ears buzzed, and the room turned gray for a minute.

"The defendant must also remain at the address on the property bond until her trial date." The judge struck his gavel.

Property bond? It had to be Lucy. She had put her house, their house up for bail.

∞ ∞ ∞

Callie sat with Lucy and Clarence at the table in the familiar kitchen. "Grandma, I can't believe you did that for me. I don't feel like I deserve it, taking your money and running away like that."

She told them on the way home about missing the bus, the robbery, and ending up in Coosa Springs. She told them about the Blue Moon, the sisters, and how she had gotten arrested. Callie had come back to her childhood home the same way she left Frogmoor, in Clarence's delivery truck, this time with Lucy and a load of Bunny Bread. Clarence had called in sick to help Lucy make the arrangements for the property bond. She'd have to stay with Lucy, but she was free for now and happy. She was out of jail and free to fight to stay free.

Lucy dabbed her eyes with a fresh Kleenex as she handed Callie a fried bologna sandwich and a glass of iced tea. "No, I'm the one at fault. I should never have encouraged you to hook up with that low down Reggie Knight. Clarence said he was seeing a woman, a married woman, and he thinks it was her husband that shot Reggie. And the money is rightfully yours, anyway. I should have spent more money on you all those years. Clarence told me about you finding that letter. I was afraid for you to go to them people asking for help."

Callie looked around the cozy kitchen with beadboard walls painted pale blue. A spring breeze from the open window ruffled white curtains. She knew now how much the little house she grew up in meant to her. "But Grandma, this little house? Twenty-five thousand dollars?"

Lucy sniffled. "You never knew this, but your granddaddy had land. Lots of land."

Callie knew the story about the kind old landowner Granddaddy Moses had worked for who died and left this house to him. But land? "Land," she asked?

Lucy nodded. "In fact, he owns the Carson's farm and all that land he grows tobacco all over. He just never collected rent from old man Carson."

That explained Snake Carson's dislike of her.

Lucy started crying again. "Like I said, I should've done better by you. But—see, it was like this." She mopped up tears and let out a long sigh. "Moses got behind on the property tax after he got sick with heart problems and had to quit working in the mill. I used some of the money your—people paid to catch up the payments. It took me nearly five years, but I did it. I could've taken in ironing or something to bring in extra money. Instead, I sat on my behind pampering myself. And then I got that letter and an offer to send you to college. I wanted you to be able to go to college. You've always been so smart."

Shame washed over Callie like a tidal wave. All the times she had called Lucy, Lucifer, taking money without asking, and traipsing off after a mother that only half cared about her. *Della!* She was supposed to have taken the bus to Detroit yesterday. "Grandma, has Della called?"

"I called her. I told her you were coming back here to straighten things out and left it at that. She seemed satisfied."

"Good. Grandma, about that college. I just didn't want to go to an all-black college. I wanted to go somewhere that is more accepting of mixed people. I guess that's what I had in mind when I headed for Memphis and Detroit, the music world."

"I should have thought of that, Callie."

"But Grandma, what if—will you lose everything if..."

"Don't even think that, Callie. I trusted things enough to take the chance."

Clarence had been quietly sitting by making notes in a small spiral notebook. "Here's where we are. Callie, Sister Mary Eunice called as I was on my way out the door this afternoon. They took the letter to Winfred Whitfield. In person."

Lucy fanned her face. "Oh, Lord, have mercy."

Clarence waved a hand. "They didn't ask for money, but he guaranteed services from an attorney. His son, your father."

"Oh, Lord, have mercy," Lucy said again.

"And indeed, it's happening. I was on the phone with Grandma in the bedroom while you two sat in here blubbering. The nun gave Whitfield my phone number. Callie, you have an appointment in the morning at ten. In Raleigh. Grandma's got the address."

"It's sister, not nun."

"Whatever. They'll set a preliminary hearing. You two go over to the house. The nun—sorry, sister, and Ruby Jean and the preacher are on their way there. Grandma made chicken pot pies. Ask the preacher trucker guy about being a witness. It's weak, but it's all we have for now. But I'm going to try to crack this case before any hearing. I'm on my way to Tarboro."

"You be careful over there, Clarence. Take my car. What you gone do with all that bread?"

"Deliver stale bread tomorrow, I guess."

"Well, I can make us some bread puddins' if somebody don't want it."

"I'll keep that in mind. Thank you, Aunt Lucy." Clarence took her keys.

Callie hoped and prayed Clarence knew what he was doing.

She wished she could go with him and work on a way to prove she was innocent. But she was out of jail, Ruby Jean was coming, and she would be surrounded by the ones she loved and cared about. And tomorrow she might come face to face with her real father. She held Lucy's hand and helped her down the path to Aunt Lettie's house.

Chapter 32

Ruby Jean couldn't take her eyes off her best friend. She had fought the vision all the way to the Wake County courthouse. She wanted to see Callie in person, not in a vision. And now here she was, back in Frogmoor having supper at Callie's great aunt's house.

When they had ridden past the familiar landmarks of Frogmoor Ruby Jean fought to keep the countryside beyond—the tobacco fields, the Carson house, and Callie's bungalow on the other side of the railroad tracks — out of her thoughts. She hoped the sister and preacher Prescott didn't ask if she wanted to call or go to her house. All that mattered was Callie and getting her out of trouble.

She had to go to a trial, but for now, Callie was out of jail. Clarence was off working on finding the real killer, and tomorrow, Callie would meet with a lawyer, her real daddy. Ruby Jean couldn't imagine what that must feel like. Thank goodness for that letter and thank goodness Sister Mary Eunice thought up a way to use it to help Callie. And thank goodness too, Callie had called and told her and Trudy to go get it.

"Mrs. Truelove, this chicken pot pie is simply divine." Sister Mary Eunice held her plate out as Clarence's Aunt Lettie made the rounds with seconds. "Thank you so much for having us to dinner. And Mrs. Gibbs, what you did for Callie is so admirable."

"Humph! Not as admirable was what you and the preacher did, Sister. Taking that letter straight to Winfred Whitfield in person? I couldn't have done that. No siree." Callie's grandma followed behind Aunt Lettie pouring cold sweet tea. "And call me Lucy, and my sister is Lettie."

"Thank you, both so much. It means a lot to me," Callie said. "And Grandma is an angel to do what she did."

Callie had called her grandmother Lucifer, but now she was an angel. She was glad, and she could tell from the look the sister gave Callie that she was glad, too. Her grandma had turned out to be a good person after all.

"It was my duty to come," the sister replied. She told them about her idea to help test the public accommodations act at the Edgefield Inn and how Callie and Trudy got arrested. "And Matt said it had bothered him that he didn't see the girls more safely on their way down the road, so here we are."

Miss Lucy sat the tea pitcher back on the counter. "Well, I'm right proud of Callie for that. Ain't you Lettie?"

"Yes, I am. 1 `ve been watching the news. And to think Callie and Ruby Jean were right there in the middle of it." Aunt Lettie sat a double fudge chocolate cake on the table, slicing fat pieces to put on her pretty dessert plates. She gave Callie the first piece.

Callie took a big bite of cake. "I sure am glad to be out of jail. The food was awful."

"Did they give you a court date, Callie?" the preacher asked.

"I'm supposed to call Monday to find out the court date."

"I'm surprised they didn't already set it," he said.

"That's Wake County for you," Lucy said. "You have to do all the work."

"In the meantime, I guess I meet with my father tomorrow." Callie's face lit up. "He'll get me a preliminary hearing, soon I hope."

"Yes, it's my understanding those get set pretty quickly. Look, if there is anything I can do, be a witness about picking you girls up, or anything, don't hesitate to ask."

"Clarence did tell me to mention that to you, Matt. You're about all I've got. You, and the people at the Blue Moon. I'll be sure to let you know what my father says."

There it was again—that glow. Callie was going to meet her real father.

"My boy Clarence is gone find the real killer," Aunt Lettie

said. "He's working on it right now. He's in criminal justice school, and he knows what he's doing."

"I sure hope so, Aunt Lettie. I'm scared." Callie's lower lip trembled.

Sister Mary Eunice reached across the table for Callie's hand. "Try not to worry, Callie. Stay positive. You're innocent, and you'll get out of this. Look how much you have going for you. Friends and family."

Callie sniffled. "I know. And I'm glad."

"What will you do after everything is resolved, Callie? Have you thought about that?" Preacher Prescott asked.

"Well, I suppose I'll have to go back to Coosa Springs, somehow. I have the disorderly conduct charge to take care of. And my things are there. But it's all stuff I can live without, I guess."

"That charge might be something we can take care of with a phone call, Callie. Don't you agree, Matthew?"

"I do. The court is more than happy to take care of minor charges these days."

"What about going to join your mother in Detroit? Are you still planning on that?"

"I don't know, Sister. I can't answer that right now."

Sister Mary Eunice turned her attention to Ruby Jean. "Ruby Jean, you're back close to your family. Don't you want to call home?"

She figured that was coming. Ruby Jean concentrated on her piece of cake. "Not really," she answered quietly.

"If it's your father you're worried about, Matt and I can both be with you. Since both of us are sharing the driving, we don't have to hurry back to Coosa Springs."

"I don't really want to." How could she explain that she was afraid of running into Aunt Peggy? Or Snake drunk? Or both? Not to mention being ashamed of the run-down house with its peeling paint.

Preacher Prescott broke the silence. "You know, I've been thinking of something. On the way up, I was telling the sister about needing to hire a caretaker for my daughters." He explained Hannah Grace and Anna Faith's disabilities to Miss Lucy and Miss Lettie. He looked at Ruby Jean. "If Ruby Jean would like the job, it's hers. We have a spare bedroom, and we'll fix it up pretty for her. And later on, we can get her into a program for training to be a nurse's assistant. We wouldn't take her away from making a life of her own."

"That's a wonderful idea, Matt." Sister Mary Eunice took her hand. "It's something to consider, Ruby Jean."

Miss Lucy began clearing the dishes. "Ruby Jean, why don't you stay here with us for now while you decide? You'll be here with Callie, and I suppose these two will come back to testify." She turned to the preacher and the sister. "Right?"

"Exactly," Sister Mary Eunice said.

"Of course," Preacher Prescott added. "Whatever happens, we'll make sure the girls get to wherever they want to go."

The sound of it, a nurse's assistant. Could she really become one? Whatever happens? The words scared her. She only hoped, whatever happened, wouldn't mean prison for Callie.

Dark was almost upon them when Miss Lucy got her key from under the floor pot by the door and let them in. Her house was as pretty as her sister's. She turned on the lights and drew the drapes. The sun had set on a day Ruby Jean had begun before sunrise.

Miss Lucy plopped down in a huge easy chair. Callie and Ruby Jean sat on the edge of the matching sofa.

"Sit back, girls. Get some rest. Lord, I'm so glad to have you home, Callie. Come give me one more big hug."

Ruby Jean watched as Callie embraced her grandma, so much like the last hug she had given Mama. It had been so hard, knowing it would be the last.

Miss Lucy soothed Callie, rubbing her back and patting the

springy hair on her head.

"You like my new 'do, Grandma?"

"I do. Don't worry Callie, you're gone be all right."

Ruby Jean closed her eyes. She was hugging Mama and kissing her on the check. *Don't worry, Mama, I'm gonna be all right.* The vision was trying to creep in.

Callie sat down beside Ruby Jean and took both her hands in hers. "RJ, are you trying to have a vision?"

Ruby Jean shook her head and opened her eyes. "No."

"RJ, maybe you ought to call Roy."

"What if Aunt Peggy's there?"

"If she answers, hand the phone to me. I'll ask for Roy."

"Ruby Jean, you really ought to," Miss Lucy said. "What's this about having visions, Callie?"

"Ruby Jean has visions, Grandma. She gets it from her mama. She used to use them to keep RJ from killing Snake. She helped find a little lost boy, one time, and she knew when her mother was dying in Tennessee. Then one afternoon RJ brained Snake with a frying pan. She ran off and had a vision of her own. She had a vision about Reggie being shot and me in jail. That's what made us both decide to leave. That and her mother dying, not being able to stop RJ from killing her own daddy anymore."

"Humph!" was all Miss Lucy said.

"If you don't want to call Roy, RJ, then have the vision," Callie said. "Get it out of the way, and you'll know what to do. Maybe your mother is already—resting peacefully. Just get in touch with that third eye you told me about and do it."

"Callie, I've been trying not to have visions anymore. That first vision I had ended up getting us in trouble. We left because of it, and now you're under arrest. Maybe if we had stayed, the real killer would've been caught. And if you had been at home, it might not have happened at all."

"I don't think so, RJ. It could've been worse. We don't know how things would have turned out. You had that vision for a reason."

Ruby Jean's shoulders drooped. Callie was right. Maybe she

ought to get it over with. The vision would only keep nagging at her. She pressed her eyes with her palms. Then it came, the swirls turning into a bright light above a hospital bed. Mama's face, eyes closed, lips apart, breathing heavy.

She sat up. "Mama's alive. She's in the hospital."

Miss Lucy stood up. "Lord have mercy. Call the hospital and ask for Ida Carson's room. It's the only way you'll know for sure."

"Here, I'll do it for you, RJ." Callie picked up the phone on the table by the sofa and dialed. "May I speak with someone in Ida's Carson's room please?" She looked at RJ and nodded a yes. She waited. Then she handed the phone to RJ.

"Roy?" Ruby Jean's voice quivered.

"Ruby Jean! Where are you?"

"I'm here, Roy. In Frogmoor, at Callie's grandma's house."

"Thank God. Mama keeps hanging on, Ruby Jean. Aunt Peggy's here, and she keeps saying your name to her. She knows something's wrong because you're not with her. It's like she can't let go. Can you come? Room 302."

"I'm on the way." Ruby Jean hung up the phone, "It's true. She's been waiting for me before she goes."

"Let's go," Callie said. "Oh wait, oh no, Clarence is off in Grandma's car."

They all paced the floor until a few minutes later when, miraculously, they heard a car pull in and shut off its engine.

Thirty minutes later, they pulled into the dark, almost empty hospital parking lot. Ruby Jean's heart throbbed in her throat. Clarence said it was probably past visiting hours, and their best bet was to go through the emergency room. He pulled in close to the entrance and parked. A night watchman opened the big glass door for them.

"Callie, you and Clarence wait down here, okay? God knows

what Snake would say if you two came up with me."

"I definitely agree, RJ. Go. We'll be here until you come back."

Ruby Jean took a deep breath and hugged Callie. "Thanks, Callie. I love you."

"I love you too, RJ. Now go. And don't let Snake or your aunt intimidate you."

Ruby Jean gave Callie one last quick hug and went to the front desk. "Hey, look, I just got in town. My mother is dying in room 302."

A girl with an angelic face smiled at her. "Go ahead, honey." She pointed. "The elevator's right over that way. Just hit three."

The hallway was silent. Ruby Jean walked past doors looking at the numbers. She saw 299, and on the other side, 298. She kept walking. She came upon 296. On the other side was room 295. She was going the wrong way. Room 302 had to be the other way. She turned and walked back past the elevator and down the hall past room rooms 300, 301, and across the hall to room 302. She opened the heavy wooden door. Mama was there in a hospital bed just like her vision with lips parted and her breathing heavy.

Roy hugged her. I'm so glad you're here, Ruby Jean. Mama doesn't want to seem to let go," he whispered. "I think she wants to say goodbye to you."

Snake stood by the window. He had on a clean long-sleeved plaid shirt with the sleeves rolled up above leathery arms. His dark hair was slicked back, and he had a close shave. Ruby Jean could see the sour whiskey on his breath. The twins huddled in the corner glaring at her. Aunt Peggy sat in a chair by Mama's bed with her high heels off.

"Well, looky here, Daddy. It's Ruby Jean, the runaway."

"Shut up, Junior, you brat," Ruby Jean snarled.

Snake just stood there not moving. "Where the hell have you been, Ruby Jean? You're supposed to be with Peggy."

"I don't owe you any explanation, Daddy. I'm a grown woman."

Aunt Peggy uncrossed her legs and leaned forward. "You're a disabled girl, Ruby Jean. What in tarnation got into you, running off like that?"

"Shut up, Aunt Peggy. I don't owe you any explanation either."

"My God, how disrespectful. I'm glad my own children don't talk to me like that."

"Your own children are two mean and nasty girls, Aunt Peggy. Now leave me alone, I'm here to talk to my mama." She sat on the edge of the bed and took Mama's hand. "It's me, Ruby Jean, Mama," she whispered. "I'm sorry I didn't go to Aunt Peggy's. But things turned out all right. In fact, they turned out real good. I got a job working as a waitress in a motel café. Oh, I had to do a little housekeeping, but mostly, they wanted me to be a waitress, so I did. I took orders, brought people their food, and got paid wages and tips. A couple of times, I even ran the cash register."

Mama's eyes flickered, and Ruby Jean was sure she smiled. "And get this. I've got an even better job offer. This man—he's a preacher — he has two little-disabled girls. He wants me to live in and be a caretaker. And he seems to think there may be a way I could go to a school to learn to be a nurse's assistant. I think it might be a real good opportunity for me."

Mama squeezed her hand.

"You know, I ran off with Callie. We were going to find her mother Della and become singers. But I'm beginning to think this caretaker's job would make more sense for me. I've just got to find out what Callie's going to do. It's hard to part with her."

Aunt Peggy came over and started petting her, stroking her arm. "Ruby Jean, come home with me. You can help me out and keep the house clean while I'm working. You're disabled, you know. You deserve a check from the government."

She brushed Aunt Peggy's hand away. "No thanks, Aunt Peggy. I don't need a check from the government. I can make my own way."

Ruby Jean held one hand, and Roy held the other until Mama

drew her last breath. It was the first time she ever saw Snake Carson cry. The nurses came to prepare mama's body. They all were asked to leave the room. Ruby Jean stayed behind to give Mama one last kiss.

Thank goodness Callie had talked her into having one more vision. Mama was gone from this earth, and the gift was gone with her. A gift Ruby Jean no longer wanted.

Chapter 33

Callie knocked softly on the door and went into the bedroom Lucy had fixed up for Ruby Jean. She looked so frail, sprawled out on the big feather bed, her dark hair fanned out. Poor RJ. Lucy had sat with them in the living room after they got home talking to RJ about her mother. In Frogmoor, everybody either knew everyone or knew of them. Lucy knew of Ida Carson.

They had helped a cried-out Ruby Jean to bed. She fell asleep, exhausted. She didn't even ask to have a light on anywhere. This time, it was Callie who didn't want to sleep in the dark. She laid wide awake going over in her mind what Clarence had talked about in the hospital waiting room.

The married woman Reggie was seeing was a real slut, the kind that liked to run around on her husband. She would come to Frogmoor to babysit for her sister who worked late at the King's Inn over on the highway to Raleigh. Clarence had found out her name after pretending to befriend one of the regular bar customers. The guy said she babysat, all right. Right up until the kids got good and asleep. Then she would hit the bar, and her sister would go home a couple of hours later.

Last night, Clarence went to Tarboro to a place pretty much like Ledford's. He found out the husband's name: Johnny Albright. The guy he talked to knows him well. He was with him one Sunday night about a month ago at the King's Inn when he and some guy were about to fight. They both got kicked out of the bar. He said his friend didn't show back up, and he had to bum a ride back to Tarboro after the bar closed.

It had happened about the same time she and RJ left. And on

a Sunday night, the night before Reggie's two days off. Someone had shot and killed Reggie for some reason. It must have been either him or somebody to do with hauling liquor and cigarettes for Al Ledford. They had to find the real killer. Her life depended on.

Ruby Jean sat up and half-opened her eyes. "Hey, Callie."

"Hey, sleepy head." She sat down beside her and brushed her bangs out of her eyes. "We've got to trim those bangs later. How are you feeling?"

"I'm okay, Callie. I'm just so glad I got to say goodbye to Mama."

"Me, too. And from what you said last night, she knew you were there."

"She did. Did I tell you she squeezed my hand when I told her about maybe learning to be a nurse's assistant?"

"You did. You know, that sounds like a good opportunity for you, RJ."

Ruby Jean nodded. "I'd miss you, though. I had started looking forward to what life would be like for us in a place like Detroit. Do you think you're still gonna go when..."

"When all of this is over? That's just it. I can't think of anything else until all of this *is* over." She sighed. "I'm really scared, RJ."

"Try not to be. Think about what Sister Mary Eunice said yesterday. You've got all of us to help. I don't guess I can do anything but pray. But you thought of the letter and Sister Mary Eunice, and the preacher were good enough to do what they did. Clarence is working on stuff. And now your real daddy is going to be your lawyer. Are you excited, or nervous?"

Callie shrugged. "A little of both, I guess. But I don't think he'll be overjoyed to reunite with me."

"He's probably a little nervous, too."

"I thought about that. In fact, he may set me up with another lawyer in the firm. That might be best for both of us. They'll try to get me out of this and then be done with me."

RJ looked at her sadly. "It'll be okay Callie. You've got plenty of people to love you."

"Thanks, RJ." She gave her a hug. "You're the best. Well, I'm gonna go finish getting ready." She stood up. "I've got to go find something to wear." She looked down at her raggedy shorts and t-shirt. "I found these in my old room, and that's about it. I didn't want to ask Grandma to wash my old stinky jail clothes and nothing else. Clarence is picking me up early to go by the bungalow. He says we're probably not supposed to, but I've just got to find something to wear."

"I don't guess I'll see you until after your meeting."

"It shouldn't take long. Make yourself at home around here."

Callie slid on an old pair of flip-flops and grabbed the purse Lucy was letting her use. She walked out the door just as Clarence pulled up. Damn, not the bread truck again. Couldn't he borrow Aunt Lettie's car? She walked up to his window. "You want me to go ask Lucy if we can borrow her car?"

Clarence nodded toward the back. "Don't be mad. I just got one quick delivery."

She hopped in. What choice did she have? "Don't forget, I have to go to my old place and grab something to wear."

He looked down at her shorts and flip-flops. "How could I forget? And about the bungalow. I had an idea." He reached for a cigarette. "Want one of these?"

She shook her head no.

"I thought a cigarette was the first thing a person wanted after being locked up."

"No, it didn't bother me. I wasn't smoking that much where I worked. And quit talking like I'm a criminal."

"Sorry. I'll be a good boy and not smoke." He stuck the pack back over the visor. "Anyway, about the bungalow. I'm sure they looked everywhere for Reggie's missing gun, but you should look around and see if you find anything strange or different. You lived there, and only you would know. Maybe something he dropped."

"But you said I might get in trouble if I've been over there."

"Yeah, I changed my mind about that. You had an appointment with your lawyer, and you had no clothes to wear. You'd gone straight from one jail to another. You had to get your things, and we just happened to find it, if there is something lying around. I don't think we'll have anything to worry about."

Callie tensed as Clarence turned onto the dirt road by the post office and drove over the tracks to the bungalow. The first thing they saw was the yellow crime scene tape that had blown down in the wind.

The little cinder block house sat sad and forlorn, overgrown with new spring grass. Callie had, at least for a little bit, planned to fix up the house really cute for them, and maybe a baby. The cycle would be broken. She would have a husband and kids that knew who their daddy was.   Now it was a crime scene. She grew misty-eyed, but she didn't cry. That dream had been short-lived.

"By the way, Clarence, have you seen my cat? I thought you were going to take Blackjack for me."

"I took him home, he left."

The second thing they saw was the padlocked door. They walked around to the back. That door was padlocked too. Callie looked down at her clothes. "Oh crap, what am I going to do? Have you got a few bucks for some clothes?"

Clarence scoffed. "If you can find something for two dollars."

Callie sighed. "Great. Wait, a minute. The bathroom window lock is broken. Or it was. I remember one time Reggie locked me out. I got in through the bathroom window." It was a tiny window, and it had been a struggle, but she had gotten in. "Help me get the window up, and I'll go through and let you in the front window."

Callie held her breath while Clarence pushed on the solid glass window, palms flat. She prayed no one had noticed and fixed the lock. After a full minute struggle, the window creaked, and Clarence opened it as wide as possible. He lifted her up. She barely escaped getting stuck before popping inside.

Empty beer cans were strewn everywhere, and the stench

of rotten food reeked from the kitchen. Reggie's parents had already stopped paying the power bill. She let Clarence in the front window.

"Shoo… this is awful. Get your stuff, Brown Sugar, take a look around, and let's go. If you find anything, don't touch it. I've got these." He pulled a rubber glove and a baggie from his pocket.

Callie looked in the bottom cabinet in the kitchen where she had kept empty grocery bags. She fought off the roaches for three of them. She went through the bedroom drawers and the closet, stuffing in the few clothes she had left, picking out a black skirt and white blouse to wear to meet her father. She shuffled through beer cans and everything else on the floor. She didn't see anything unusual. There was nothing on the table, nothing behind the TV, and nothing but dust and one of Reggie's old socks behind the dresser. There wasn't much place else for anything to be. "I can't find anything, Clarence. You can keep looking while I get dressed."

She put the skirt and blouse on and checked herself in the bathroom mirror. Shoes. She needed shoes. She still had on flip-flops. She had bought a new pair of loafers a while back that she forgot to take. She looked in the bottom of the closet and found one of them. Where was the other one? She looked around. Maybe under the bed? The bed was a mattress, and box springs on cinder blocks turned sideways. She had to get on her belly to look, but there it was. She pulled the shoe out, and a shiny object caught her eye. "Clarence, come in here."

"What is it?"

"There's something under here. It looks like—it's a cigarette lighter."

"So?"

"Reggie didn't have a lighter, he used matches." She scooted up further to look at it. "It looks like it has an initial on it. I can't see what it is."

Clarence handed her the glove. She scooped up the lighter and slid out from under the bed, still on her belly. She stood up and dusted off her clothes. Clarence opened the baggie, and she dropped a plain silver Zippo with a gold initial J on it.

"Come, on. We've got just enough time to make this bread delivery and get to Raleigh. We'll talk on the way."

Callie tossed the bags of clothes out the front window and crawled out. Clarence followed and got the bags. She hopped in the bread truck without looking back.

"So what are you going to do with it? The lighter I mean. Are you going to give it to my—the lawyer?"

"No, I don't think we should yet. Not right away. Sure it's got a J on it. Johnny Albright. But J can stand for lots of other names, too. And even if I dust it for prints, and find out they're his, the prosecution could come up with all kinds of other scenarios: they frequented the same bar, or his wife could have had it while she was with Reggie."

"You can do fingerprinting?"

"Yeah, and I've got a fingerprinting kit."

"So who's to say I didn't wear gloves when I supposedly shot Reggie? And they found the gun?"

"Then they would try to pin the murder on you with circumstantial evidence. It would go to trial, and a jury would decide. All we would have is testimony from the bartender about the fight. And testimony from your trucker friend. *If* we could only recover the gun and find Johnny Albright's prints on it. Along with the lighter, we'd have him. I could go straight to Chief Price, and he'd have to drop the charges. He might want to do his own investigating, but I can guarantee you, he'd hurry it up. So, the answer is no, don't say anything about the lighter yet."

At five minutes past ten Clarence parked in front of the Grayson Whitfield Law Firm. Callie's insides were in a knot as they walked into the plush, carpeted office. An older lady behind a desk greeted them curtly.

"Your name please?"

"I'm Callie Gibbs," she managed to squeak out, "and this is my cousin Clarence Truelove. We have an appointment at ten o'clock."

"Do you know which attorney?"

Did she? Should she say with Mr. Whitfield? "Um, not really."

"That's okay. I can look." She flipped through her clipboard. "Ah, here you are. Mr. Sutton. Jeff Sutton will see you. Come with me."

"It was just as she thought it might be. She wouldn't be meeting her father after all."

Jeff Sutton stood and shook their hands. "I'm Jeff Sutton. I was asked exclusively to take your case. I'm honored to meet you both. Sit down, let's talk. First of all, I was able to get you a preliminary set this morning. It's next Tuesday afternoon at two. You don't need to worry about calling for a court date. I'll take care of all that. Now, what I need for you to do, is to tell me what's going on. What's your side of the story?"

Clarence interrupted. "First of all, Mr. Sutton, I'm Callie's cousin, and I'm a criminal justice student."

Jeff Sutton nodded. "Good," he said, seemingly not very impressed.

Clarence continued. "Callie left home two days before Reggie's body was found." He explained why she left and where she ended up. "Unfortunately, she missed the bus she was supposed to take, so the only witness she has is a truck driver who gave her and her girlfriend a ride. She was able to locate him, and he can be a witness."

"I understand there is also the matter of a stolen driver's license. Now I need you to tell me the truth, and I need to hear it from you, Miss Gibbs."

Jeff Sutton swiveled back and forth in his office chair as Callie told him the whole story. She told him about why she took Nellie Wilson's ID, the robbery, and working at the Blue Moon.

He listened as she told him about getting arrested, questioned about the robberies Babs and Dale had committed and then extradited back to Frogmoor for questioning in Reggie's murder.

"So let me get this straight. They found probable cause to arrest you because of the stolen ID, your history of not getting along with Reggie, and no solid proof of exactly when you left town."

"That's correct. That, and my grandmother told them I was headed for Detroit, but I was going in the wrong direction."

Clarence spoke up. "The Frogmoor police are trying their best to pin this on Callie, Mr. Sutton since Reggie was one of their own." He told him about how Reggie's dealings running liquor and cigarettes was kept under cover, about Reggie seeing a married woman, the bar fight, everything except the lighter they found."

Jeff Sutton chewed on his thumbnail. "Interesting. I know how things can be out in the country with these small sheriff's offices. It sounds like more investigation needs to be done. To be honest, we don't have a lot going for us at this point, as far as defense. It would be a lifesaver if you could get proof of the actual time you left. Forensics might be able to pinpoint the time of death and exonerate you. And unless your trucker friend can produce a dated Polaroid shot of you, it's a pretty weak argument. He could be anybody. We could establish Reggie's reputation as bad, but that might backfire. It would provide a motive for Callie. Especially the fact that Reggie was cheating on her. Listen. Let me work on things. Meet me at the courthouse at one before court. The good news is, I feel pretty confident we can get this reduced to voluntary manslaughter. Then we can make sure more investigation gets done." He turned to Callie. "I'd make sure you stayed out of jail until your trial. I'll argue that you have roots here and aren't a flight risk. And you have no prior criminal record. Is that correct?"

Callie's heart sank. "Correct." That was it. The best the Grayson Whitfield Law Firm could do. Callie was about to stand when a knock came at Sutton's door.

"Come in." The door opened, and he walked in. She recognized him: Grayson Whitfield, her father. He introduced himself and shook hands with her first, then Clarence. Callie decided that the description tall, dark, and handsome fit him perfectly, except, of course, he wasn't quite as dark as her. But she had his eyes, and when he looked at her, she could tell he noticed.

"Are things all set, Jeff?" he asked.

"Yes, sir. I got the info I need, and I'm meeting Callie, and Clarence here, before court on Tuesday."

Callie's head reeled with questions. What had Winfred Whitfield told him?

"That sounds good. Callie, I'd like you to stop by my office." He glanced at Clarence.

"I'll wait for you in the truck, Callie."

Grayson Whitfield closed the door behind them. "Sit down."

He sat down behind a huge desk lined with framed photos of his wife and children. Callie sat across from him. He laced his fingers together. "When I asked Jeff to take over your case, I hadn't planned on—getting involved. But the things Dad said about you kept haunting me, about your identity crises, and your problems with your husband. I knew I wouldn't rest easy if I didn't talk to you."

Callie sat speechlessly. What could she say?

He went on. "So you left to find Della."

"Yes, sir. I wanted to go find her and join the music world. I was tired of the teasing and taunting around here. I can sing pretty well, and I felt like I would fit in better."

"And you didn't want to take up Dad's offer of attending the Negro college."

"Yes, sir. That's right."

He let out a long sigh and looked off into the distance. "The truth is, Callie, I liked Della. I liked her a lot. I used to catch her singing while she cleaned. She'd see me, turn around, and stop, looking embarrassed. She had a beautiful voice. Then one day she was sitting out in the garden behind our house drinking lemonade, taking a break. She asked me if I wanted a glass. She had just made a fresh pitcher. I said, yeah, that would be nice. She brought out the whole pitcher and another glass. We sat drinking lemonade and talking for the longest time. We laughed when the whole pitcher was gone."

He paused for a minute. Callie was dumbstruck and had no idea what to say.

"After that, first one thing led to another. Then I decided it needed to stop before I got any more feelings for her. Interracial marriage was illegal. It still is in most states. Our relationship would never be accepted. I started going out with other girls. I knew it hurt Della, but at the same time, I felt like she understood. Then she quit working for us. The next thing I knew, she had given birth to a baby. Lucy demanded a blood test, and, well here we are. Dad was determined nobody would find out."

Callie sat as still as a stone statue.

Finally, he spoke again. "Listen, Callie, I know you realize the importance of my father's political career. Mine as well. Let me make a deal with you. Mail the original letter to me. I'll tell Dad to see to it that you can go to a college of your choice. Just get accepted. We'll pay for it, and we'll do all we can to help you out of this trouble. As long as you respect our careers."

As long as she kept the secret. Nothing had changed; nothing except that she could go to any college. Like Frampton University, near Boston, where Vivian had gone to school and met Sammy Lucas.

"You don't have to make your decision right away. You can let me know by mail."

She stood up and found her balance. "I'll do that, *Mr. Whitfield*." She shook her father's hand and left. An idea had been turning over in her mind since this morning when RJ said she guessed all she could do was pray. She didn't think RJ would want to, but she was ready to try it.

Clarence cranked the bread truck when she walked out. She hopped in.

"Clarence, we've got to find that gun."

"No shit. Any ideas how?"

"Ruby Jean."

"Ruby Jean?"

"Yeah, Ruby Jean has visions. She gets it from her mother, Ida Carson. She saw a vision of Reggie shot and me in jail. That's why I left when I did."

Clarence slammed on the brakes and pulled over. "Ida Carson. I remember hearing about her. She helped find a lost boy in the woods a few years ago. Why didn't you tell me before? Private detectives love psychics."

<h1 style="text-align:center">Chapter 34</h1>

"It's hard to explain, but I don't think I have the gift anymore, Callie."

"How do you—how could you know that?" Callie stammered. "What do you mean?"

"I felt it leave with Mama last night."

"You can, Ruby Jean. You have the gift. Your mother left it to you." *Please, dear God.* Callie prayed she was right. "You've had three that turned out to be right."

"Yeah, but they just sort of came on without me trying. Or the last two did, anyway."

Clarence scooted up closer to Ruby Jean. "Tell us about the first time, RJ. Why were you trying to have a vision, and how did you do it?"

"It was right after I was afraid I might have killed Snake with Grandma's big heavy skillet. Mama was real sick. I knew she was dying, and I didn't want to go live with my Aunt Peggy. Then I remembered what Mama told me one time. She said the way to have a vision was to think of a problem and ask for a picture to help you. She said to pretend to have a third eye in the middle of your forehead. That's what I did. That's when I saw Reggie shot and Callie in jail."

"Then that's what you should do now, RJ," Clarence said. "We have the problem, a big one. Your best friend might go to prison for a crime she didn't commit."

Callie had reached the point of begging. "Please try, RJ."

"Okay then, I will, Callie, for you. I'll try my best, I promise. But what if I see something else? Something—worse."

"We'll cross that bridge when we come to it, RJ. Besides, if you see me in prison, I need to know. Think of it this way. Your mama used to use her gift to keep you from killing Snake. If I know prison is in my future, we work harder on getting me out of this."

They waited until Grandma and Aunt Lettie left for their Friday night bingo game at the American Legion and gathered around the mahogany dining room table. The sun had set, and the evening star shone through the lace curtains. The light from the kerosene lantern on the buffet cast three giant shadows on the wall.

Ruby Jean nodded. "Okay, I'm ready." She took a deep breath and pressed her eyes into her palms like she had last night.

Callie and Clarence watched her like she was a lizard sprouting wings.

Clarence perched on the edge of the chair. "Think, RJ. The third eye."

"I am."

"Shut up, Clarence, let her think. I'm the one that did this with her last night. Think, RJ."

Ruby Jean sat up. "You know what? I think I could do this better alone."

"Okay, you got it. Come on, Callie."

Clarence and Callie paced the living room floor wringing their hands. The house was silent except for the ticking clock and the little spring chorus frogs trilling in the distance. Then Callie thought she heard RJ saying something. They looked at each other. Clarence must have heard it, too. She said something again, louder this time. And again, louder.

"I see it. Callie, I see it."

Callie's ears pounded inside. She and Clarence raced into the kitchen. Callie pulled a chair up and sat in front of her. "See what, RJ? What do you see?"

"A gun. I see a gun."

Clarence sat down on the other side of RJ. "Focus in RJ. What do you see around the gun?"

"Water. It's in water."

Callie grabbed two handfuls of her hair. "Oh, no. He threw it in a lake somewhere. How will we ever find it? And if we do, the fingerprints will be washed off."

"No, they won't," Clarence answered. "The edges of our fingers sweat a lot. Our feet and hands do, too. That sweat has oils that water takes a while to wash away. They may be faint, but we've got the Zippo you found. The prints on it will be clear. We can match them up. A crime lab can do an even better job retrieving the prints. We'll have him. *If* we can just find the gun."

Callie took RJ by the hand. "Try to see if you can see anything else, RJ. Please." She was begging for her life.

RJ had her chin down, her eyes scrunched tight. "Round."

"Round?" Callie asked.

"Something to do with round."

Clarence snapped his fingers. "Round Pond."

Round Pond wasn't really a pond but a road named Round Pond Road. The road ran along the bogs for about a mile before the marshy water disappeared into groves of pines. Clarence parked on an old dirt side road off Round Pond Road, and they walked. A full moon, the first one since she and RJ had left, lit the bog. Stubby trees stood like soldiers in the murky water.

"Are you getting any vibes or anything RJ?" Clarence asked. "I could go through here with boots and a metal detector, but it might take days. Can you focus in on a spot? Maybe some kind of marker?"

Ruby Jean shook her head. "The place I saw has bricks around it."

"Bricks?" they both asked at once.

"Yeah. I don't think this is the place."

Dark clouds shadowed the moon for an instant. The wind

blew them aside.

Round, bricks, water, Callie thought. Round, bricks, water. "I've got an idea. Reggie showed me an old dried-up well one time. It's on their property out past the bungalow. It's hidden in a field grown up with grass, now. But a long time ago, they used it. We pulled the concrete slab off and looked. It's sided up with bricks."

"Do you think that could be it, RJ?" Clarence asked.

Ruby Jean closed her eyes. "Yeah, yeah I do. That might be it."

Callie's heart sank. "Oh, no. That's worse than being in the bog. At least we could go through there with a metal detector."

"No, no, it's not," Clarence said. "They've never dug wells deeper than thirty feet around here in the flatlands. My Uncle Clyde's got a thirty-two-foot extension ladder behind his garage, and I've got rubber boots in the back of the truck. Let's go."

Clarence parked past the bungalow as close as he could get to the edge where the tall lawn grass turned into taller field grass. Callie helped him get the extension ladder from the top of the bread truck. Ruby Jean carried their flashlights.

Clarence pushed the concrete slab away. Callie helped pull the extension ladder out and lower it. It touched the bottom, and Clarence locked it into place.

Clarence put a rubber glove on his right hand and pulled a plastic bag from his pocket with the other hand. "Here I go, ladies, wish me luck."

"Please, be careful, Clarence," they both said.

The only sound was the echo of Clarence's footsteps as he descended into the well. They waited until they heard the swish of water.

Callie yelled down. "Are you okay, Clarence? Are you there yet?"

His voice was faint. "Yeah, I'm here. I'm looking now."

They waited, listening to the swishing water.

Callie heard another sound, almost like a cat purring. Wait. It *was* a cat purring. She shined her flashlight into the tall weeds and saw two green eyes glowing. *Meow.*

"Blackjack! Look, RJ. My cat, Blackjack. Here, kitty." Blackjack ran to her at the sound of his name. She picked him up. He was skinny as a rail; skinny as a rail, with nipples. "Oh, my, gosh, RJ. Look! Blackjack turned out to be Black Jane."

"Hey," Clarence yelled. "Hold the ladder down up there. I'm halfway up."

Callie set the cat down, and they ran over to hold the ladder.

Clarence reached the top of the ladder and held up the plastic bag. "Surprise!"

"The gun! The gun! Is it the gun? Please let it be the gun."

Clarence climbed the rest of the way out and held the bag out to her. "Does this look familiar?"

"Yes, that looks like Reggie's gun, all right."

Callie and Ruby Jean jumped up and down, screaming silently into thin air.

Clarence laughed. "Don't go too crazy until we find out what condition these prints are in." He looked down at the cat. "Whoa, is that Blackjack?"

"Yes, and no. It's Black Jane." She turned the cat over and showed her underbelly to Clarence. "Look at her. She's skin and bones. We've got to find her kittens."

"Listen to you. I risk my neck to get you out of a murder charge, and all you can think about is kitties."

Callie hugged him. "Thank you, Clarence." She hugged RJ. "Thank you, RJ. I love you both. Black Jane, show us where your kitties are so we can get out of here."

∞ ∞ ∞

Clarence had a little workshop set up in the back of Aunt Lettie's garage. They stood around a plywood table propped up by two trashcans on the end. Black Jane had finished lapping up a bowl of milk and was nursing black and white spotted kittens in a box in the corner. Callie and Ruby Jean watched Clarence set up for the fingerprinting. He explained the process and how it had helped land many criminals.

"Okay, first, I'll get your prints, Callie. It'll give me a chance to practice, and you'll see the difference between yours and the ones on the gun. You never touched the gun, right?"

"Right."

"Okay, press your four fingertips on this piece of glass."

She and RJ watched fascinated, as Clarence sprinkled on a silky black powder, then brushed and blew it away with a fine brush. He took the clear tape and pressed it against the glass. He picked up the tape and pressed it on a square of white paper. He held it up. "See? There are your fingerprints."

Callie inspected her fingertips. "You're right."

"Now, this kit comes with black and white powder, black and white paper squares, and this brush. Since the gun is black, I'll use the white powder and black paper."

"What about on the cigarette lighter?" Ruby Jean asked.

"Good question, RJ. Actually, I think either one would work on silver."

Clarence carefully followed the same procedure, first with the gun, then the Zippo. "Stay right there." He took the three cards over and held them under the dangling light bulb. "Okay, come here, and I'll show you."

Callie and RJ walked over to the light.

"See here? The prints on the lighter and the gun match. And they don't look anything like yours."

Callie fell over with joy. RJ picked her up. They cried and hugged.

Callie wiped away tears. "What's next, Clarence? What do we do now?"

"I take all the evidence over to Chief Price first thing in the morning. He'll look at the prints and probably send the gun and the lighter to the real crime lab. I tell him what the bartender told me about Reggie and Johnny Albright getting kicked out of the bar for fighting, and then that's it, Brown Sugar. You'll be cleared, the charges dropped. Then you can get on with your life again."

Chapter 35

The hum of the semi's big engine had lulled Callie into a deep sleep. She woke up, stretched, and looked around.

Matthew Prescott smiled from behind the wheel. "Good morning, sleepyhead."

Good. For a split second, she thought she was riding in the back of a cop car or in jail. But she was here, and Ruby Jean's head lolled beside her. They got their smoking gun, or the wet one. The fingerprints were clear enough to match the ones on the cigarette lighter. Johnny Albright was in custody and couldn't afford bail.

By the looks of the sky, the sun would be up soon. "Good morning. Mind if I let in some fresh air?"

"Go right ahead. Maybe it will help rouse Ruby Jean. We'll be right outside Montgomery in a couple of hours."

Callie rolled the truck's huge window halfway down. A strong gush of early spring air blew in.

RJ woke up. "Good grief, Callie. Up that window. You're gonna blow my head off."

Callie rolled up the window. "Okay. I just wanted to wake you up. We'll be in Montgomery in about two hours."

"Good. Wake me up then. I'll need my energy for the march." She turned over and went back to sleep.

The truck rolled on toward Montgomery. Matthew Prescott hadn't had to be a witness after all. But he had promised to get them where they needed to go, and they needed to go back to the Blue Moon in Coosa Springs. He combined the trip with a long haul to Raleigh and picked them up at midnight on Wednesday. They talked and rode, talked and drank coffee and Pepsis. Matt talked about his girls, and how great it would be to have RJ living with them. They already had a pretty room set up for her with her own TV and radio, even a phone. Ruby Jean was beyond excited.

Callie thought about Grayson Whitfield one last time. That was it. Not Father, not Daddy, just Grayson Whitfield. She still had so many questions. Where had they been when she was conceived? Probably in one of the bedrooms of that big house Della cleaned. She decided to forget wondering about it. No doubt she would never know. She couldn't picture herself sitting down and having a heart to heart with Della anytime soon.

Callie had gone to Tuesday's hearing to clear everything up and answer to the charge of stealing Miss Wilson's driver's license. Jeff Sutton had been there, but not Grayson Whitfield. Kenneth Sawyers stood beside the bailiff, arms crossed, looking like he had a mouthful of sour grapes. Miss Wilson herself was there and didn't want to press charges. She announced dramatically that she wanted Callie to have the chance to come back and finish high school. That was exactly what Callie planned to do. Grayson Whitfield said anywhere you want to go, just mail me the letter. But she wanted to be accepted because of her grades, not the senator's money. Funny, she couldn't think of him as Grandfather. The memory of Granddaddy Moses was all she needed, and he would be proud to know she decided to go back home and finish high school. And Grandma Lucy's questionable shot at getting her a college education wouldn't be in vain.

∞ ∞ ∞

"My goodness, look at all the people. How will we find them?" Ruby Jean asked.

"We look for the sisters. They're uniquely dressed. The

others will be with them," Matthew said.

The day was cloudy, but a warm sun beat through. Jackets were tossed over shoulders. The crowd was eerily silent; the only sounds were of shuffling feet and helicopters clacking above. Here and there, groups broke out into song, singing verses from *We Shall Overcome,* and making up verses to *This Little Light of Mine.* Men, women, and children crowded the street in all shapes, sizes, and colors, and dressed all kinds of ways. Hundreds of troopers lined the street. Flags flew. Black men wore white makeup with VOTE written on their foreheads. Some carried signs saying I Am A Man. Callie had never seen so many different looking people in her life, and they were all full of joy. She would never forget it.

"Take my hand, Ruby Jean," Matthew said. "I don't want to lose you today."

RJ grabbed his hand tight and then reached for Callie's. They followed one flowing nun's habit to the next until they found them.

The sisters were with Vivian, Jerry, Trudy, and Miles. They all embraced and declared that it seemed like an eternity since they had seen each other.

"We joined the march last Sunday, Sister Mary Agatha said. "About seven miles out of town, we had to pare down the group to around three hundred because the four lanes turned to two. Those three hundred have been marching and camping out in muddy fields for four nights. People have been pouring into Montgomery to greet them."

"Man, you guys missed it last night," Trudy said. They had an outside stage show. Joan Baez, Pete Seeger, Tony Bennett. It was an absolute gas."

"And Peter, Paul, and Mary sang *The Time's They Are A-Changin,*" Vivian said. "It made chills go up my spine. So fill us in. What's going on? You don't know how glad we were when Clarence called us Saturday morning with the news. And my condolences on the passing of your mother, Ruby Jean."

"Thank you, Vivian."

"Well, Ruby Jean is now the caretaker for Matthew's little girls, and he's going to help her enroll in a program for special needs students to become a Certified Nurse's Assistant," Callie said.

"Oh, my, gosh, Ruby Jean, that's great!" Vivian said.

"Come here, my child," Sister Mary Agatha hugged RJ. You are perfect for it." She peered over her glasses. "What about you, Callie? Are you going to join your mother?"

"No, I'm going back home after this. Back to Frogmoor, to Grandma's and finish up at Wesley High. Miss Wilson has agreed to help catch me up. Can you believe it? Then I'm going to college." She decided not to say where. She wanted to tell Sammy first. If she saw him that is.

"You know what, I have an idea," Jerry said. "When school is out, come down and work at the café. You can earn some spending money and be near Ruby Jean for the summer."

"That sounds great, Jerry. I'd love that if it's okay with Grandma."

"Yay," Vivian clapped. "Then it's all set."

They turned their attention to the march, joining in on the sporadic singing.

"Hey Trudy," Callie whispered. "You don't know where Sammy is, do you?"

"Yes, he's one of the three hundred that marched the whole way. He's upfront in one of the orange jackets, right in front of Dr. King and his crowd. Don't go getting any ideas, girl. You got to stick with us and go back to the Blue Moon to spend a night or two before you hop on a bus back to North Carolina."

"Is he mad at me?"

"I don't think so. You'll see him sooner or later."

Callie looked through the thick crowd trying to spot the orange jackets.

The crowd swarmed and mingled in front of the Alabama state capital, singing songs, waiting for speakers. They joined in another chorus of *This Little Light of Mine*. Someone touched her on the arm. She turned around to see Sammy Lucas in a bright orange jacket.

"Hello, Callie Gibbs."

"Sammy! How did you find us in all this crowd?"

"The sisters. Those big headdresses. So what's up with you? Are you going to Detroit now?"

"No. I'm going back home and finish high school. Then I'm going to college. To Framington, in the fall."

"Framington? Already? How did you manage that?" He looked at her curiously. "Let me guess. The letter."

"Yep. Senator Winfred Whitfield is footing the bill.

He grinned his biggest Sammy grin. "Are you going to be a politician or a singer?"

"I don't know yet. Maybe both."

They all locked arms and joined in another spirited, impromptu chorus:

I'm so glad we're fighting to be free.
I'm so glad we're fighting to be free.
I'm so glad we're fighting to be free, singing glory, hallelujah,
I'm so glad.

*Folkway Records and Albums FH5591
Copyright 1961 by Folkway Records & Service Corp
121 W. 47th Street
New York, NY

www.ingramcontent.com/pod-product-compliance
Lightning Source LLC
Chambersburg PA
CBHW060526160726
47991CB00001B/195